S0-BNH-258

For Andrea and Leonie

First published in Switzerland under the title *Hubert und der Apfelbaum.*

First published in Great Britain, Canada, Australia, and New Zealand in 2000 by North-South Books, an imprint of NordSüd Verlag AG, Gossau Zürich, Switzerland.
First published in the United States in 2006 by North-South Books.
Distributed in the United States by North-South Books Inc., New York.
Library of Congress Cataloging-in-Publication Data is available.
ISBN-13: 978-0-7358-2044-9 (trade edition)
ISBN-10: 0-7358-2044-9 (trade edition)
10 9 8 7 6 5 4 3 2 1
Printed in Italy

Hubert and the Apple Tree

By Bruno Hächler
Illustrated by Albrecht Rissler
Translated by Rosemary Lanning

A Michael Neugebauer Book
NORTH-SOUTH BOOKS · New York/London

Hubert lived at the edge of a small town. He was a friendly man with a mop of curly brown hair, small round spectacles, and kindly twinkling eyes. His wooden house had grown crooked with age. It stood far back from the street, coyly concealing itself behind a large, spreading apple tree in a meadow strewn with wildflowers. Every morning, when Hubert looked out at that beautiful tree, his spirits rose. Every evening, when he came home from work, he would sit by his window and watch the birds in the tree's leafy crown.

There is more to watching trees than you might think, because they are constantly changing. In spring, they deck themselves in dazzling blossom while their new leaves unfurl in the warm sunshine, and bees buzz around them, looking for nectar. In summer, when the hot sun blazes down, people are grateful for the cool, green shade they offer. In autumn, the wind toys with their tawny leaves, and scatters them carelessly across the fields and streets. Then winter comes and blankets their bare branches with snow.

Hubert often lay under his apple tree, remembering how he had climbed it as a child. All too often he had hidden in its thick canopy of leaves when his mother called him to come indoors before he was ready.

Whenever he looked at his tree,
Hubert was indescribably happy.
He felt he had all he could possibly
want from life.
Sometimes people stopped outside
his fence and exclaimed,
"Look at that tree! Isn't it lovely!"
But most of them hurried past,
too preoccupied to stop.

Years went by. Hubert was growing older. Deep furrows etched his face. His hair turned white, thinned, and fell like autumn leaves. His beard grew longer and thicker. Hubert was still a happy man, and he still spent hours watching his tree and the birds.

Sometimes he caught mischievous children stealing his apples, but he never scolded them. “Forbidden fruit always tastes better, doesn’t it?” he said with a chuckle.

Then, one autumn day, something terrible happened. Stormy winds were rattling the shutters and fallen leaves whirled high in the air. Billowing storm clouds rolled over the nearby hills, turning the sky so black that people took fright and ran indoors. At the first rumble of thunder, Hubert closed his windows and watched the approaching storm from behind the glass. Raindrops clattered against the windowpanes. Then a heavy shower poured down like a waterfall on the small town. Lightning flared and crackled, and the thunderclaps grew louder and more menacing. Suddenly, Hubert's heart stood still. He saw a huge bolt of lightning strike his apple tree. There was a deafening crash. The tree groaned, and its trunk split open. Cooling rain ran into the wound.

The storm had passed. Hubert hurried out to his apple tree. How sad it looked now — as gnarled and crooked as the old house. Its trunk was split right down to its sturdy roots.

"That must hurt," Hubert whispered, tenderly stroking the tree. It seemed to sigh. To Hubert, the gleaming drops of water on its bark looked like tears.

The following spring was warm and sunny. Birds sang. Flowers bloomed. The only sad sight was the gnarled old apple tree.

A few tiny leaves had sprouted here and there, and bees buzzed around its scattered blossoms but, try as it might, the old apple tree could never regain its former glory.

Its scar still ached when the weather turned suddenly cold, or especially hot. But something even worse was happening: people now stopped and stared at it. "Look at that ugly thing!" they said. "What an eyesore!"

"Someone ought to cut it down," a woman said. The man with her agreed.
"They could park a few cars here, or make a proper lawn if they cleared that old tree away."
Hubert was angry. He loved his tree just as it was. Every evening he went and stroked its bark. If he saw people staring he shouted,
"Go away!" and ran at them, brandishing a broom. But it was no use. The next day there would be more of them, staring and muttering. Then Hubert had an idea.

Hubert rode off on his rusty bicycle, smiling mysteriously. When he came back a few hours later, he was carrying a big bundle. He fetched a spade and began to dig next to the old tree. He didn't stop until he had dug a deep, round hole. Then he planted a sapling in it: a sturdy young apple tree, scarcely tall enough to reach the end of his snow-white beard.

At last he's getting rid of that ugly old tree, people thought. But Hubert still smiled his mysterious smile. He covered the little tree's roots with soil, watered it well, and put the spade away.

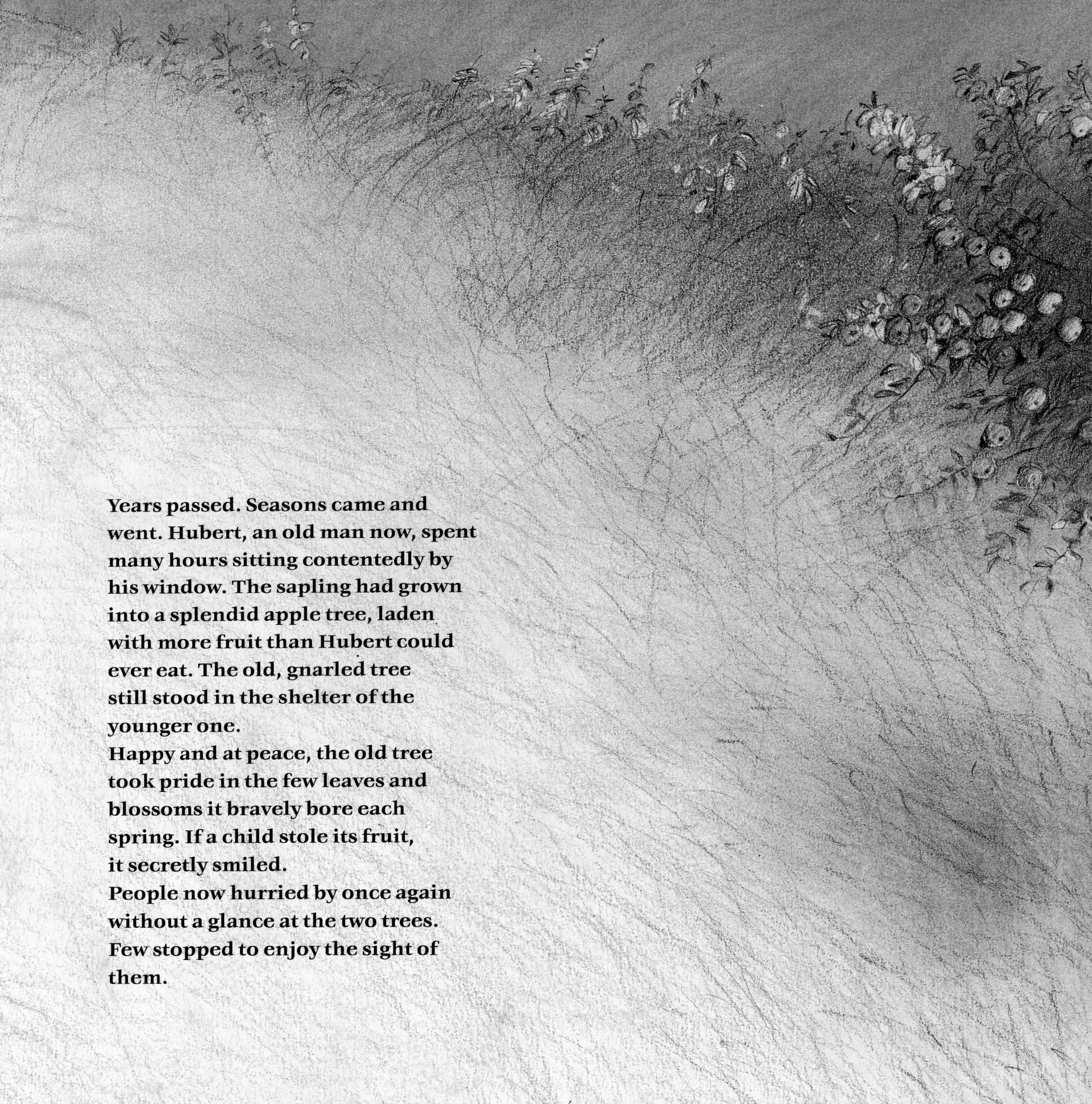

Years passed. Seasons came and went. Hubert, an old man now, spent many hours sitting contentedly by his window. The sapling had grown into a splendid apple tree, laden with more fruit than Hubert could ever eat. The old, gnarled tree still stood in the shelter of the younger one.

Happy and at peace, the old tree took pride in the few leaves and blossoms it bravely bore each spring. If a child stole its fruit, it secretly smiled.

People now hurried by once again without a glance at the two trees. Few stopped to enjoy the sight of them.

One autumn evening, the tree felt a familiar hand on its furrowed bark. Old Hubert whispered something, and the tree nodded. They had both sensed it. Winter was coming. There was snow in the air. It was time to rest.

Hubert took to his bed and, as snowflakes danced outside the window, the old tree lay down too. And they both slept peacefully, dreaming of spring.

S0-BNH-262

Glossary and Pronunciation Guide

Mandarin, the official national language of China, uses a logographic, or picture-based, writing system. The following words have been transliterated into the English alphabet and are accompanied by their English pronunciations.

Bàba 爸爸 (BAH-bah) Daddy

Huashan park 华山儿童公园 (HWAH-shan) Park and playground in Shanghai

hùkǒu 户口 (HOO-koh) A complex system of household registration used in mainland China that works like a domestic passport. A hùkǒu record identifies a person as a rural or urban dweller, based on what hùkǒu her mother has, and can limit her ability to move, hold a job, purchase food, or access government services.

Lìlíng 莉玲 (LEE-leeng) A common Chinese girl's name. Translated from the Mandarin, it means "sound of white jasmine."

lychee 荔枝 (LEE-chee) Also known as a Chinese cherry. A sweet, juicy fruit that grows in bunches. To eat a lychee, peel the reddish-pink skin, then pop the white fruit into your mouth.

Māma 妈妈 (MAH-mah) Mommy

nǐ hǎo 你好 (NEE how) Hello

Qíqi 琪琪 (CHEE-chee) A Chinese girl's name. Translated from the Mandarin, it means "fine jade."

renminbi 人民币 (REN-min-bee) Official Chinese currency

Tǔbāozi 土包子 (too-BOW-zi) An insulting term sometimes used by children. Literally, it means "little dirt bun" and is similar to the American slur "country bumpkin"—someone from the country who doesn't know anything about the city.

Yéye 爷爷 (YEH yeh) Paternal grandfather

To Dad,
who taught me
to live with integrity
and compassion

Special thanks to Chris and Gloria Hsieh, Libby Chen, and Sarah Wu, who helped make sure all the details of this book are accurate

Published in the United States by Anne Schwartz Books, an imprint of Random House Children's Books, a division of Penguin Random House LLC, New York. Anne Schwartz Books and the colophon are trademarks of Penguin Random House LLC.
Visit us on the Web! rhcbooks.com
Educators and librarians, for a variety of teaching tools, visit us at RHTeachersLibrarians.com
Library of Congress Cataloging-in-Publication Data is available upon request.
ISBN 978-0-593-18192-8 (hardcover) | ISBN 978-0-593-18193-5 (lib. bdg.) | ISBN 978-0-593-18194-2 (ebook)
The text of this book is set in 13-point Amasis.
The illustrations were rendered in pencil and watercolor on watercolor paper.
Book design by Sarah Hokanson
MANUFACTURED IN SINGAPORE 10 9 8 7 6 5 4 3 2 1 First Edition
Random House Children's Books supports the First Amendment
and celebrates the right to read.

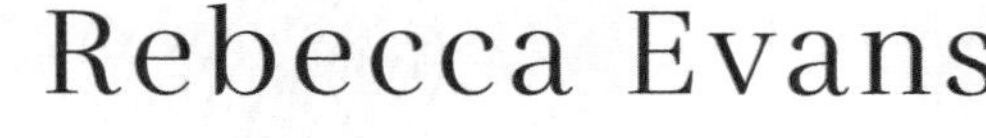

a·s·b
anne schwartz books

I used to go to school in the mountains of China, where I was born, but since we moved, my desk there is empty. My parents can't afford to pay for school here in the crowded city.

Most days I go to work with Māma, but little girls don't belong in the sewing factory. "Be quiet. No wiggling," they say.

Sometimes Bàba takes me to work. But the can factory isn't a place for little girls, either. "No running," they say.

One day I go shopping with Māma. She holds my hand tight because little girls don't belong at the busy market. There are so many people. Baskets bursting with hot peppers. Pools of fish, turtles, scorpions, and frogs. Piles of steaming dumplings. Puppies bark-bark-barking at bright birds in cages . . .

and a girl in a yellow coat, who smiles at me.

Māma pulls me away before I can smile back. "Hurry, Lìlíng," she says. "We have lots to do."

I look for the smiling girl everywhere—behind the spices that make my eyes water,

by the barrels of sweet lychees . . .

under the tables of rainbow fabric.

She's gone.

That evening, Bàba takes me to Huashan park when he gets home from work. “Little girls always belong at the park,” he says.

“Nǐ hǎo.” I smile at the children, but they laugh at my old red coat and dirty shoes.

“Tǔbāozi!” they call me. Little dirt bun.

I climb under the slide and pretend I'm a dragon with diamond scales. Dragons don't need new friends.

Back at our tiny apartment, I stand on the balcony and watch the big busy city. Down between the tall buildings, thousands of teeny-tiny cars and bicycles zip around and around, on the streets, all full of people, people, and more people.

Something flashes below—sunshine yellow.

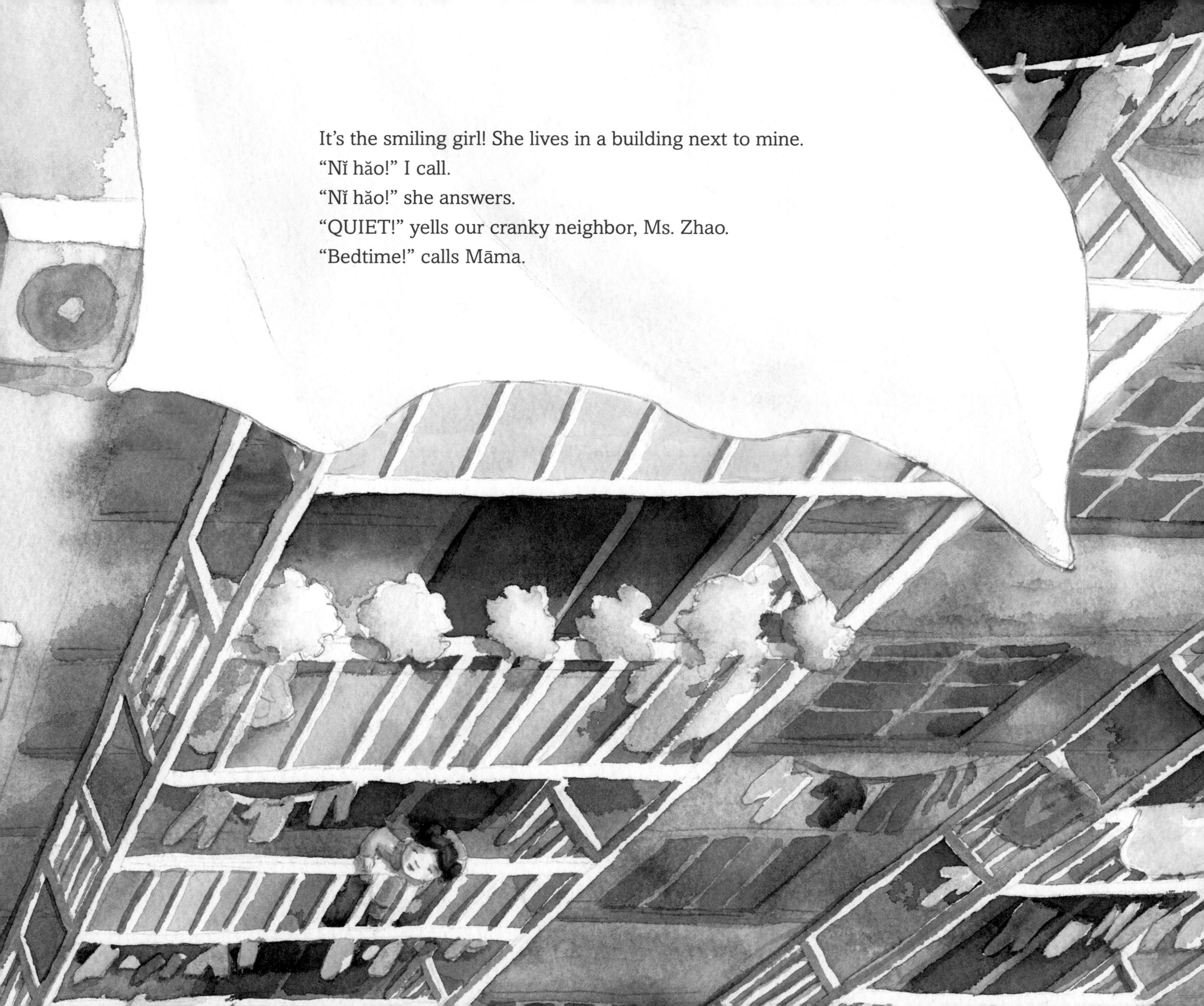

It’s the smiling girl! She lives in a building next to mine.
“Nǐ hǎo!” I call.
“Nǐ hǎo!” she answers.
“QUIET!” yells our cranky neighbor, Ms. Zhao.
“Bedtime!” calls Māma.

The next day, I wait forever while the sewing machines clickety-clickety-click. Finally, it's time to go home.

I run to our balcony. The girl is on her balcony, too. She smiles up at me.

"What's your name?" I shout.

"NO YELLING!" hollers Ms. Zhao.

Now, every night, just before bed, the girl and I smile at each other from our balconies.

I look for the girl when Māma takes me to the market, but she's not there.

I beg Bàba to take me to the park. The girl is not there, either. The kids throw sand at me. “Go back to your farm, Tǔbāozi.”

I'm quiet as Bàba and I walk home.

I climb back into my hiding hole under the slide and pretend it's my secret dragon cave. Even dragons need a place to cry sometimes.

Quiet as we eat dinner. Quiet as I climb into bed. If the smiling girl had been at the park, would she have played with me?

And then I have a big idea!

The next morning, I draw a picture of my old home and friends in the mountains. I write, **Nǐ hǎo, I am Lìlíng.**

I stick my note in a can and tie a string around the outside. That night, I lower it over the balcony into the girl's hands.

The next day, I write a new note. **Your yellow coat is pretty. It makes you look like a little yellow ricebird. From your friend Lìlíng.**

I lower the can again, and when I pull it back up, there's a new paper inside with a drawing.

I am Qíqi. I used to live on a mountain, too. It was covered in giant snowflakes, it says.

Qíqi and I start writing every day. In the morning, she goes with her yéye to help clean sidewalks. Qíqi thinks it's funny that I call her a yellow bird. She calls me a red ginger flower.

One day, Qíqi writes a special letter that makes me happy.

Dear best friend,

Tomorrow Yéye can take us both to the park. Can you come?

Little Bird Qíqi

I run to ask Bàba so I can write back right away!

Dear Little Bird Qíqi,

Bàba says I can come! But what if the other kids are mean?

Red Flower

Dear Red Flower,

We can be fierce tigers and CHOMP their mean words.

Little Bird Qíqi

Dear Little Bird Qíqi,

We can be mighty dragons roaring over the clouds. Not afraid of anything!

Red Dragon Flower

Today, I take a deep breath and squeeze Qíqi's hand tight at the entrance to Huashan park.

"Remember, we are dragons!" Qíqi whispers.

"Or tigers," I growl.

And we are brave, together.

Author's Note

In 2014, when first I visited Hangzhou and Guangzhou, China, I was captivated by what I saw and experienced—temples built thousands of years before my country even existed, teeming outdoor markets, bicycles that greatly outnumbered cars, and people who actively sought to speak with us. I especially loved the hidden alleyways alive with activity and filled with the rhythm of bike wheels against the pavement. One day, back at home, I painted a picture of an image that had stuck with me from our trip—a little girl perched on a bicycle seat, riding among a sea of other bicycles. I could remember her sad face vividly, because we had not seen many children during the day in the cities. I wondered why. I began to ask questions and do research, to try to understand China better. That's when I heard about the hùkǒu system.

In China, when a child is born, the government gives her papers called hùkǒu, which she keeps for her whole life. The papers state that the only place she can legally have access to free public school, get a job with benefits, or buy a house is in the town where her papers were issued. Because public services in the cities are superior, those with urban hùkǒu papers attend better schools and receive better health care than those holding rural hùkǒu papers. When someone moves, it is possible to get new hùkǒu papers, but it is hard; there are many rules, and each city has different laws.

As China's economy grows stronger, the wealth gap between rural and urban Chinese is narrowing, and more people from the country are able to afford to move to the city. The hùkǒu system is changing as well; it is less restrictive than it was in the past. However, there are still many people who don't meet the requirements or don't have the money to get a new hùkǒu, making it difficult for families to relocate. If children come to the city without new hùkǒu papers—like Lìlíng in this fictional story—they must pay expensive fees to attend public school and may be discriminated against because they are considered second-class citizens. Because of this, most parents who move to the city are unable to bring their children with them. They make the hard choice to leave their children behind in the country with grandparents or neighbors.

When I learned about how difficult the hùkǒu system can make life for poor families, I wanted to share this with others. I know I have much to learn, but I believe the more people strive to understand and respect one another, the more we can work together to make the world a better place.

I also wanted to share a universal story about loneliness and hope. Everyone feels lonely sometimes, but you never know when a new friend might walk into your life and change it forever.

Resources

- abc.net.au/news/2016-09-06/millions-of-chinas-children-left-behind/7816010
- china-briefing.com/news/china-hukou-system-shanghai-benefits-eligibility-application-process
- cnn.com/2014/02/04/world/asia/china-children-left-behind/index.html
- pbs.org/newshour/show/millions-of-chinese-children-fend-for-themselves-when-parents-must-follow-work-far-away
- studio-anrikevisser.com/child-friendly-factory-spaces-in-china
- thoughtco.com/chinas-hukou-system-1434424

ARTISAN FARMING

Lessons, Lore, and Recipes

Richard Harris with Lisa Fox • Photographs by Trent Edwards

Gibbs Smith, Publisher
TO ENRICH AND INSPIRE HUMANKIND
Salt Lake City | Charleston | Santa Fe | Santa Barbara

First Edition

12 11 10 09 08   5 4 3 2 1

Published by
Gibbs Smith, Publisher
P.O. Box 667
Layton, Utah 84041

Orders: 1.800.835.4993
www.gibbs-smith.com

Designed by m:GraphicDesign / Maralee Oleson
Printed and bound in China

Library of Congress Cataloging-in-Publication Data

Harris, Richard, 1947–
Artisan farming : lessons, lore, and recipes / Richard Harris with Lisa Fox ;
photographs by Trent Edwards. — 1st ed.
p. cm.
ISBN-13: 978-1-4236-0133-3
ISBN-10: 1-4236-0133-5
1. Agriculture—New Mexico. I. Fox, Lisa, 1950– II. Title.

S451.N554H37 2007
630.9789—dc22

2007017326

ACKNOWLEDGMENTS

First of all, very special thanks to Ellen Kleiner of Blessingway Authors' Services, a world-class editor without whose enthusiasm and continuing encouragement this book would never have seen the light of day.

Thanks to all the wonderful folks at Gibbs Smith, Publisher, especially to Leslie Cutler Stitt for her thoughtful editing and her patience, which I know we tried sorely—and, of course, to Gibbs Smith himself, a true visionary.

Thanks to those who have provided insights and inspiration during the writing of this book: Emigdio Ballon of Tesuque Pueblo; Jo Ann Baumgarther of Wild Farm Alliance; Eric Biderman (Ribera); Teague and Kozma Channing of Gemini Farm (Truchas); Nancy Nathanya Coonridge of Coonridge Organic Goat Cheese (Pie Town); Les Crowder of Sparrowhawk Farm (Socorro); Tom Delehanty of Pollo Real (Socorro); Lana and Monte Fastnacht of La Mont's Wild West Buffalo (Bosque Farms); Doug Findley of Heidi's Raspberry Farm (Corrales); Charles Gore of the New Mexico Agricultural Statistics Service; Rick Kingsbury of Pecos Grass-Fed Beef (Ribera); Willem Malten of Cloud Cliff Bakery (Santa Fe); Antonio Manzaneres of Shepherd's Lamb (Los Ojos); Becky Mullane of Dixon Apples (Cochiti Lake); Joanie Quinn, Marketing and Education Coordinator for the New Mexico Organic Commodity Commission; Matt Romero of Romero Farms (Dixon); Danny and Joey Sam of the Picuris Buffalo Project (Picuris Pueblo); Monte Skarsgard of Los Poblanos Organics (Los Poblanos Historic Inn & Cultural Center, Los Ranchos de Albuquerque); Gordon Tooley of Tooley's Trees (Truchas); Dr. Ron Walser, New Mexico State University Extension Fruit Specialist; and to the New Mexico Farm and Ranch Museum and the pueblos of Santo Domingo, Taos, San Ildefonso, Tesuque, and Picuris.

Thanks also to all those who have granted Lisa interviews for *Farming Through the Seasons,* including Estevan Arellano, Carl Berghofer, Daniel Carmona, Michael Combs, Stanley Crawford, Richard Deertrack, David Fresquez, Brenda Fresquez, Gonzalo Gallegos, Miley Gonzalez, Aaron Greenwald, Funny Hendrie, Bob Maldonado, Fred Martinez, Gail Minton, Randy Murray, Patty Nelson, Lynda Prym, Emily Romero, Miguel Santistevan, Lan and Charlotte Slater, and Eduardo Velarde.

I also want to express my appreciation to Remington, my cattle dog, who traveled thousands of miles around New Mexico with me on research trips for this book, played in all the orchards and barnyards, chased the goats and bison, and peed on fence posts from Costilla to Las Cruces.

And finally, a great big burst of thanks to Cultural Energy, the Taos-based nonprofit group creating media voices for youth, arts, and activism. They present Lisa's radio show *Farming Through the Seasons*, for which many of the people in this book were originally interviewed.

May they all live long and prosper.

CONTENTS

INTRODUCTION

UNDER THE SUN

Artisan: "One who produces something (as cheese or wine) in limited quantities, often using traditional methods."

Merriam Webster's 11th Collegiate Dictionary

Beautiful things spring up in the most unlikely places. It used to be that you could recognize organic small-farm produce by the wormholes. As Joni Mitchell sang back in the day, "Give me spots on my apples but leave me the birds and the bees—please!" ("Big Yellow Taxi"). But that's no longer the case. One factor that helps today's small growers make a living where past generations of farmers could not is that their produce is a sensory feast. It not only tastes better but looks better than the stuff you find in supermarkets. The artisan produce that's available in farmers markets today, dazzling in its array of greens, whites, oranges, reds, yellows and occasional blues, tantalizes the eye as much as the taste buds. A fresh-picked tomato, shallot, or crookneck squash, or even a lowly turnip, can be an aesthetic wonder when grown with love.

This book got started at the other end of the food chain—the messy part. I drove down to Albuquerque for the annual New Mexico Organic Farming Conference. Held shortly before the start of the spring planting season, the conference drew hundreds of farmers—Anglo, Hispanic, and American Indian, of all ages from student interns to octogenarians—who had obtained organic certifications for their farms or were interested in doing so. The lineup of some forty presenters ranged from New Mexico Secretary of Agriculture Miley Gonzales to Emigdio Ballon, the Incan elder from Bolivia who had been recruited to revitalize agriculture at Tesuque Pueblo. There was also a trade expo where vendors were selling live earthworms by the pound, natural concoctions for controlling grasshoppers and other pests, jugs of compost tea (which you use to fertilize soil but wouldn't want to drink), and actual dirt, a rarer commodity than you might think in New Mexico.

Inspired by watching our local farmers market in Santa Fe grow over the years from a handful of hippies selling carrots and variously colored eggs into a busy community gathering place that draws as many as 5,000 people during peak season, I went to the Organic Farming Conference with an eye toward writing about where the food at the market came from. The conference opened my eyes to the unexpectedly large number of organic farmers in New Mexico. I would later learn that the state has far more organic farms than surrounding southwestern states. In fact, the New Mexico Organic Commodities Commission provides inspectors to certify farms in more populous neighboring states, like Arizona, which has no such agency of its own.

Why, I wondered, would small farmers, organic or otherwise, choose to struggle with the exceptional challenges of growing crops or raising livestock in New Mexico, of all places, where the landscape is mostly a boundless landscape of clay and sandstone with absurdly little water? In the months that followed, I would pose

above: Emigdio Ballon at Tesuque Pueblo

this question to farmers who had moved here from much more fertile places like Virginia, Wisconsin, and California. Their answers revealed what makes New Mexico farming unique.

New Mexico has been spared from the ravages of big agribusiness by the fact that most farms here are tiny—sometimes as small as two to five acres, rarely larger than fifty. There is neither enough flat ground nor enough irrigation water to plant larger acreages. Furthermore, most farms along the 450 miles of the Río Grande—the state's only major river—date back to seventeenth-century Spanish land grants that had been split up between heirs over many generations until, in the mid-twentieth century, a new generation of the old families left the old Spanish-speaking villages to seek better-paying urban jobs. It would be impossible for a large corporation to buy up enough contiguous small farms to put together a section of land suitable for farming with big modern machinery. By the same token, it was fairly easy for young, idealistic, educated aspiring farmers to find parcels of land small enough to be worked independently.

The absence of large-scale farming means that most New Mexico farmland has remained unpolluted by the pesticides and herbicides that have ruined the groundwater and exterminated honeybees and other beneficial (and essential) wildlife in other states where farming is a big industry. It has also kept New Mexico farms safe from the kind of "pollination pollution" that has put small organic farmers out of business in many states where their produce has been unintentionally crossbred with genetically altered, often sterile crops. It has also prevented the standardization of produce into a few strains. With literally hundreds of varieties of beans, apples, and so on, New Mexico would be far better able to survive a pandemic crop blight than any of our nation's "breadbasket" states.

No large-scale farming also means an absence of lobbyists in the halls of the state legislature to advocate for burdensome agricultural regulations like the ones that force small operators elsewhere to do business only with industrial food processors, distributors, and other middlemen who take the profits out of farmers' pockets.

Traveling several thousand miles around New Mexico in pursuit of the story in this book, I discovered that the preservation of small farming makes the state a microcosmic open-air laboratory for techniques that can help shape the future of humankind. Organic foods are only part of the story. After all, today the supermarket demand for premium-priced organic produce has given rise to vast organic farms in other parts of the country whose operations have many of the same ills—exploitation of migrant workers, for example—as conventional agribusiness. In fact, I would learn while researching this book that some small farmers, while continuing to farm organically, have eschewed the "organic" label entirely, finding that the marketing advantage is not worth the reams of government paperwork. Instead, the key words today are "sustainable" farming and "local" food.

Sustainability is a broad philosophy that touches many aspects of life, such as bringing your own canvas bag to the farmers market so as not to create a demand for plastic. Eating locally grown food is sustainable because it means less fossil fuel is used to transport goods for your consumption. Most supermarket food across the country or even around the world requires unimaginable amounts of energy, which can be saved by eating food grown by local farmers who sell it at farmers markets. As the world's population grows and the supply of oil dwindles, eating local food gains importance. As the standard of living rises in places like India and China, it becomes essential that we in the United States present a different model for them than the one we followed through the twentieth century. If we fail to do so, the lack of sustainability could soon bring humankind to the brink of extinction. Developing a different way of getting food from farm to table is one aspect of that challenge, and, when you consider the importance of food to every person on the planet, an essential one.

But losing our sources of fossil fuels is not the only specter facing the world in the next few decades. Even more threatening is the possibility—or, some experts say, inevitability—that we will run out of fresh water. Again, New Mexico is a proving ground for a different method of water use in agriculture. This method returns the water used for irrigation to the same aquifer where it would naturally flow. Unlike the present laws in the United States and most other countries, it does not try to apportion water as a property right (whether the water actually exists or not) but instead depends on sharing whatever water is available. Known as the *acequia*, it was developed in the arid deserts of North Africa and brought here by the Spanish conquistadors, who were surprised to discover that the local Indians did the same thing. This method is used only in New Mexico.

Our Spanish and Indian heritage also makes New Mexico foods and agriculture unique. Traditions that continue on small farms today date back to the arrival of the first Spanish colonists, nearly a generation before the *Mayflower* landed on the far side of the continent. Before that, the ancient Pueblo Indians had been growing crops

above: a seed spreader, San Ildefonso Pueblo

and living in permanent towns for millennia. The knowledge of farming came up from Mexico very early and did not spread to the Indians of what is now the northern and eastern United States until thousands of years later. And the farming ways of the Spanish and Indians lived on, unknown to settlers in other parts of America, isolated by distance and by Spanish law, which prohibited Anglos from even entering New Mexico until rather recently. That's why you find exotic foods like green chile and blue corn in New Mexico and nowhere else in the United States.

A few people pooh-pooh the trend toward eating local on the basis that it would limit our choice of foods to pre-twentieth-century subsistence levels. In some cases that might be true if we were to eat *only* food grown close to home, but we're a long way from that. We can do our bit to save the earth even if we allow ourselves dispensations for lobsters from Maine or mangos from Mexico. Yet it's surprising to find how many fruits, vegetables, herbs, and spices can be grown in our own neighborhoods, once we rid ourselves of the limited choices production-line agriculture has imposed on us. Farmers markets place a premium on growing novel and unusual crops. It takes a lot less energy to transport seeds around the world than fruits, vegetables, and livestock. Dragon beans, Russian finger potatoes, Egyptian onions, and French shallots simply earn more money for growers than their plain-Jane supermarket counterparts would.

The catch, of course, is that you have to know how to cook well with them. Toward that end, we decided early on that it was important to include a good supply of recipes in this book, introducing ancient Indian foods and traditional Norteño (northern New Mexican) dishes as well as some new gourmet foods to try, and some ways of cooking vegetables that many people aren't familiar with. I contributed a few of my own favorites since, although I'm not a farmer, I do fancy myself to be a gourmet chef. Lisa, too, has an impressive collection of recipes and knows how to use them. And a couple of chefs from Santa Fe restaurants who participate in the farmers market's Shop with the Chef program volunteered theirs.

What we really wanted, though, was recipes from the farmers themselves. We did manage to gather some, but our biggest discovery was that most farmers don't use recipes. That makes sense, when you think about it, because they're used to working with ingredients that change from week to week—as you will be, too, if you do a significant part of your food shopping at the farmers market. Ask most market vendors what their favorite recipe for summer squash is, and you'll get an answer like, "Well, I like to scoop out the seeds and wrap it in foil and put it on the grill for a while, or sometimes I chop it up and stir-fry it in olive oil and maybe put in a little buffalo sausage if I have some, or maybe I'll put it in the blender with some red chile and maybe some cilantro and make soup. . . ." If you come back another week and ask what to do with a bulb of fennel, you're likely to get exactly the same answer. So why not join them in going beyond traditional cookery into the creative realm where recipes don't matter, the keys are fresh ingredients, and creativity and simplicity are the secrets?

The more I learned about small farming in New Mexico, the more the subject unfolded like the petals of a rose, reaching far beyond farmers markets. Before long, it became clear that I needed help from someone who not only knew much more about New Mexico farming than I could learn in a year but also had the confidence of traditional farmers in remote villages where outsiders are looked at with distrust and met with stony silence.

In the nick of time, I met Lisa Fox. Lisa and her significant other, Pete, live in a hand-built hobbit house in the wild foothills north of Questa. Her business, Southwest Chutney, takes her around to many small farms and orchards in the northern New Mexico mountains to gather ingredients, giving her the rare opportunity to make friends with many traditional growers there. She sells her products at farmers' markets in Taos, Santa Fe, Los Alamos, and Dixon. In the world of small farming, she knows . . . well . . . everybody.

Since 2004, she has also hosted a radio talk show called *Farming Through the Seasons,* which is syndicated to public radio stations by Cultural Energy in Taos. Current shows can be heard on KRZA 88.7 FM (Taos), KLDK 96.5 FM (Dixon), and KUNM 89.9 FM (Albuquerque). Past programming is archived on the Web site at www.culturalenergy.org. Some of the material in this book comes from interview tapes originally made for her radio show.

Lisa says:

Living in this high desert valley, seemingly on top of the world, I've had a wonderful opportunity to get to know some of the special people who live and farm in its nooks and crannies. Tucked high in the mountains or hidden deep in the canyons or out in the vast openness, each farm I visited faces unique challenges that this diversity poses.

I did not grow up on a farm, but my mother had quite a green thumb. We always had planting projects going on. We had doors lined with black construction paper. Beans hung between the dampened paper and glass so you could watch as they sprouted. Magically, the roots would emerge, the bean would crack open and send its tiny shoots upward toward the light. Way back then we had a small front yard, carefully planted so we could know the joys of pulling a carrot out of the ground. There was a huge honey locust tree, my best friend and confidant. I spent hours circling its magnificent trunk, my hands brushing alongside it.

Through visiting farms and interviewing farmers, I have found a chance to reconnect with that little girl who was fascinated with nature and her mysteries. I have likewise found that the farmers I visited are blessed through their work. They share that sense of wonderment.

The challenges and inspirations that farmers face daily are enormous. It requires mindfulness, openness and constant attention. I am in awe of the dedication that farming requires. As Colin Henderson of El Sagrado Farm told me, "One listens to Mother Earth, she responds open-heartedly and, working with her, we show our gratitude by being of service."

The process of improving soil through cover crops, mulching and consciously composting our kitchen waste allows Mother Earth to breathe through soil that is alive. It takes an enormous amount of energy to sustain us all. We take so much—and take so much for granted.

And so Lisa, photographer Trent Edwards, and I offer this, our book of discoveries from the hidden corners of New Mexico, exploring the distant past and possible future of the foods we eat. ❁

above: a cultivator

SEEDS

In New Mexico, corn comes first. From the monumental Indian pueblos of ancient times to the blue corn enchiladas served at popular Santa Fe tourist restaurants, all find their beginnings in a handful of corn kernels that arrived in New Mexico in some wandering trader's pack around the same time that, on the other side of the world, Moses was leading his people out of Egypt.

At Santo Domingo Pueblo, between Santa Fe and Albuquerque, each year on August 4—the feast day of the pueblo's patron saint—more than two thousand people come together to take part in the corn dance. A huge drum carved from the trunk of an old cottonwood tree rolls through the streets of the village, and singers chant hauntingly in Keres, the local language. People of the pueblo and their invited guests crowd the rooftops of the adobe houses until the roof beams creak. The feast day carnival rides on the outskirts of town grind to a halt. An eager hush falls over the spectators, Indians and non-Indian visitors alike. Heavy-built "clowns" wearing nothing but breechcloths and stripes of black-and-white body paint circulate through the crowd of onlookers, disciplining the unruly with smacks of their sticks and confiscating the cameras of tourists unwise enough to try sneaking past the pueblo's photography ban.

Then the dancers, men and women side by side, glide through the dusty streets in measured two-beat steps. Graceful koshare "spirit" dancers and tribal elders lead the files, as younger men and women follow, down to the smallest children at the end. The men, bare to the waist, wear turquoise and shell jewelry, fox pelts, and aprons embroidered with rain cloud and corn symbols. They carry rattles, and strings of smaller rattles are wrapped around their ankles. The women wear plain black dresses with the left shoulder bare and turquoise-painted headdresses with white feathers, and each carries evergreen sprigs. The dancers wind through the streets all afternoon, with intermittent breaks, and slowly, imperceptibly, the energy level rises until the dance becomes an outpouring of pure emotion.

This is the largest of the corn dances held at most New Mexican Indian pueblos during the summer. It is not staged for tourists, nor is it a contest dance like those at powwows. Instead, it is a prayer. Some observers in earlier times labeled dances like this as "rain dances," believing their purpose was to entreat the gods for rainfall to water their crops. But in fact, in the first week in August—the middle of New Mexico's brief monsoon season—it's a rare day when thunderstorms don't come anyway. The purpose of corn dances is more subtle: to bring the people of the pueblo into harmony with the corn, which will ensure not only a bountiful crop but also physical and spiritual health among the people who eat it. (In winter, animal dances serve the same purpose, bringing the people into harmony with the wild game that once supplemented their food supply.)

The irony of the corn dance is that, like most pueblos, Santo Domingo actually grows very little corn or any other crop, except a few fields of alfalfa for animal feed. The minute quantities of blue corn that are planted are for use during the corn dance or other religious ceremonies, or for cooking special meals for the feast day. At other times of the year, the people buy blue corn preground and packaged in the supermarkets, just as most other New Mexicans do. Yet corn is so inextricably woven into the Pueblo people's history for the past four thousand years that the corn dance has become a celebration of pure spirit, not food. It is an acknowledgment by the tribe as a whole that corn is their origin, their sacrament, to be kept alive even though their agricultural way of life has largely been lost.

In the annals of agriculture, New Mexico is unique. Corn—and the whole concept of planting seeds and harvesting crops—came here thousands of years before it spread to other regions of what is now the United States. It spurred the building of ancient "cities" unlike anything found in other northern regions. And even today, the magic of blue corn survives, as you'll see later in this chapter when you meet some New Mexicans who have been inspired by corn to return to the land as a new, intercultural generation of small farmers, seed-savers, and seed-swappers.

Because of blue corn and other seeds, New Mexico continues to play a unique and vital role in American agriculture. Most of the state is unsuitable for big agribusiness operations. There just aren't acreages large enough to cultivate huge quantities of crops using heavy machinery and toxic chemicals. Small farms—often only a few acres—still dominate the agricultural scene.

And that's more important than ever today. Since 1990, major agricultural regions such as the Midwest and California's Central Valley, already poisoned by insecticides until the water is undrinkable, have been taken over by homogenous, genetically modified crops. Corn has been in the forefront of this movement, too.

Not only is most corn grown today of a few homogenous strains, but it has also been altered by gene-splicing from other animal and plant organisms to grow despite the application of Agent Orange–like herbicides called glucophosphates that kill every other plant in sight—including the neighbors' heirloom varieties. Worse yet, some of these "Frankenstein" crops are planted with terminator seeds, from which future generations of seeds will never germinate. Genetically engineered terminator corn can pollinate other strains of organic, rare, or heirloom corn up to five miles away, ending the possibility of seed-saving forever. This places farmers who plant large acreages of corn in a state of serflike dependency on big chemical companies that own patents on the genetically altered seeds, since they must buy new seed each year along with the herbicide that helps it grow at the expense of all other living plants in the area.

Thanks to the absence of large-scale commercial agribusiness, many areas of New Mexico remain essentially GMO-free zones (GMO means "genetically modified organism"). Here, small farmers continue to grow multiple crops in the same fields in the traditional manner used by Indians and Spanish colonists for centuries. Free from outside contamination by GMOs, these farmers can not only perpetuate the thousands of local seed variations that assure crop diversity for future generations but also develop new adaptations of seeds traded from almost every other nation on earth.

The genetically modified seed issues began with corn, though they have spread within a remarkably few years to encompass many other patented crops sold in supermarkets without identifying labels. Looking at corn not only in a historical context but also from the viewpoint of small farmers and others who grow it today, we can discover the epic story of all traditional farm crops and the drama inherent in preserving them today.

A BRIEF HISTORY OF CORN

5000 BC—Prehistoric people living on the savannahs of southern Mexico and Guatemala first developed corn from a grasslike wild grain using seed selection. Almost nothing is known of the people who first cultivated corn. They lived thousands of years before the Olmec, the first Mesoamerican Indians to leave archaeological traces of their civilization.

2000 BC—Knowledge of corn reached what is now New Mexico and Arizona. Anthropologists recently established this date, which is older than previously thought, by carbon-dating corn kernels found in a cave in the Gila Mountains of southwestern New Mexico. The prevailing theory is that corn was carried from Mexico by traders, who may have used it as currency or a medium of exchange. Some scientists believe the Indians of that era moved northward from central Mexico and brought corn with them.

The identity of New Mexico's first farmers is also lost in time. Archaeologists do not know what language they spoke or whether they were related to earlier groups of hunters and gatherers, such as Clovis Man (circa 8200 BC), Folsom Man (8900–8200 BC), and Sandia Man (10000–8000 BC), who lived in New Mexico much earlier, when it was a lush climate zone teeming with exotic animals such as mammoths, camels, and giant turtles at the southern extent of the glaciers of the last ice age.

The first corn growers in New Mexico apparently planted kernels in the floodplains where mountain creeks spilled into small fertile valleys, moistening the earth beneath the surface enough for the corn plants to thrive on their own.

They may have taken the first steps toward abandoning a nomadic way of life by setting up semipermanent camps in these areas to protect the corn from birds and animals.

1500 BC–AD 250—During the "preclassic" archaeological era in Mexico, the Olmec and early Maya people developed corn that grew much larger ears and more kernels. The new breed of corn, however, depended on humans to cultivate it in rows and could not pollinate in the wild. This required permanent human settlements and generated food surpluses that freed many people from the need to hunt, gather, and farm full-time, allowing opportunities to develop such hallmarks of civilization as art, architecture, astronomy, and mathematics.

AD 250–900—In Mexico's "classic" period, Mayans and other groups built large cities centered around plazas, stone pyramids, temples, and palaces, and surrounded by communal fields where corn, beans, and squash grew together. They developed community cisterns and irrigation systems to sustain their crops through the long, dry tropical winters.

Meanwhile, in New Mexico, new irrigation methods such as rainwater runoff ditches and small dammed reservoirs enabled permanent communities to form. The typical residential group consisted of about twelve families living in pit houses—the optimum number of people needed to grow and process corn with the technology of the time. Agricultural settlements began in the Mimbres and Mogollon regions of southern New Mexico and spread northward to the Four Corners region.

Creation mythologies, which show striking similarities in Central America, Mexico, and the American Southwest, probably came to New Mexico along with agriculture. Central to these myths is the belief that the first human beings were made from corn. Even today, many traditional Indians live almost exclusively on corn and recognize its spiritual, as well as dietary, importance.

AD 850–1150—Known as the "late classic" or "early postclassic" period, this time of rapid transition saw the decline of the Mayan world and the rise of other advanced agricultural civilizations in Mexico—especially the Toltecs (an Aztec word meaning "ancient ones"), who established a trade empire extending from the Yucatán to New Mexico.

Many artifacts found in New Mexico, such as macaw feathers from Central America and copper bells from South America, show that Toltecs traded with the people in the north, as do finds in Mexico of turquoise from the ancient mines around Cerrillos, New Mexico. Toltec traders may have brought the new, improved strains of domestic corn to New Mexico.

Thanks to advances in corn technology, agricultural communities grew suddenly, within a few generations, from ranchos of a dozen or so pit houses into palatial cliff dwellings such as the ones at Mesa Verde National Park and

above: corn doll

even larger pueblos with hundreds of residential units, broad plazas, and cathedral-like great kivas for religious ceremonies. This new civilization—known by the archaeological term *Hisatsinom,* the Navajo word *Anasazi* ("enemies of our ancestors"), the more politically correct term *Ancestral Puebloans,* or the common Pueblo Indian name *Ancient Ones*—culminated in the building of the Chaco Canyon site, where numerous pueblos, built close together and occupied at the same time, included Pueblo Bonito, the largest multifamily residential building ever constructed in the world before the twentieth century. Parts of the Four Corners region supported larger populations in AD 1000 than they do today.

Around AD 1000, corn also began to spread eastward from New Mexico to tribes beyond the Mississippi River for the first time.

AD 1150–1600—About 850 years ago, the center of ancient Pueblo civilization at Chaco Canyon, New Mexico, was abandoned. Nobody knows why. Theories include crop failure due to drought, disease, or soil depletion, as well as other possible disasters such as war, overpopulation, religious fragmentation, or invasion by nomadic tribes. In the same time frame, the decline of the Toltec civilization may have put an end to trade between New Mexico and the great Mexican civilizations. Other pueblos in the Four Corners region were also abandoned, leading up to the depopulation of Mesa Verde a century later.

While the exact migration patterns are unknown, it is clear that the majority of the Pueblo people resettled in the Rio Grande Valley of north central New Mexico, where they established smaller villages that often mixed walled pueblos with cliff dwelling complexes, sustained by communal fields of corn grown alongside beans and squash. The migration of the Pueblo people coincided with the development of more sophisticated irrigation techniques like river water diversions (similar to the Spanish acequia systems described in chapter two) and waffle-style walled cornfields that used mulch to retain moisture. Parts of the region, such as the Pajarito Plateau around Bandelier National Monument and Los Alamos, had larger populations by AD 1500 than they do today.

As self-defense became less vital, the largest Pueblo groups moved down from the canyons and plateaus to more fertile cropland fronting on the Rio Grande, where they were living when the first Spanish explorers arrived. Conquistador Francisco Vásquez de Coronado, who led the first officially sanctioned expedition into New Mexico in 1540, described how the Pueblo people of western New Mexico drew magical lines of cornmeal around their buildings to fend off the Spaniards who had armor, horses, and steel swords. Most of the corn grown in New Mexico was blue corn, unlike the yellow and white corn Coronado was familiar with in Mexico, although archaeologists have found that the ancient Pueblo people grew other colors in earlier times.

The conquistadors discovered some puzzling facts about the seed trade between Mexico and New Mexico that have never been fully explained. Although local Indian farmers had been growing corn, squash, and beans since ancient times, other common Mexican crops like chile and tomatoes were unknown in New Mexico until the Antonio Espejo expedition of 1582–83 brought them. Yet the same explorers found Indian farmers growing melons that the Spaniards had imported to the New World from Asia within the previous fifty years. Somehow, the native trade in melon seeds reached New Mexico before the conquistadors did.

AD 1600–1848—By most accounts, the members of the Spanish ruling class who colonized New Mexico had little interest in farming. While large land grants were parceled out to Spanish military officers, the landowners relied on the thousands of Indian workers from central Mexico to do the actual growing. Franciscan priests organized baptized Indians to grow food for their missions, and the Spanish settlers at first required the people of the pueblos to tithe a portion of their crops. More than this taxation, though, it was the sporadic banning of corn dances at the pueblos that finally led to a bloody revolt in 1680, when the Pueblo people and their nomadic allies drove the Spaniards out of New Mexico.

Upon the return of the Spaniards eleven years later, many Pueblo people, fearing reprisal, moved west to live among the Athabascan nomads who had recently arrived in the Four Corners region after a long migration down the Rocky Mountains from Canada. The Puebloans brought corn with them, and it was the knowledge of corn farming that separated the Navajos (a Tewa Pueblo word meaning "cultivated fields") from the Apaches, who were of the same race but did not grow corn.

The Spanish government gradually adopted a live-and-let-live approach, respecting the tribes' autonomy for more than a century and a half. The Rio

above: ceremonial corn, Tesuque Pueblo

Grande Valley was shared peacefully by missionaries, Pueblo people, Mexican Indians, and *mestizos*, unaffiliated Indians known as *Genízaros*, and Spanish farmers whose ancestors were often Sephardic Jewish, Gypsy, and other Middle Eastern people who had converted when Spain became Catholic. They moved to remote areas of the New World to avoid the threat of the Spanish Inquisition, which tended to view these converts with suspicion and to try them for heresy on the thinnest of excuses. By the time of Mexico's independence (1821) and the Mexican War (1846–48), all of these various groups were sharing the same foods, recipes, and farming techniques, giving birth to the unique, traditional New Mexican cuisine we know today.

KEEPING TRADITION ALIVE

The Man Who Sold the Corn

"I was the first person to put blue corn on the market."

Richard DeerTrack, speaking at a recent partnership conference hosted by the Taos Economic Development Corporation and Taos Pueblo

The founder and current director of the Cross-Cultural Communication Project and of DeerTrack and Associates, a consulting firm on Indian affairs, and president of the New Mexico Environmental Law Center, tribal elder Richard Deertrack has served at the highest levels of tribal government at Taos Pueblo for over twenty years.

> *I was out in Santa Cruz, California, when my partner and I first had the idea. We were eating blue corn mush cereal in the morning, with bananas and raisins and nuts and all the goodies. I was sitting looking at that blue corn, and I looked at her, and she said, "Why not?" and I said, "Why not?"*
>
> *We bought two hundred pounds of blue corn, took it back to California, hand-roasted it, hand-ground it, and put it in crude packages. How much can you buy blue corn for now? Ninety-eight cents a pound? Maybe on sale for fifty cents a pound? It might surprise you that I got five dollars a pound when it first came on the market. The niche for selling this blue corn was that it was Native American Indian grown, from Santa Ana.*
>
> *Why am I telling you this story? Because when I talked to Joe Sandoval, the Taos Pueblo governor at the time, he said to me, "You know, son, this is the best project that could ever come to our community. We want it." The whole governor's staff agreed on it.*
>
> *I said, "Governor, do not take it to the tribal council until I am present."*
>
> *But he was so enthused about it that he took it to the tribal council anyway—and it was shot down. Somebody said, "What are we going to do, sell our tribal foods?"*
>
> *That person was not aware of the fact that when we were growing up as young children, our grandfathers used to put sacks of blue corn on horses and take it into town and sell it or barter it.*
>
> *Now see how tradition has been used to block the development of our lands, to stop the intimate connection that we as traditional people have to our lands. The intimate connection, the spiritual connection we have to the food. Our lands are lying fallow. Everything related to that blue corn is gone today.*

Richard DeerTrack's Blue Corn Trading Company lasted until 1989. After that, while Santa Ana and Ohkay Owingeh pueblos continue to grow some blue corn for commercial sale through local stores and via the Internet (www.cookingpost.com), traditional farming methods have been unable to compete with large-scale, non-Indian blue corn growers and processors such as Sunny State Products, located off Interstate 40 near the town of San Jon in eastern New Mexico.

Several New Mexico pueblos have recently started experimental agriculture programs, trying to grow everything from amaranth to llamas as well as the traditional blue corn. These programs are typically funded by nongovernmental organizations matched by proceeds from Indian casinos. One of the first such grants came to Santa Ana Pueblo from an unlikely source—the Body Shop, a socially conscious British beauty products company.

Today, saving seeds and the growing traditions that go with them are the special province of a new generation of farmers—Indian, Hispanic, and Anglo alike. For many, outside funding is not available. For all, it is a grassroots effort.

The Corn Teacher

"I first got really excited about agriculture because of maíz azul, blue corn."

Miguel Santistevan

Taos native Miguel Santistevan experiments with seed saving, water harvesting, and drought adaptation techniques, using traditional methods to grow landrace crops of northern New Mexico such as native corn, bolita beans, garbanzo beans, fava beans, amaranth, tomatoes, and garlic at his Sol Feliz Farm in Taos Canyon. Like most younger-generation farmers, he brings a strong educational background to his work. He holds a bachelor's degree in biology, cum laude, from the University of New Mexico and a master's degree from the University of California–Davis. He has been certified in permaculture design by the Traditional Native American Farmers Association, a mutual support organization headquartered at Tesuque Pueblo that draws its membership from eighteen tribes in New Mexico and Arizona.

above: cornfield, Tesuque Pueblo

I knew nothing about planting. I really didn't ever plant. I used to watch my grandfather work his little garden, but it was never part of my reality. My reality was playing drums in a punk rock band, skateboarding around Albuquerque and being a political activist, doing demonstrations.

Then I ran into these guys from the Atrisco land rights council, part of La Merced de Atrisco in Albuquerque, the main land grant there. They had a community garden in the South Valley, and I knew nothing about it, but it sounded like something interesting, and when I found myself with that blue corn in my hand and putting it in the ground, it was magical. Something inside that has a connection to maíz, and it awoke that day in May of '93. It redefined my life. I've planted every year since then, and I'll plant until I die.

Santistevan went to the University of California–Davis to study maíz. "It became the icon of my life," he says. "Everything you need to know in life, you could learn from maíz. It's a very awesome cultivar."

At UC–Davis, Santistevan worked with Dr. Steve Brush, who was studying maíz in Chiapas. Santistevan was offered a full fellowship to go along to Mexico and study the relationship between the crop diversity of maíz and language diversity in the Maya Indian region. But a family health crisis called him back to New Mexico instead. He does not regret the lost opportunity.

Sure, I could go to Chiapas and become an expert in maíz there. But then I would come back to New Mexico, where I'm going to stay because this is home, and I'd have to start all over again. So I thought I should just study what I need to study from the outset.

My professor said, "We can still work out a research plan, and I'll still be your advisor, your professor, but you have to find your own funding now." So I said okay. I applied for a grant, and they gave me eight thousand dollars. I stretched that grant money over two years, paying for my gas and all the incidental fees for doing research. Those were some of the best times of my life.

I cruised around in my truck and I just looked for cornfields for two summers, and talked to everybody I could about corn, and everybody opened their doors. I'd say, hello, my name's Miguel, I'm doing some research and I was wondering if I could ask you a few questions. Sure enough, they would invite me in. I didn't need a food budget because everybody opened their houses to me, they fed me, they gave me all this information. More than a hundred families shared information with me.

There are all the different varieties of maíz azul. *There might be blue corns from ten different villages, but all of them different soils, different angles of the sun, different growing seasons and microclimates. And then there are differences in how the farmers plant. I met farmers who don't even irrigate. I know one particular farmer who plants early and deep, and if he doesn't see his corn in about a month, then he irrigates. I found a relationship between irrigated corn and dry land corn of the past. It was the same seed grown under two completely different strategies.*

Looking back on his first awakening to the magic of maíz azul, he adds, "I still have those original seeds, and now I'm getting seeds out—especially to young people. Especially to people who belong to that tradition. I don't just give seeds to anybody, but people who care about the culture here and the land and the seeds. They need to be shared."

Toward that end, Santistevan serves as project coordinator for the New Mexico Acequia Association's Sembrando Semillas Youth Project. (*Sembrando semillas* means "sowing seeds.") "I wonder sometimes whether the kids have a similar feeling to what I experienced in Albuquerque when I first planted corn. I was older when I did that. I was already twenty-one. These kids are younger. We do not fathom the impact that satellite TV has had on our young people. They have been trained to be consumers. But nevertheless, the kids want to work the land. They don't know they do, but once you get them out there, and they see the fruits of their labor, any kid would rather take care of animals, take care of crops, than flip burgers at McDonald's."

above: Gilbert of San Ildefonso

The Archaeologist Farmer

"Our first priority must be to preserve our land and water, our way of life. How do we get this message to consumers, which is what marketing is?"

Lynda Prym

Lynda Prym, a graduate of Penn State University in ethnobotany and cultural ecology, came to New Mexico in 1977 to do field archaeological work at Fort Burgwin Research Center near Taos Pueblo. Having previously lived on a farming commune in the heart of Pennsylvania's Amish country, she brought with her an interest in traditional agriculture that has led to her involvement in many aspects of small farming in New Mexico. She served as editor and publisher of The Farm Connection, "a forum for New Mexico farmers to exchange information for an environmentally sound, economically workable, and socially just agriculture," and she is cofounder of the New Mexico Organic Farming and Gardening Expo. This interview took place while she was managing Resting on the River, an herb farm in Abiquiú owned by film star Marsha Mason, who also chairs the New Mexico Organic Commodities Commission.

I can't really separate seeds from the culture of human beings. People gathered seeds for sustenance and then learned how to cultivate and propagate them. Seeds have been with human beings since human beings walked the earth.

My mother's from Syria, and my maternal grandparents were farmers there. They raised food for their family, although they wouldn't have called themselves farmers when they immigrated, and I was raised on gardens and gardening. They brought seeds from the old country, and food was not separated from growing food. They talked to me a lot about the land.

Down the street lived some of my other relatives from Syria, who also had brought seeds from the old country and grew varieties like cousa squash [cousa means "summer squash" in Arabic] in their gardens. Growing food was tied to a lot of different aspects of life. Seeds were always drying on the porch at certain times of the year, and there were little jars full of seeds in the pantry.

Later, when I lived in Amish country, it seemed that agriculture was culture. It wasn't separated from daily life, and there were rituals, spiritual practices, routines, and daily life all put together to maintain what would sustain the family and the community—the very key to human happiness, self-reliance, self-sufficiency, all those things I think we're seeking desperately in our world right now.

I also started thinking a lot about seeds. When I went on to do fieldwork in anthropology near Taos Pueblo, it just kept coming up. I could see that the seeds were being kept for ceremonies, even though in 1977 only the older generation was still farming and gardening at all. But people would bring out these seeds from the ceiling of an abandoned house on the pueblo where seeds were kept and protected. Even if people weren't farming, seeds were being kept culturally alive with ceremonies. We still see it today, how seeds are part of ceremonies. There's really no separation. There's still an understanding of how connected people are to seeds.

I went to work at Ghost Ranch in the '80s on a genetic preservation project under the guise of a small working farm called the High Desert Research Farm. We were working with hulless barleys, dry-land wheat, a lot of beans—about five hundred different beans gathered in the Four Corners area. We grew those and shared them with other farmers. Again, it was the seeds keeping the culture alive and the culture keeping the seeds alive.

There's a lot of diversity in the Southwest that I think people are unaware of. Each tribal group had its own particular strains of chile or corn or beans. There were a lot of varieties of the bolita bean alone around northern New Mexico. Everybody didn't just eat pinto beans. Pintos were dry-land beans grown in the mountains around Albuquerque. The Dove Creek area, for instance, has an incredible diversity of legumes. Native Seed Search [www.nativeseeds.org], a great organization in the Southwest, has maintained seeds all the way from the Sierra Madre in Mexico to the Four Corners area, focusing a lot on northern New Mexico.

For many years I participated in the Seed Savers Exchange [seedsavers.org], a network that began as a group of people saving seeds for the public domain. It's now grown into an international grassroots organization with thousands of members who are keeping these seeds, doing selection the way farmers have for thousands of years to keep their genetic potential alive and maintain genetic diversity.

With more GMOs [genetically modified organisms] being introduced and more industrialized commodity-type chemical agriculture spreading globally, seeds are lost as people are disconnected from the land base where they grow them. Seeds contain the potential to be taken elsewhere and adapted as long as people can do on-farm selection. But when people are displaced from the land, they can't grow the seeds. They eventually go to work in a city or for industrialized agriculture. The seeds are lost, but what's also lost is a culture. So to me it's cultural genocide when you start separating people from their seeds and the land where they grow those seeds.

Seeds are the genetic potential for our future. If we genetically engineer all that potential, if we homogenize and narrow the gene pool, we're not just

above: horno, Taos Pueblo

losing our food base but the potential for resistance to disease and to insects. In the case of global climate change, too, we will need seeds that can adapt to natural selection.

For so many centuries, spirit and seed were not separated. Farmers selected their own seed. Only within the last forty years has agriculture begun to become industrial and those values have started to be lost. The more we narrow that gene pool, the fewer resources we'll have for adaptation in the future.

My most hopeful vision would be that more people would be drawn to farmers markets, artisanal food products, truck farming, market farming, and home gardening, because those are the places where heirloom varieties are being kept alive. We can still grow a lot of our own seeds, and that helps the farm to keep its costs down as well as keeping the seeds out there adapting to their environment and available to other farmers.

So I see a lot of hope in the small-scale agriculture movement, all the interest in food security, all the interest in artisanal foods, because that's what will keep these people growing heirloom varieties. If growers can go to farmers markets with, for instance, an heirloom tomato that's different than the heirloom tomato your neighbor's growing, it provides more diversity in the market, it's a good marketing technique, and it provides people with more awareness of the incredible flavors, textures, and qualities that are out there.

Even in fruit production this is so important. New Mexico used to have many varieties of apples, for instance. Then people started looking at getting more into commercial markets. But those varieties can't compete with other apple-growing states. Now there's a growing interest in heirloom varieties of apples, and people are showing other people how to graft. Promoting those heirloom varieties also provides a broader market. You can sell a winter keeper or a cider apple or a dessert apple. All that diversity enriches the quality of life of consumers (which all of us are), to have all those wonderful flavors.

I think small farming is a connecting point to the earth for us. We might not notice until it's gone. As far as helping farms to be more sustainable and economically viable, it does offer new hope, because it creates marketing niches and ways for people to be competitive without putting their neighbors out of business. You just have a different variety. And so that's where I like to find hope.

WHAT HAPPENED TO INDIAN CORN?

New Mexico became United States territory in 1848 as part of the treaty ending the Mexican War. The federal government praised the Pueblos as an example of tribal prosperity through their use of traditional agriculture in an attempt to persuade migratory tribes like the Utes of southwestern Colorado to settle down to a farming lifestyle. At the same time, a new wave of Anglo settlement in the Rio Grande Valley was putting the communal farmlands and water rights of the Pueblo Indians in jeopardy.

The situation was made worse in 1876, when the U.S. Supreme Court ruled against Taos Pueblo in the case of *United States v. Joseph* (94 U.S. 614, 4 Otto 614, 24 L.Ed. 295), finding that the Pueblos were not "Indian tribes" within the meaning of the federal law that protected other native people from real estate swindlers. The arrival of the railroad four years later touched off a land frenzy along the Rio Grande that threatened Indians and small Spanish farmers alike with invasion of their traditional growing lands. The decision would not be overturned until 1913, when a flurry of reversals in policy led to land and water rights disputes that have not been settled to this day.

In the 1920s and '30s, Commissioner of Indian Affairs John Collier adopted a policy of pressuring the Indian pueblos to accept modernization, including large machinery, progressive farming methods, and agricultural education programs, all of which clashed with the native people's traditional, spirit-based beliefs about farming the land. During the Great Depression, most of the Rio Grande Pueblos accepted farm reform to one extent or another.

Then came World War II. As most Pueblo men went off to serve in the U.S. Armed Forces, tribal farmlands fell into disuse. When the men returned, fewer of them were interested in resuming an agricultural lifestyle. The GI Bill presented new educational opportunities, the boom in construction and manufacturing industries held out the promise of higher-paying jobs away from the reservations, and federal relocation programs were designed to encourage assimilation of Indians into mainstream urban culture. Central to the Indian programs passed by the conservative postwar U.S. Congress was a new policy known as "termination," aimed at ending tribal dependence on the government by forcing a choice between two options: accepting government help or holding to traditional lifestyles and tribal sovereignty without outside sources of income in a world where money had become essential. All farm aid to the tribes was cut off. Indian Affairs Commissioner Collier resigned, outraged at a policy he saw as the death knell for the Indian agricultural renaissance he had hoped to start.

From 1938 to 1964, the number of acres under cultivation at most New Mexico pueblos declined by as much as 85 percent. Only Sandia and Santa Clara pueblos, both adjacent to non-Indian urban areas, expanded their agricultural output. Nine of the nineteen pueblos grew no crops at all except small corn gardens for ceremonial purposes. Among the pueblo cultures, only the reclusive Hopi people of northern Arizona still rely on corn for their subsistence.

THE HEIRLOOM SEED BANK

When a small farmer has grown a rare or heirloom crop, he or she can put aside part of the harvest as seed and keep it viable for more than a human lifetime. The farmer then takes on a key role in preserving seed diversity and defending the kind of disaster that many fear could happen if a chemical-resistant blight were to wipe out a large part of the world's crop production.

But first you have to get the heirloom seed, and that's not always easy. They don't sell it at the local feed-and-seed store.

New Mexico growers got a head start in the business of growing unusual fruits, vegetables, and herbs in 1989, when a new experimental farm called Seeds of Change got its start near Gila, New Mexico, the same area where archaeologists discovered the four thousand-year-old corn kernels considered the first known domesticated seeds in the United States. Formed by a group of passionate gardeners in a remote area where cross-pollination or other contamination from large agribusiness enterprises was highly unlikely, the company tested hundreds of varieties of open-pollinated organic seeds and offered them for sale to other organic farms in New Mexico and beyond.

Soon, exotic vegetables began to appear among the chiles, tomatoes, chicos, and apples for sale at farmers markets around the state. On any given Saturday morning you might find someone selling dragon beans, Russian finger potatoes, or bright red carrots, all grown from packets supplied by Seeds of Change.

By 1996, Seeds of Change had grown into a nationwide enterprise and the primary source of temperate-zone rare and heirloom seeds. Finding it necessary to set up a business office in Santa Fe, they relocated their experimental farm—now called Rancho La Paz—to the small, scattered farming community of El Gulque, on the west bank of the Rio Grande just north of Ohkay Owingeh Pueblo in northern New Mexico. Though less remote than Gila, the new location was surrounded by traditional farms and just as far from big operations that used pesticides, let alone genetically modified seeds. The land had previously been cultivated by Tewa Indians for at least eight hundred years.

Rancho La Paz may be the hardest small farm in New Mexico to visit. A locked gate with a white concrete wall blocks the driveway, and you can only get permission to enter by stating your business through an intercom speaker. The best chance of seeing what lies beyond the gate is one of the two days when it is opened for public tours (advance reservations required) led by field coordinator Kelle Carter in late August and early September.

Although Rancho La Paz is only six acres in size, approximately one thousand varieties of plants are grown there during the summer. Some are outdoors, in colorful fields where each row is planted with a different cultivar. Others are inside the 3,600-square-foot greenhouse and 2,000-square-foot pollen isolation tent. The water for irrigation, including misters and drip irrigation, comes from a centuries-old acequia diverted from the Rio Grande.

Only a couple of dozen people take the tours each year, though. For most small farmers, the Seeds of Change Web site and professional seed catalog are the focus of interest. It's here that they can find the latest in never-before-seen rare and heirloom niche vegetables, fruits, and herbs such as red stalk celery, Oaxacan green dent corn, Hopi pink corn, Peruvian purple potatoes, French breakfast radishes, pizza jalapeños, Canadian snow apples, monster spinach, Incan yacón, twenty-foot-tall Jack and the Beanstalk beans, cinnamon basil, licorice mint, Munstead English lavender, and fifty different varieties of heirloom tomatoes. Next year the selection will be different.

[For catalogs and information, contact Seeds of Change, P.O. Box 15700, Santa Fe, NM 87592; 888-762-7333; www.seedsofchange.com.].

above: mano and metate

SEED SWAPPING—GROW LOCALLY, TRADE GLOBALLY

Seed saving leads to seed swapping, the same kind of activity that brought corn to New Mexico in prehistoric times. Today, much seed swapping happens at local grassroots events. In Belen, for instance, the Valencia County Xeriscape Club sponsors seed swaps at the local recreation center. Participating in an organization called Organic Seed Partnership [www.plbr.cornell.edu/PSI/OSP%20home.htm], the ag school at New Mexico State University not only hosts large seed swaps but sends representatives to university swapping events as far-flung as Maine, West Virginia, and California. Tesuque Pueblo, too, recently hosted a seed swap in connection with its recent Symposium for Sustainable Food and Seed Sovereignty.

And closer to home, a guy named Yoga Bill (Bill Sudkin) often shows up at New Mexico farmers markets searching for seeds to bring back to GE-Free SLV (Genetically Engineered-Free San Luis Valley), the group he helped organize in the nearby San Luis Valley, just over the Colorado state line near the headwaters of the Rio Grande. "I'm not a scientist," Yoga Bill admits.

> *I'm not a farmer, but I eat food, and when I go to the market I want to know what I'm putting into my body. With that idea I started to research what's happening. One of the facts I found was that as late as 1900, food for the planet's hungry was provided by as many as fifteen hundred plants, each further represented by thousands of different cultivated varieties. But today over 90 percent of the world's nutrition is provided by only thirty different plants, and only four—rice, corn, soybeans, and wheat—provide 75 percent of the calories consumed by man.*

GE-Free SLV meets once a month, with e-mail communication between meetings. Some local farmers are involved, but most members are concerned citizens and gardeners, people who are seed savers who want to keep a diverse food base going. They are presently spearheading an effort to declare the New Age southern Colorado village of Crestone a GMO-free zone.

The seed swap that is most global in scope is sponsored by Slow Food International, an eighty thousand-member nonprofit "eco-gastronomic" organization, at its conferences in Italy and other parts of the world. New Mexico has an exceptionally active Slow Food chapter, thanks largely to the efforts of prominent food author Deborah Madison (*Local Flavors: Cooking and Eating from America's Farmers' Markets*), who lives in Galisteo. A sizable contingent of New Mexicans attended Slow Food's Terra Madre conference, a four-day gathering held in Torino, Italy, in 2005.

Among the attendees was David Fresquez of Monte Vista Organic Farm, which has fields near Española, New Mexico; in La Mesilla; and higher in the mountains near Peñasco:

> *I've been trying to get seeds from every corner of the world, in different books or else visiting different countries. To me it's real interesting to see what they do in France and Italy and Bolivia and Mexico and . . . there were people from 131 different countries, and they all had something to offer and their own traditions.*
>
> *I grow close to a hundred varieties of tomatoes. Each one has a different taste, and no two taste the same. There are green ones, black ones, purple ones, orange, yellow, pink, brown, some that are variegated yellow-red, and then there's one that's yellow, red, and green—partly zebra, you know, zebra is green, but they crossed this one. I have a lot of seed that I save, and it's hard to save a lot of seed when you have that many varieties.*
>
> *One time I had a tour of students at my farm, and one of them said, "That's a big tomato there!" I said, "Sure, you can have it. Pick it." Then I saw how big it was, and I said, "Maybe I should save the seed." It's always been very hardy, prolific, and reliable. I save the seeds on that one.*
>
> *And then pumpkin seeds—I save all I can get, and now I'm getting some from Australia, from Italy, France, Germany, Guatemala. And then we have our own. There's going to be fifteen varieties of pumpkins and squashes this summer.*

Recalling the Slow Foods conference in Torino, Fresquez notes some uncertain attitudes about international seed swapping.

> *What struck me funny was that I tried to get some corn seed from a vendor from Bolivia who was selling wool, but he also had corn that they were selling. I saw some kernels that had fallen on the floor from the display he had there. So I said, "Can I have some of this seed?" and he said no. He definitely didn't want me to have anything. And then in the Italy section, in another part of the* salon de gusto, *the food area, I was looking at some corn. I asked the guy if he would sell me an ear of corn, and he said no. I offered him ten euros an ear, which is more than ten dollars, and he reluctantly sold me the corn. I got two ears of corn for twenty dollars.*

Other attendees had more positive experiences. As Lynda Prym describes it:

> *I was fortunate to go to the Slow Food gathering in Torino. Globally, that event is very important because it's so tied to food security. I didn't hear all*

the speeches translated until I read them, but it was almost always referred to. From the Prince of Wales to representatives from Africa, everybody saw this as part of the crisis in agriculture.

There were plenty of seed swaps going on all over the place. We all stayed on some kind of agroturismo*—a vineyard or a farm or a food processor, and everywhere we went, people were exchanging seeds. It's a very important language in agriculture, and I think people recognize its importance, so it was a big theme.*

We were in the Piemonte region of Italy, and it wasn't unlike northern New Mexico in the scale of agriculture, but it seemed a more valued way of life. It's an older culture, and also there weren't Wal-Marts and big corporate grocery stores, so people relied more on farmers markets, and you saw more heirloom varieties. Artisanal foods didn't have to become a "movement" in Italy. They're very much a part of life there.

TRADITIONAL CORN RECIPES

For people who have tasted New Mexico-style corn only in the form of store-bought taco shells and restaurant enchiladas, here's a collection of time-honored recipes offering a taste of what *maíz* is really all about.

When Dennis Liddy bought Bode's Store, the general store in the small Spanish-Indian village of Abiquiú, back in the early 1990s, he noticed that tortillas were conspicuously missing from the refrigerated foods section, so he decided to start carrying them. "I thought I'd be selling a lot of tortillas here," he recalls, "but it turns out I don't sell any. People buy cornmeal in fifty-pound sacks and make their own." Similarly, traditional farmer Estevan Arellano of Embudo says he "won't eat tortillas from the store because they taste terrible."

Any of these recipes makes a conversation-sparking addition to a Thanksgiving Day feast. They might be equally appropriate served alongside other traditional Indian dishes like Three Sisters Stew or bison steak, to celebrate October 12, known to many New Mexico Hispanics as Día de la Raza and observed with feasts and protests by many American Indians as Native American Day. (In other parts of the country, it is known as Columbus Day.)

Indian Blue Corn Tortillas

When it comes to ingredients, this recipe couldn't be simpler. Making the tortillas takes a little more practice. I learned to make thick corn tortillas like these by hand from a Guatemalan village woman, who started with whole corn kernels and ground them into flour with a roller-shaped stone on a concrete slab (see mortar and pestle on page 12), a process that took more than an hour. Fortunately, you can buy ready-ground blue cornmeal at many New Mexico farmers markets and grocery stores, as well as over the Internet.

Makes 12 to 18 small, filling tortillas, serving 6 people

1 cup coarse-ground blue cornmeal (harina azul)
½ teaspoon salt
1¼ cups water

Put the cornmeal in a mixing bowl and mix the salt into it. Bring the water to a boil, and then stir it into the cornmeal. Mix well. Cover the bowl with a cloth and let it stand at room temperature for one hour. All the water should be absorbed, and the dough should be stiff and dry to the touch.

Roll the dough into one-inch balls. Pat each ball back and forth in your hands and press it between them as you would hamburger patties until you have flattened it as much as you can (about 1/4-inch thick and the diameter of a large cookie). After three tortillas, rinse your hands with water and pat them dry with a towel to remove any accumulation of cornmeal, which will cause the next tortilla to stick to your hands and break. For serving company, you can make the flattened tortillas uniformly circular by trimming the edges with a cookie cutter or jar lid about three inches in diameter.

On a hot, ungreased griddle or Teflon frying pan, cook each tortilla for four minutes, turning with a spatula once per minute. It's done when brown spots appear on each side.

Remove from griddle or skillet and serve warm.

Blue Corn Atole

This souplike corn beverage is a staple food of traditional Indians throughout the Southwest, Mexico, and Central America at both morning and evening meals because of its ease of preparation and versatility. New Mexican and northern Mexican curanderas *(healers) often limit sick patients to a diet of atole during treatment (sort of a native equivalent to chicken soup).*

Basic atole recipe (per serving):
½ cup milk
½ cup water
4 teaspoons fine-ground blue cornmeal
(harina para atole)
2 teaspoons honey

In a saucepan, mix cold milk and water. Stir in cornmeal and continue to stir until it is dissolved and free of lumps. Bring to a boil over medium heat, stirring constantly. (Atole thickens suddenly as it nears the boiling point, so if you don't keep stirring, it will form a thick lumpy layer at the bottom of the pan.) Remove from heat, let cool slightly, and add honey. (Don't boil honey—it destroys much of the nutritional value.) Serve in a coffee mug or soup bowl.

Variations: Native people use a wide variety of different flavorings for atole. Try any *one* of the following:

- cinnamon
- red chile (coarse ground)
- lavender
- anise seed
- juniper berries (crushed)
- squash blossoms (as an edible garnish)

Note: Some people make a thicker version of atole as a hot breakfast cereal similar to Cream of Wheat by increasing the amount of cornmeal in the recipe to 2½ to 3 tablespoons per cup.

Traditional Pueblo Piki

Usually associated with the Hopi people of northern Arizona but also made by other Pueblo people in New Mexico, this distinctive, paper-thin, rolled flatbread is a delicious appetizer or stand-alone conversation dish. Developing the skill to make it takes practice. Once you've tried this yourself, you'll have a new appreciation for the women who sell piki at the annual Santa Fe Indian Market.

Makes 4 to 6 piki rolls

1½ tablespoons powdered ash (chamisa, juniper, or dried bean pod ash is usually used)
¼ cup cold water
2 quarts water, divided
3 cups fine-ground blue cornmeal (harina para atole), divided
Olive oil (or bone marrow)

Strain the ash through a strainer or screen to a fine powdery consistency. In a small bowl, mix it with cold water and set aside. Boil 4 cups of water. Put 2 cups of cornmeal in a large mixing bowl. Pour 2 cups of boiling water into it and mix well. Then stir in the remaining 2 cups of boiling water until the batter is moist and firm. Slowly stir the ash water into the mixture. (The ash will make the cornmeal cook to a dark blue color instead of turning concrete gray.)

Let the dough cool, and then knead it until smooth. Gradually knead in the remaining cup of cornmeal. Slowly mix in 3 cups of cold water until the batter becomes thin and runny with no lumps. Save the additional cup of cold water in case you need to add some to keep the batter thin enough. Meanwhile, heat a large pancake griddle and oil it lightly with the olive oil (or, if you're really traditional, rub it with the marrow bone). Dip a tablespoonful or so of the batter and spread it quickly in a very thin layer across the griddle from one side to the other. Dip another spoonful and spread it onto another layer next to the first, repeating until the griddle is covered with a layer of piki 12 to 16 inches wide.

When the piki is cooked, it will separate from the griddle. Carefully lift and slide it onto a large plate. (A spatula will help.) Repeat, making a second layer of piki like the first. When it is cooked, place the first layer on top of it, causing it to soften again. With a spatula, fold the sides of both layers toward the center until the edges just touch. (This way, the flat piki is four layers thick.) Then gently roll the piki away from you lengthwise until it is completely rolled like a burrito. Remove it from the griddle and place it on a plate to cool. Unless you plan to serve it soon, you may wish to protect it by wrapping it in plastic wrap.

Oil the griddle again and repeat the whole process, diluting the batter with more cold water if necessary. If you tear a layer of piki, you can dissolve it back into the batter and reuse it. Continue repeating the process until all the batter is used.

Chicos

Unique to New Mexico, the smoky-flavored young corn kernels known as chicos (little ones) are hard to find in supermarkets or gourmet shops, but you'll often see them for sale in late summer at farmers markets and roadside stands. They are also available, though quite expensive, via the Internet. Chicos are harvested three weeks earlier than mature corn, while the kernels are still soft and sugary sweet. They are then roasted in a horno oven until golden in color and sun-dried. Traditional Hispanic farmers in northern New Mexico divide their cornfields, harvesting about 40 percent as chicos, 40 percent the following month as posole, and 20 percent as seed to exchange or plant the following year.

Chicos are traditionally cooked without other ingredients to interfere with their sweet, subtle flavor.

Serves 6 to 8

Place two cups of chicos in a cooking pot or Dutch oven. Fill it with water and let soak overnight.

Drain the water. (It is traditionally thrown out, though some people like to save it for use as a base in vegetarian soups.)

2¼ quarts fresh water
1 tablespoon olive oil
Pinch of salt
1 teaspoon anise seed (optional)

Add above ingredients to the chicos. Bring to a boil. Lower the heat and simmer for 3 to 4 hours or until the kernels are tender.

Variations: New Mexico locals often cook chicos and Anasazi beans together, since both have a sweet taste and are cooked for the same amount of time. They can be soaked, boiled, and simmered together in any proportion from 50/50 to three parts beans and one part chicos.

Three Sisters Posole

Posole is the local Spanish word for corn that has matured until its sugar content has turned to starch. The thick-skinned whole kernels are rarely eaten alone without being ground into cornmeal first. Preparation of whole posole kernels means cooking them all day, so why not add other ingredients and make a stew of it? The recipe for traditional Hispanic posole stew, with red chile and meat appears in chapter two. What follows is a Pueblo Indian version.

Since prehistoric times, Indians have cultivated the "three sisters"—corn, beans, and squash—together in the same fields, providing shelter for one another during the growing cycle. Beans and squash seeds probably spread northward from Mexico and eastward from New Mexico along with seed corn. The three complement each other, making for a balanced diet, so Three Sisters Stew became a standard communal meal for native people across the continent. Legends relating the three crops together are found in many Indian mythologies, though neither of the other vegetables shares corn's mystical importance in New Mexico.

There are many regional variations of the traditional Three Sisters Stew. In New Mexico, the stew invariably contains chile peppers, which can't be grown in most other parts of the United States and Canada. Today, Three Sisters Stew is a favorite among vegetarians, who concoct endlessly creative recipe variations for it. Alas, to their horror, you can make a great buffalo stew simply by adding bison stew meat or thin-sliced bison sirloin steak to Three Sisters Stew.

Posole is sold in two ways: packed in liquid in plastic bags in the refrigeration cases of supermarkets or dried in stores and farmers markets. If you buy dry ones, look at the label or ask the market vendor whether they have been prepared with lime (powdered limestone, not the fruit). Growers often, but not always, do this step before removing the kernels from the cob. This process, traditionally used throughout Mexico and New Mexico, is called "nixtamalization" (from the Aztec word for lime). It softens the tough skin of the corn kernels and makes nutrients such as niacin, calcium, riboflavin, and amino acids in the corn accessible by the human digestive system. It also eliminates potentially harmful mycotoxins and enhances flavor and aroma.

To nixtamalize posole, mix a small amount of powdered lime (known as cal in Spanish, widely available in New Mexico markets and at Mexican grocery stores in the United States) with water—1 teaspoon of lime and 2 quarts of water for 2 cups of posole. Add the posole and bring it to a full boil. Cook over medium heat for about one-half hour. Then turn off the heat, cover the top of the pot with a cloth, and let the corn steep at least overnight and preferably for 24 hours. Drain the kernels in a colander and wash them thoroughly to remove the lime residue.

Serves 6

1 (2-pound) butternut squash or other winter squash
1 medium sweet onion
2 or 3 cloves garlic, minced
1 tablespoon olive oil
2 cups Anasazi beans or pinto beans, soaked overnight
2 cups posole, either bagged in liquid or nixtamalized and soaked overnight
½ cup roasted, peeled, and chopped fresh or frozen green chile, (or try strips of fresh padrón chiles or poblano chiles)
1 cup vegetable broth
1 teaspoon cumin
1 teaspoon sage
2 cups (1-inch chunks) vine-ripened tomatoes
Salt and pepper
Fresh chopped cilantro

Preheat oven to 350 degrees F. In a large pot or Dutch oven, steam the squash just long enough to tenderize for slicing. While the squash is steaming, sauté onion and garlic in olive oil in a small skillet until the onion is transparent. If you are using unroasted frying chiles such as padrón or poblano chiles, sauté them at the same time.

Carefully remove the hot squash from the pot, pour out the water and, in the same pot, put the soaked beans and posole in 1 quart of water. Bring to a boil, cover, and reduce heat to medium. As the beans and corn cook, add the green chile, onion, garlic, vegetable broth, cumin, and sage. Cover and continue cooking.

When the squash is cool enough to handle, slice it in half. Remove the seeds from the center. Slice the squash into bite-size chunks and peel them if desired. Place the chunks in a baking dish or wrapped lightly in aluminum foil, and bake for 40 minutes.

When the squash chunks are baked, add them to the pot. Reduce heat and simmer for at least 1 hour, adding more water as necessary. Add the tomatoes and simmer for another 20 minutes. Salt and pepper to taste. Garnish with chopped cilantro leaves before serving.

WATER

"Sin agua, no hay vida." ***This traditional saying, which translates as "Without water, there is no life," reflects a fundamental New Mexican reality.***

The most valuable commodity in New Mexico is not gold. Despite early explorers' fanciful tales of Indian cities whose streets were said to be paved with gold, very little in the way of precious metals has ever been discovered here.

Nor is land the most treasured commodity. The fifth largest state in the United States, New Mexico has vast expanses of land—an arid sea of crackled clay and sand punctuated by island-like evergreen-clad peaks reaching down from the southern tip of the Rocky Mountains near Santa Fe.

The most prized gift of nature in New Mexico, without a doubt, is water. The average precipitation in five representative cities and major towns near the Rio Grande—Taos, Los Alamos, Santa Fe, Albuquerque, and Las Cruces—is 13.25 inches a year. This is not a great deal of moisture. But according to the common meteorological definition of a desert (ten inches or less), New Mexico is not a desert at all. The state receives about the same amount of rainfall as Los Angeles and three times as much as Las Vegas. However, it is not simply a lack of rainfall that makes the landscape so dry.

Several factors besides rainfall combine to give New Mexico's terrain its desert character. At lower elevations, almost all the annual precipitation comes during the two-month monsoon season, from early July through August. In the winter, most snow falls on the high mountains, accumulating until the spring thaw, when it runs off into flash-flooding arroyos, swollen creeks, and raging rivers that are dry the rest of the year. The water rushes away down sunbaked slopes with little time to soak into the earth. Although much of the water is captured in large reservoirs along the Rio Grande and Chama rivers, this water is not available for use by either rural or urban New Mexicans. It is reserved for downstream big agriculture in Texas.

As a result, water is a surrealistic commodity in New Mexico. The water captured in man-made lakes is only available for fishing and boating. As far as drinking water or irrigation water are concerned, it might as well not exist. On the other hand, legal water rights claims often relate to "dry water"—water that in fact does not exist.

For many reasons, New Mexicans already face the kind of freshwater problems that will become more acute around the globe in the near future: conflicts between urban and rural users, conflicts between indigenous users and post-colonial governments, and conflicts of law about how water rights are defined, to name just a few.

facing: acequia at Dixon's Apple Orchards

New Mexico's small farmers live on the forefront of all these issues, and sometimes the unpredictable rainfall can make their lifestyle tenuous. In the years 2002 through mid-2006, the worst drought since weather records began struck New Mexico. Precipitation declined to less than half the seasonal norm, and the normally semiarid landscape became one of the driest deserts in the United States. Streams and acequias dried up, and small farmers were forced to install drip irrigation to survive. Trees died by the hundreds of thousands. Cities like Santa Fe imposed draconian water restrictions that banned all outdoor uses of water, including gardening, landscaping, and even car washing. Yet suburban housing development continued unabated, taking it on faith that the rainfall would return one day.

And it did. In July and August 2006, after a dry spell when no trace of moisture had fallen in eight months, drenching storms came and lasted for two full months, breaking records for rainfall. Acequias, the traditional irrigation ditches that crisscross the farmlands, backed up and flooded crop fields. Hardest hit were the chile fields around Hatch in southern New Mexico. This and other areas of the state were declared federal disaster areas because of flood damage.

Be careful what you wish for . . .

ACEQUIA CULTURE

From the Middle East to the New World

Acequia is the Spanish version of a Yemeni word for "irrigation ditch." Like many aspects of life in Spanish colonial New Mexico, such as adobe brick homebuilding, acequia technology flowed here from the Middle East by way of Spain. More than water delivery systems, acequias became the basic building blocks of rural society, linking New Mexico's farmers to those who came before across vast expanses of distance and time. Today in the United States—except for a handful of historic curiosities at some restored Spanish mission churches in Texas and California—acequias exist only in New Mexico.

When the first Spanish farmers arrived in New Mexico four centuries ago, they found that the Pueblo Indians were diverting water into their fields from earthen reservoirs by means of irrigation ditches that looked very similar to the ones their families back in Spain had used. The essential difference was that the acequia system of old Spain and Arabia used gates to let water onto one farmer's property and then the next, while the Indians worked all their cropland communally. Both systems allowed water to be shared equitably in a climate where water availability was often unpredictable or scarce. As the settlers knew, the acequia system had been working in the Middle East since biblical times.

The first Spanish farmers came to New Mexico for the same reason as the English-speaking Pilgrims, who founded their smaller colony thousands of miles away on the continent's east coast a generation later: to escape religious persecution. Since AD 711, Spain had been occupied by the Moors—Islamic North Africans whose armies had invaded across the Strait of Gibraltar. The Moors, as well as the Sephardic Jews who migrated into Spain in search of vacant land during the centuries that followed, were educated in ancient Middle Eastern agricultural methods dating back to around 8000 BC. Efforts by Christian armies to reconquer Spain began almost immediately and continued in different provinces, with varying degrees of success, for nearly eight centuries.

Spain was finally united under the Catholic monarchs Fernando and Isabel in 1492. The end of the war against the Moors freed up funds to finance exploration and colonization efforts. Just seven months later, the king and queen commissioned navigator Cristóbal Colón (known in his native Italy as Cristoforo Colombo and later, in the English-speaking world, as Christopher Columbus) to lead an ocean expedition across the Atlantic.

Neither religious tolerance nor the separation of church and state was recognized in European nations at that time. Jews and Muslims living in Spain after the reconquest were required by law to become Roman Catholic converts or to leave Spain. Those who stayed, including an estimated one hundred thousand converted Sephardic Jews—a large percentage of the country's total population at that time—were called *conversos* (converts), or, more pejoratively, *marranos* (swine), a double entendre mocking their dietary prohibition against eating pork. Despite persecution in some provinces of Spain, conversos often held on to past positions of wealth and power, which fostered further resentment. In the sixteenth and seventeenth centuries, the Spanish Inquisition—a court originally designed to prevent the "heresies" of Protestantism—turned its attention to the problem of the conversos. In a series of trials, Jewish converts were charged with privately practicing Judaism, prosecuted for heresy, and publicly burned at the stake in the Inquisition's notorious *autos-da-fé*. By the time of the colonization of Mexico, secret Jews had become the main focus of the Inquisition. Extortion by neighbors, along with the church's confiscation of land, property, and money as part of the punishment for those convicted of heresy, made Spain a dangerous place for conversos—wealthy aristocrats and subsistence farmers alike.

The solution for many was to leave Spain, booking passage for remote areas of the Spanish-speaking New World. In places like New Mexico, the church was represented by Franciscan missionaries. Preoccupied with bringing the Gospel to local Indians, the Franciscans had no interest in whether Spanish farmers had sincerely relinquished Judaism or not. Fray Angélico Chávez (1910–1996), a renowned New Mexico historian best known for his genealogy of the origins of New Mexico families during the Spanish colonial period, asserted that more than half the settlers who came to New Mexico in the 1600s—including his own ancestors—were of Jewish descent.

New Mexico's Semitic roots matter because the Spaniards who conquered the New World on behalf of Spain were predominantly military men, nobility, and bureaucrats. They knew little of farming. Under the feudal system in Mexico, army commanders and government functionaries were rewarded for their service with land grants while the actual work of growing crops and livestock was performed by the same native people who had always lived on the land. But in the remote land of New Mexico, the situation was different.

How Colonial Farmers Came to New Mexico

At the end of the sixteenth century, the king of Spain decided to establish a northern outpost that would serve as a buffer between Mexico, then known as Nuevo España, and the vast, largely unknown lands to the north. The colony would protect Mexico from invasion not only by nomadic Indian tribes but also by English-speaking adventurers. Although no British colony had yet been established anywhere in the Americas, the recent defeat of the Spanish Armada meant that it was only a matter of time. Having decreed the colonization of Nuevo Mexico on the northern outskirts of the desolate Chihuahua Desert, the crown offered leadership of the expedition to the highest bidder. The winner was Juan de Oñate, a silver baron in the town of Zacatecas, New Spain. One of the richest men in the country, Oñate was the grandson-in-law of conquistador Hernán Cortés and his mistress, La Malinche, Aztec king Moctezuma's daughter. Oñate was to organize the expedition at his own expense, buy all needed provisions, and recruit colonists. In exchange, he would receive a large tract of land, including "ownership" of all the Indians that lived on it.

When Oñate's expedition set out in the year 1598, it consisted of about 130 farmers, mostly conversos, and their families, along with 200 soldiers and ten Franciscan missionaries. They brought 1,100 cattle, 4,000 sheep, 1,000 goats and 300 horses—the first livestock to be raised on New Mexican farms. Before that, the Pueblo Indians had kept dogs and turkeys, but there is no evidence that they used either one for food. Turkeys were raised as a source of feathers for ceremonial decoration and blanket weaving, and dogs were apparently used only as hunting companions and household pets.

Oñate, though a rich businessman, proved to be a poor leader. Hoping to find a route up the Rio Grande to the mythical Straits of Anian—a passage thought to connect the Mississippi River with the Pacific Ocean—Oñate brought a full complement of sailors and shipbuilding equipment, but he did not bring enough supplies for his farmers, soldiers, and priests, who were forced to appeal to the local Indian pueblos for food and blankets to survive the unexpectedly harsh winter.

Oñate established his capital, San Gabriel, at the confluence of the Rio Grande and Rio Chama north of present-day Española, and parceled out small plots of farmland called *suertes* (Spanish for "luck") along the riverbanks to his farmers through lottery-style drawings. Those whose small farms thrived would be rewarded with up to five additional suertes, creating farms called *multifundias*. The finest small farms in New Mexico were honored as *joyas*, or jewels, and today it is common to find rural back roads named La Joya.

After establishing San Gabriel, Oñate set out on a six-hundred-mile exploration that spanned from Oklahoma to the Gulf of Mexico, leaving the colonists unsupervised and unprotected. The Spanish farmers seemed to get along well with their Indian neighbors, working together on an extensive acequia system to irrigate the new farms. Oñate and his soldiers took a tougher approach to subjugating the Indians of the Southwest, however. In one particularly notorious February 1599 incident, he found seventy Indians at Acoma Pueblo guilty of battling with a small contingent of his men. As punishment, he ordered all Acoma men over age twenty-five to have their right feet cut off and to serve as slaves for twenty years; males age twelve to twenty-five had their right feet amputated but were not enslaved. (Almost four centuries later, when a bronze statue of Oñate was erected at a visitor's center near the site of his original capital, vandals came in the dead of night with a cutting torch and removed his right foot—a lasting reminder of that colonial atrocity.)

Many more instances of Oñate's cruelty to Indians followed, endangering their friendship with small Spanish farmers, whose lives became increasingly difficult and isolated. Deserters from the failing colony, mostly adventurers disgruntled because they had found no silver or gold, carried stories of the bad conditions in New Mexico back to Mexico City, where the Spanish viceroy ordered Oñate to stand trial for the atrocity at Acoma, wrongfully executing Indian and Spanish prisoners, and adultery. As the viceroy and the king of Spain discussed whether to terminate the Nuevo Mexico colony, the Spanish farmers and missionaries carried on without a government. Eventually, a new governor, Pedro de Peralta, was appointed, with instructions to abandon the old capital and establish a new one farther south at the site of present-day Santa Fe, which has remained the capital ever since.

But the farmers who had put forth so much effort to irrigate and work the land clung to their suertes in the north, and this area—from the confluence of the Rio Chama and the Rio Grande north to Velarde and Dixon—remains the foremost center of small traditional farming in New Mexico today. The Spanish farmers of northern New Mexico, like their Indian neighbors, continued to rely on themselves, growing local crops and assimilating new crops imported from Mexico, living independently and sustainably, avoiding contact with the colonial government.

More than two centuries later, after Mexico won its independence from Spain, the rural people of this area staged an unsuccessful rebellion trying to win their independence from Mexico. Soon afterward, when Mexico ceded New Mexico to the United States in settlement of the Mexican War, unidentified people from the same area assassinated Peralta, the first American territorial governor. Their way of life changed very little until the 1940s, when World War II meant the drafting of most young male Hispanics and Pueblo Indians into the military and the presence of the huge, top-secret government research base at Los Alamos introduced a new cash economy to northern New Mexico.

TRADITIONAL FARM HERITAGE

The Descendent

"We're buying back some of the land that belonged to us."

Eduardo Velarde

Eduardo Velarde grows peaches, apples, plums, apricots, and nectarines on his farm in the rural northern New Mexico village that bears his family's name.

Recounting his family's legend, Eduardo Velarde says:

> *When Don Juan de Oñate first came on his expedition, my tenth-generation-back grandfather was his personal secretary. For his valor, they deeded him 52,000 acres, and he got to pick what he wanted. Then back in 1870-some, they took it all back, because it was a gift from a foreign country, and the United States doesn't recognize foreign gifts.*
>
> *But something, I understand, called the Homestead Act—President Taft signed it, and he deeded this piece of land to my grandfather. It's about six acres since they cut the highway. It used to be about ten acres, and then when they made the four-lane in the '60s they cut a bunch out. We're buying back some of the land that belonged to us, and a lot of our relatives still have a lot of the land.*
>
> *The acequia on this particular orchard is the Chicos Ditch. The other ones are on Garcia and Medio and there's another one down there, I can't remember the name. They're all gravity flow from the Rio Grande. Ninety percent of the ditch is still in the original place where they dug it out. From what I understand, my relatives got a lot of Native Americans to help dig it out around 1608 or 1610, somewhere around then.*

The Traditionalist

"Making foods and sharing them with your neighbors . . . sharing water . . . sharing labor . . . all these are things of the past."

Estevan Arellano

Estevan Arellano works an ancestral farm in the Embudo Valley, which has been in his family since 1725. Arellano is also a lecturer, journalist, and Spanish-language author. He is the translator of the first English-language version of Gabriel Alonso de Herrera's *Obra de Agricultura*, a 1513 farming instruction manual used by Spanish colonists in the New World, now published under the title *Ancient Agriculture* (Salt Lake City: Gibbs Smith, Publisher, 2006). His farm has orchards, vineyards, and mixed fields grown in the traditional way of the first Spanish settlers. He also raises churro sheep, the original sheep the Spanish brought to the New World, and *corrientes*, the original cattle. He has been searching for the descendants of the original pigs that came from Spain but has not been able to find any. He recalls the early twentieth century and the changes that have taken place in northern New Mexico farming during his lifetime.

> *We would trade our fruits and vegetables by* cambalache, *which means barter, for other crops or for hunters' meat like elk or venison. It was something like today's CSAs* [community-supported agriculture], *except that we mostly dealt with relatives. Once, I remember, we traded a truckload of apples for a truckload of piglets. Those pigs will eat whatever you can't sell or whatever falls on the ground. Now, today, I keep churro sheep. They eat apples, too.*
>
> *We also used to sell from the back of a pickup truck or go house-to-house in Taos, but when we'd do this, we would mostly get Anglos who wanted to buy apples in one-pound bags. We Hispanics had larger families, so we sold to each other by the bushel.*
>
> *You have to understand your own microclimate. People move in from outside the acequia culture and don't understand it. This makes for a clash of cultures with outsiders, because they think they know more about sustainable agriculture, permaculture, and all that. It offends the local people, who have been farming the land for as much as four hundred years. How much more sustainable can you be?*
>
> *In those days the farmers lived by certain principles. One of them was* convicte de comida, *which meant making foods and sharing them with your neighbors—anything from butchering an animal to making* biscochitos. *This is fading away as people shop individually at stores instead. Then there was* apartamiento de agua, *the Arabic concept of sharing water, and* cooperación, *or sharing labor. All these are things of the past. Los Alamos brought a cash economy to northern New Mexico, and then everything changed. People are too busy working or going to Indian casinos.*

Farming has also changed in that many people have switched over to drip irrigation, often considered better in times of drought because it requires less water. But Arellano says this is an illusion. There would be enough water if the acequias were better maintained.

> *The banks of acequias were used as roads or trails between villages. Today we can't do that because they're overgrown with Russian olives, cottonwoods, and Chinese elms, so a lot of water is lost from the acequias. A single Chinese elm consumes two hundred gallons of water a day. And with all the vegetation, you can't find the gopher holes that leak water out of the ditch. Priests used to parade along the acequias to bless them on San Antonio's feast day, but now you can't walk along the acequias any more, so the tradition has disappeared within my lifetime.*

Drip irrigation, he claims, limits the range of crops that can be grown in a field because only the seeds planted in rows along the irrigation hoses get water. The traditional Spanish farmer's field was more like a forest. A canopy of large trees protected smaller trees, which in turn protected grapevines, all sheltering lower crops from late and early frosts, down to the tiniest plants. One of his favorite things about traditional farming is the tiny, tasty volunteer plants like *calite* (lambs quarter) and *verdulagas* (purselane), which are used as herbs in traditional farm cooking. "We used to get huixtlacatle, a fungus that grows on blue corn, but hybrid corn doesn't produce the fungus, so it has been lost. Other mushrooms also don't grow because of the changes in the riparian environment as the acequias have gotten overgrown."

ACEQUIA CULTURE TODAY

The Acequia Activist

"Traditionally we measure water in time."

Miguel Santistevan

Miguel Santistevan, the Taos-area farmer and educator we met in the previous chapter, is among the leading figures in fighting to preserve New Mexico's acequias through his activities with the New Mexico Acequia Association, founded in 1990 to provide a unified presence for the thousand or so individual acequias. Here he explains how acequia culture has shaped northern New Mexico and speaks of the challenges that confront acequias and the small farmers that depend on them today.

You hear complaints about people hoarding water or fighting over the water, but back in the day, water was the central thing that was shared. We had an age-old tradition, thousands of years of sharing water, all the way back to the Middle East. You always share what you have with others. I came across stories that during the Depression or during hard times, one family would make soup with a bone, and then they would take the bone to their neighbor so they could get a little bit of protein and get that flavor in their soup as well. Back in the day, when you were making chicos, it was a community event. Everybody would come and help out, and then the next weekend you would be at someone else's house helping. You could always rely on your neighbors and your extended family to help.

Nowadays it's everyone out for themselves. Even in agriculture, in the sustainability movement, sharing is the part that's lacking. We're not figuring out how to work with each other and how to rely on each other. To me, that's a so-called luxury—it could also be called a sickness—of the modern economy. Everybody takes care of their own selves. How many people are living in two- to three-thousand-square-foot houses, and they're just a couple without kids? And they're not even living here year-round. They consider having an empty house a luxury. Then other people look at that and say, if I work hard I can have that.

But I say, if I work hard, I can be planting another half acre or another acre. To me, that's wealth—having more seeds, more animals, more connection to my system, whether it be the water, the animals, the soil, the crop diversity, the insect life, the wildlife, the fruit trees. To me that's the wealth of what I really have going on here, because as I see it, money comes and goes. I could buy some beer, I could go to the movies, and I'll still have money to do that later, but if I don't plant this corn, that can't be replaced and there's no money that can get that back.

If you look now, our acequias are irrigating a lot of hay and alfalfa. But the traditional Native American crops—the maíz*, that's definitely Native American, the* calabaza *(squash) is also Native American, the* frijoles *(beans) are also Native American. And other crops are also important—the frost-tolerant crops: the* alverjon *(peas), the* lentejas *(lentils), the* garbanzos*, the* havas *(fava beans)—so we get a jump on the season that the Native Americans didn't necessarily have. We can be planting in February or March because those crops went through that breeding process in the Old World. So you put those together—the Native American depth of agriculture and land management with the Arabic, Middle Eastern, and Spaniard land management.*

When the Spaniards came, they brought a whole crew of Claxcalteca Indians from what is Veracruz now. People envision the Spaniards coming over here and building the acequia system, but they didn't do that. They hired the Mexicanos *to put in the acequias. People like me, I would say that at least half of my blood is Mexican Indian, because that's who came up here with the Spaniards. And then there's also other native blood in my veins. I have a great-great-grandmother from Taos Pueblo, and there are stories of Apaches and Comanches stealing kids and all these things that happened. And the* genízaro *phenomenon—there was a time when renegade Comanches, Apaches, and Utes would come into a village and steal kids and sell them to Spanish landowners. Those people would be baptized and would lose their native identity and become hispanicized Indians or* genízaros.

above: acequia gate

I have Vargas in my name; my grandmother's maiden name is Vargas. So one of our cousins says, "Oh, we're a direct descendant of Diego de Vargas [the Spanish governor who led the reconquest of New Mexico after the Pueblo Revolt of 1680]." And I say, "Well, that's excellent, but it could be that we're a direct descendant of Diego de Vargas's house servant, for all we know." A lot of people freak out when they hear that. They say, "Oh, my god, I'm from Spain, I'm a Spaniard, I'm pure Spaniard." Then they get upset when I say there's not even a pure Spaniard in Spain. I'm proud of being Mexicano, and I welcome all these immigrants, because they're my cousins. We're all—Somos gente de maíz ["We are people of the corn"]. The other day this Mexicano came out here, and I was honored to have him here, and he saw my cornfield and said, "Hey, this reminds me of home." And I said, "You are home, man—Nuevo Mexico."

Acequias are mostly a northern New Mexico thing, and southern Colorado. There are a whole bunch of them tucked away around here that the state engineer doesn't know about, that nobody knows about except the people who are working them.

These water systems come from both the mountain and the river. A lot of people consider the acequia to be just the actual channel, but the way it was originally set up, the acequia is connected to the entire watershed, so any springs you have in the watershed, even on private property, belong to the acequia. Some people think that because a spring is on their property, it's theirs, but it's not. It's communal property—all the water belongs to everybody. When people try to privatize a spring, it's unacceptable. It's a continuation of colonization, in my opinion.

Acequias are connected to the entire watershed, and the upper watershed is like a sponge. The snowmelt dissolves into the soil, into the aquifer. When you see the river, the river isn't water flowing on top of the ground, it is water that is upwelling from the aquifer underneath the river. So we divert some of that water into the acequia, and most of that water returns to the aquifer, creating a hydrological cycle between the river and the acequia, extending the flood plain, extending the riparian area beyond what would otherwise exist.

Acequias are all about gravity flow. You don't need any fossil fuels. Nowadays a lot of people are saying, well, I want to pipe my acequia. There's no reason I should be cleaning out this ditch, because I can just put a pump in the river. But that's dangerous, because the acequia . . . it's not just the ditch and the water, it's the whole system of water sharing.

For example, I have an acre of land, so I get the water for a certain amount of time. If everybody needs the water, then everybody gets that amount of time, typically four hours for an acre. If there's a lot of water, I get a lot of water. If there's a little bit of water, I get a little bit of water, and I'd better figure out a good way to use that water.

But now people say, "I could just put a pump in the river. The state engineer says I have 3.2 acre-feet of water, so I'm just going to pump that out." That's where the logic falls apart, because they're measuring that water in volume, and traditionally we measure water in time. It's a huge disconnect. That's what's creating this discrepancy between what is the reality of the water situation and what the engineers and lawyers think is going on in their air-conditioned offices in Santa Fe. Because it has to rely on water pressure. You know, there are some acequias that are level or even flow uphill, and they rely on the whole hydrological system to push that water along.

As we start running out of water, they might adjudicate these systems and say, "Okay, there are ten people on the acequia and five of you aren't using it, so you lose that water right. You five that are using it, you can only divert this much water."

They have all these equations, they call it the PDR—the Project Delivery Requirement—which equals the amount of water that each irrigated parcel requires according to their equation plus the amount of seepage that is lost to deliver it, and that's the amount of water you're allowed to divert. On paper that looks good, but if you cut down the amount of irrigation that can take place, you're looking at a situation where there can be just a little bit of water in the acequia, like I saw in July—there was some water, but by the time I blocked it and diverted it, it only made it about a third of the way down the row because it all got consumed by the soil—so that's not going to work for us. We need to divert the water so there's enough pressure in the acequia so we can get the water on the land and do a good irrigation.

Some people say, "Well, you should go to drip irrigation," but again that's not respecting the original setup of the acequia. Drip irrigation is almost like putting your plants in a feed lot; you're just irrigating this plant, it's just getting little drops of water, but you stick a shovel in that soil and it's just dry everywhere else. When you're flooding an entire field, look at all these verdulagas, all these calites. I'm maintaining an agricultural ecosystem—there are things I didn't plant that are coming up just because the water's there, and I can use a lot of them for food, for medicine, for shampoo—I've got yerba de la negrita growing out there.

So there's a more intense relationship I can have with this land by maintaining it as a flood ecology situation, plus recharging the aquifer so my neighbors down here who have wells are eventually going to get the benefits of me flooding my land here. It's all part of that system. That's not to say I'm

against drip irrigation; I think in some cases it's okay, but if it impacts the traditional functioning of the acequia, to where people say, "Well, I'm using less water than all you guys, so I should be able to pump out water whenever I want," I say no, that's not acceptable. You get water when it's your turn, and you can put it in a tank and do drip irrigation later, but we cannot compromise the integrity of what it means for all of us to share this water and to have it equal within the acequia.

I don't want us in a situation here where we're hoarding the water. There's plenty for everybody. I used to get all upset if people were stealing the water, because that's such a shortsighted, limited viewpoint.

I've already gone through two hard years where there was just no water but at the precise moment it rains. You have to remember that another part of our culture here in northern New Mexico is our reverence toward God and our faith in God. We do not control the water. The water belongs to the earth, and the earth belongs to God.

In 2003 I had the most pathetic-looking cornfield you can imagine. More than half of it died. But the half that lived, I have that seed, and I planted some of that in this field when there was no irrigation. I planted twenty-four plants, and thirteen of them gave me corn, and I watered them once. So I never see it as a loss if I lose some of my crops; I can still go to the store, at this point, but I think those days are numbered to where the store is really going to serve our needs.

I have the luxury to adapt my crops. But in terms of the acequia systems here, most people agree that we need to share, that it belongs to everybody, and that's traditionally how it was, and I'm hoping we go back to that. And we will. We're going back to that because we'll need to. If the water policy keeps going as it's going, we're going to run out of water. We're only going to have water in the spring and whatever water we can get off the roof and whatever water we can recharge into the aquifer. It's going to be a challenge—a crisis—but it's also going to be an opportunity for us to work together.

DRY WATER WARS

The acequia system served Spanish and Indian farmers well for centuries, apportioning available water equitably among everyone who needed it. Unique to New Mexico, it continues today with about one thousand acequias still in active use. On behalf of small farmers, the acequia associations have assumed a role as one of several competing power blocs struggling with a strange, ever more complicated, tangle of water laws.

While New Mexico state law follows a variation of the "first in use, first in right" theory of water rights that prevails in most western states, the rights of Indian pueblos and rural acequia associations are in direct conflict with state law. The state measures water rights in terms of quantity, vesting owners with a right to use a given number of acre-feet of water each year. The acequia system, on the other hand, measures water rights in terms of time, giving users their share of the water flow in the ditch for a certain number of hours each week.

In 1913, the U.S. Supreme Court in the case of *United States v. Sandoval* overruled its previous 1878 *Joseph* decision and held that New Mexico's Pueblo Indians were, in fact, Indians. That created a new problem, because the court had ruled just five years earlier that Indians were entitled to "prior and paramount rights to waters that border, originate in, or pass through a reservation." During the thirty-eight years when Pueblo people were not considered Indians, about twelve thousand non-Indians had either bought plots of Indian land in good faith or simply squatted on them long enough to claim property rights. Restoring the Indians' original water rights meant that the Pueblos and their non-Indian neighbors owned conflicting rights to the same water.

Piecemeal litigation over Indian versus non-Indian water rights kept New Mexico's federal court occupied for decades, while growing population, increased urbanization, pollution, and interstate water compacts all placed increasing demands on the limited supply of water in the Rio Grande and its subsurface aquifer. Meanwhile, farmlands that had been in the hands of old Spanish farmers had been split up between heirs over many generations, always dividing plots into narrower and narrower strips so that each would keep its rights by fronting on a river or acequia. This translated into a multiplying number of wells and acequia gates, placing still more demands on the severely limited water supply.

The problem of water came to a head in 1966 with the filing of *New Mexico v. Aamodt*, which was a lawsuit brought forward to define the respective water rights of "non-Indian entities, Indians, federal agencies, state agencies, municipalities, and water associations" in the Pojoaque Valley. At the time, the demand for water in the valley exceeded the available supply by 50 percent in normal years and far more in times of drought. It was the ultimate dispute over "dry water"—legal rights to water that did not exist.

For many years, the Aamodt case lingered because a fluke of federal law allowed the judge to authorize payment by the federal government of legal fees incurred by most nongovernment parties to the lawsuit. Not surprisingly, hundreds of attorneys came forward to represent the hundreds of parties in the case, collecting millions of dollars in legal fees and hopelessly confusing the case with paperwork that filled entire rooms of the federal court clerk's office. By the time the court ordered an end to the payment of interim legal fees in the early 1980s, the Aamodt case had become truly unsolvable. The court ordered the parties to agree on a settlement.

above: corn seedlings

In 2004, the parties drafted a settlement agreement that begged the question of competing water rights by creating a regional water system that would satisfy everybody's needs by piping additional water over the Continental Divide from the San Juan River to the Rio Grande. The sticking point was who would pay the costs of the water diversion. When it became clear that its share of the settlement cost would be more than $200 million, the federal government balked, and as of this writing, the case remains unresolved, making it the longest-lasting trial court litigation in United States history.

Added to the conflicting claims of Indian pueblos, private landowners and acequias, other factors have arisen to complicate the water situation. The rapidly growing cities of Santa Fe and Albuquerque have outstripped their ability to meet water demand by drilling wells into the Rio Grande's underground aquifer, and as the aquifer level declines, the cities have sought to buy unused water rights from upstream owners such as the Jicarilla Apache Reservation and unappropriated water piped from the San Juan River. So far, little progress has been made in actually building a diversion project to carry the water from the Rio Grande to the city's water systems.

To complicate matters further, for years New Mexico has been making up for water shortfalls by running a deficit on its obligations under an interstate water compact that requires the state to allow a certain amount of water to flow south to the big cotton fields and citrus groves in Texas. By law, New Mexico cannot divert water from any of its Rio Grande reservoirs when the water level in the largest of them, Elephant Butte Reservoir, falls too low to supply the water debt to Texas. Furthermore, the courts have ruled that water cannot be diverted from the Rio Grande system if it would cause part of the river to temporarily dry up, threatening a tiny native fish called the silvery minnow, which is on the federal endangered species list. For these reasons, the newly acquired water rights from the San Juan diversion, which Santa Fe and Albuquerque depend on for continued growth, may well prove as "dry" as other northern New Mexico water rights.

Ultimately, Indian pueblo sovereignty may make competing water rights meaningless because the state lacks power to enforce the law on tribal land. Faced with the endless Aamodt litigation, one of the smallest pueblos, Pojoaque, has responded by simply ignoring the water rights issue and building a lavish casino resort that includes three 18-hole golf courses, draining many times what their share would be under any proposed water settlement. This *fait accompli* makes a final agreement about water rights in the Pojoaque Valley all the less likely. At the same time, judges have showed no inclination to bring the Aamodt case to trial because, whatever decision the court might make, its precedent would profoundly affect water rights throughout the state.

The future of water in New Mexico is unforeseeable. Real estate developers have tended to proceed on the assumption that as cities and agribusiness require more water to avert disaster, the law will somehow find a way to provide this water at the expense of the Indians, the acequias, and the environment. But tribal and small agriculture interests, by digging in their heels, may yet prevail.

All that can be said for certain is that the water rights drama gripping New Mexico today is a microcosm of the twenty-first-century developing world, in which a growing, more urbanized population competing for increasingly scarce fresh water supplies will present a global crisis even more serious than the depletion of fossil fuels. New Mexico's experience may or may not hold the answers; it certainly stands as a cautionary example—especially if it ultimately means that the acequias run dry.

THE NEW MEXICO CHILE STORY

While the early Spanish farmers' most significant contribution to regional agriculture was undoubtedly hoofed livestock, which spread from the Rio Grande across the West over the next two hundred years, they also introduced a unique crop for which New Mexico has been famous ever since: chile.

Like most chile peppers, New Mexico chile evolved from a small, round, bright red berrylike fruit known as a *chiltepín* that grew on bushes in the foothills of Peru and was traded into Mexico in ancient times. It is the forerunner of the many different species of chiles found throughout Latin America and other tropical and subtropical parts of the world today, of which the most common is *capsicum annuum*, whose cultivars range from sweet bell peppers to jalapeños, poblanos, serranos, and New Mexico chiles. (A few common chiles, such as habaneros and cayenne peppers, are other species less closely related to New Mexico chiles.)

One remarkable aspect of *capsicum annuum* chiles is their ability to adapt to a wide variety of growing conditions. Early Spanish explorers brought chile seeds from Mexico and traded them to the Indians in the 1580s. A generation later, colonist farmers brought their own chile seeds. But while the same seeds in Mexico grew into a large perennial bush that bore chiles for up to ten years, in New Mexico with its winter freezes it became an annual that had to be replanted each year. The long, tough-skinned new strain looked and tasted different from other Mexican chiles. In fact, New Mexican chiles grown in different areas, such as Hatch in the south and Chimayó in the north, taste differently. In 1896, Emilio Ortega—a member of the Ortega family whose name graces a leading brand of canned Hatch chile—moved to Ventura, California, bringing a supply of New Mexico chile seeds with him. The chiles grew well in the southern California climate and became what are known today as Anaheim chiles. Although they look the same as New Mexico chiles, the taste is so different that they cannot be used in traditional green chile recipes.

New Mexico chile is sold in its green and red phases. (Besides naming chile as an official state vegetable—though botanists will tell you it's technically a fruit—the New Mexico State Legislature has formalized an official state question: "Red or green?")

In general, New Mexicans prefer to eat chile in its green state, before it has fully ripened, as a vegetable. The chile pods are roasted in rotating wire mesh cages over a gas flame until the indigestible outer skin hardens and starts to blacken. The skin will slide easily off the soft flesh inside, which is then split open, the veins and most of the seeds are removed, and the green flesh is cut into strips or diced. After roasting, it can be frozen at any stage in the process. Chile roasters from Hatch with semitruck trailers full of green chiles are a common sight on roadsides, street corners, and supermarket parking lots in all New Mexico cities during the late August and September harvest season.

By mid-September, the chile pods turn red and are no longer eaten as a vegetable. Instead, the pods are tied together in long *ristras* and hung out to dry in the sun. In the southern part of the state, they are also spread on rooftops to dry. The dried red chile is finely ground and cooked into a smooth sauce that tastes completely different from green chile. It can also be coarse-ground for use as a spice in stews and other recipes. Fine-ground red chile is also mixed with powdered cumin, oregano, and garlic to make chili powder. New Mexico produces virtually all the supply of this spice in the United States.

Most chile is grown in two distinct regions of New Mexico. The Hatch area, which has grown to include the outskirts of Las Cruces, La Mesilla, Deming, and smaller villages like Arrey and Derry, has long been reputed to produce the best chile, thanks to the proximity of the agricultural college at New Mexico State University.

In 1907, Fabián García, a professor of horticulture at the university, dedicated himself to developing new strains of New Mexico chile by interbreeding pods from different valleys nearby. Before then, chile's piquancy was wildly unpredictable. One pod might be bland, while another plucked from the next bush might be mouth-blastingly hot, and there was no way to predict which was which until you tasted it. He developed a new strain called Fabián García's, the first to deliver crops with even, predictable heat. Since then, NMSU has steadily improved chile crops, releasing new strains such as Nu Mex, NuMex, R Naky, Nu Mex Joe Parker, Rio Grande 21, and the popular Big Jim, or New Mexico 6.

At the same time, chile growing in southern New Mexico has grown increasingly industrialized. The small farmers of generations past have been bought out by large landowners, and the few mom-and-pop farms that still operate there are at the mercy of chile-processing plants such as Bueno, Biad, Cal-Compack, and Cervantes. Growers employ about fifteen thousand Mexican guest workers to harvest the chile for low piecework pay, amounting to about ten cents per pound for picking, carrying, and unloading the chile, without health care or workman's compensation. Because of epidemics of chile crop diseases such as chile weevils and the curly-top virus, in recent years Hatch-area chile growers have used more and more pesticides, fungicides, and herbicides, which not only pose a health threat to fieldworkers but also contaminate the groundwater throughout New Mexico's largest agribusiness farming area.

At the opposite extreme, around the northern village of Chimayó, east of Española, farmers have been growing the same strain of chile from the same seed source for four hundred years. Production is on a small scale—you will see vendors at farmers markets with a half-dozen one-pound baggies of roasted chile for sale. The hotness of Chimayó chile is as unpredictable as always, and the taste is quite different from chile grown in the south. For that reason, many people think Chimayó chile is best when it is allowed to turn red, dried, mixed to homogenize the hotness, and powdered for red chile sauce. Chimayó chile is the closest we can experience to the original chile that Spanish settlers and Indians grew in the 1600s.

COOKING WITH CHILE

Here is a selection of traditional chile recipes, along with a few not-so-traditional ones we've developed over the years or come across in our travels around New Mexico.

Red chile, powdered or crushed, is available in supermarkets or Mexican groceries in most parts of the United States. Green chile is ubiquitous in New Mexico but can be hard to come by in other parts of the country. Many a New Mexico–style restaurant in places like New York and Miami has failed because of the problem of getting good green chile.

Fresh roasted green chile does not travel very well. In the car, its tantalizing smell can be way too much of a good thing, and if it is not thoroughly wrapped and sealed, the juice can stain or cause caustic burns on fabric and other surfaces. It is not allowed in carry-on baggage on airplanes. Dried or canned, it loses much of its distinctive flavor.

Green chile does keep well frozen. In fact, many New Mexicans buy a bushel of roasted chile in the fall, put it up in sandwich-size freezer bags and thaw as needed, providing a year-round supply of good-as-fresh green chile. We have successfully sent containers of frozen green chile to students and wandering New Mexicans in other parts of the country on dry ice via FedEx, but the cost factor makes this a solution of last resort.

You can order frozen green chile shipped via FedEx or Airborne Express from Wholesale Hatch Chile (www.wholesalechile.com; 888-336-4228) or Bueno Foods (www.buenofoods.com; 800-952-4453). Again, the issue is cost. For example, Bueno sells packages of six 13-ounce containers of green chile by mail order for $25.99, which is only slightly more than a New Mexico supermarket would charge; the catch is that shipping and handling costs an extra $50.

The best solution we've found is to find a supermarket where you live that also has locations in New Mexico, such as Albertsons, Smith's, or Whole Foods. These stores will often special-order frozen chile at prices that are not much higher than you'd pay in New Mexico. The minimum order quantity is likely to be around fifty to sixty pounds.

If you can't find an affordable and practical source of New Mexico green chile, use oven-roasted, peeled, and chopped Anaheim chiles and add a few Serrano chiles (split these small green chiles, remove the inside core and seeds, and chop finely) for flavor—a poor substitute for the real thing, but tasty enough.

Traditional Green Chile Stew

This is the most traditional of all New Mexico dishes, the one that defines the state's cuisine. Elsewhere in the Southwest, you may find something called green chile stew in restaurants, but it is not even remotely the same.

Serves 6

2 pounds cubed pork
1 tablespoon olive oil
1 large onion, chopped
2 cloves garlic, minced
2 cups water
2 cups roasted, peeled, deveined, and chopped fresh or frozen green chile
4 medium red potatoes, diced skin-on
1 teaspoon salt
1 teaspoon dried oregano
1 tablespoon fresh chopped or dried cilantro

In a large cooking pot or Dutch oven, brown the pork in olive oil. Add the onion and garlic and continue to sauté until the onion becomes transparent. Add the water, green chile, and potatoes. Bring to a boil, and then reduce heat. Add the salt, oregano, and cilantro. Simmer for 2 to 3 hours, adding more water as necessary. Serve with warm flour tortillas.

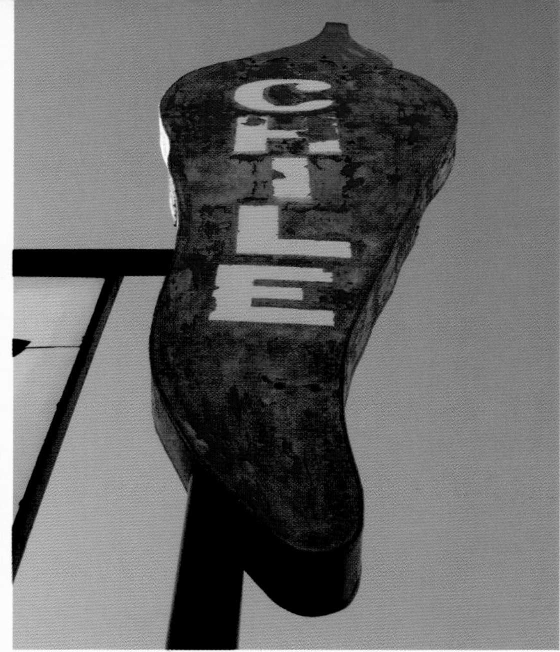

Richard's Green Chile Bison Stew

Variations on the basic green chile stew concept are endless. We've seen it made with everything from piñon nuts to chorizo, and then topped with sour cream, raw onions, or avocado slices. Feel free to use your own ideas and experiment, as many New Mexicans do. It's a hard dish to really screw up. Here is my personal green chile stew recipe, which I've been serving for twenty years.

Serves 8

1 pound ground bison
1 tablespoon olive oil
1 large onion, chopped
4 cups vegetable broth or beef broth
2 cups roasted, peeled, deveined, and chopped fresh or frozen green chile
1½ cups soaked and precooked posole, or 1 can white hominy
1½ cups soaked and precooked black beans, or 1 can black beans
1 small can (4.25 ounces) sliced black olives, drained
2 tablespoons chopped fresh cilantro
1 teaspoon cumin
1 teaspoon cinnamon
2 teaspoons vanilla extract
3 Roma tomatoes, quartered and sliced into chunks

In a large cooking pot or Dutch oven, brown the ground bison in olive oil, and then add the onion and continue to sauté until the meat is crumbly and onion pieces are transparent. Add the other ingredients except the tomatoes. Bring to a boil, reduce heat, and simmer covered for 2 hours, adding water if necessary. Add the tomatoes during the last 20 minutes of cooking. Serve with warm flour tortillas.

Traditional Posole Stew

This is the "other" traditional New Mexican stew dish besides green chile stew and Three Sisters Stew. It is especially popular during the Christmas season, when many village households keep a pot simmering on the stove to serve to drop-in guests.

Serves 6 to 8

2 pounds boneless pork loin, cubed
1 tablespoon olive oil
1 medium onion, chopped
4 cloves garlic, minced
4 dried red chile pods, crushed, or 2 tablespoons crushed red chile
2 cups white or yellow posole, either bagged in liquid or nixtamalized and soaked overnight (see Three Sisters Posole on page 19)*
5 cups chicken broth
1 teaspoon dried oregano
1 teaspoon salt
2 medium tomatoes, quartered and sliced into chunks
Chopped cilantro

In a large skillet, brown the pork in the olive oil over medium high heat, stirring constantly. Lower the heat to medium, add the onion and garlic, and continue to sauté until the onion is transparent.

Place the cooked meat, onion, and garlic in a large cooking pot or Dutch oven. Add all remaining ingredients except the tomatoes and cilantro. Cover and simmer for 4 to 6 hours, adding liquid if necessary. Add the tomatoes during the last half hour of cooking. Garnish with cilantro and serve with flour tortillas.

*For a quick version, substitute a large 16-ounce can of white or yellow hominy for the posole.

above: Crescencio Ochoa

Traditional Enchilada Casserole

Blue corn enchiladas filled with cheddar cheese, ground beef, shredded chicken, or turkey, are the most popular dish served at New Mexican restaurants in Santa Fe, Taos, and Albuquerque. We were surprised to learn that this familiar dish bears little resemblance to the enchiladas traditionally made in northern New Mexico. In our interview with Estevan Arellano, he described how different the enchiladas his mother used to make on the farm were from the kind served in New Mexico restaurants today. Based on his description, we surveyed a number of longtime traditional farmers in the Velarde and Embudo areas and developed this recipe for the kind of enchiladas old-timers used to make.

Serves 4

10 dried red chiles
3 cups water
2 cloves garlic, minced
1 cup chopped onion
Olive oil
12 blue corn tortillas, preferably homemade (see page 15)
1 pound cooked, deboned, and shredded chicken
1 cup stewed and crushed tomatoes
4 eggs

To make red chile sauce:

Rinse the chiles and place them in a cooking pot with the water. Bring to a full boil, reduce heat, and simmer for 20 minutes until soft. Meanwhile, sauté the garlic and onion in olive oil. Add to the chiles. Do not drain. Put the chiles, water, onion, and garlic in a blender and purée until smooth. Salt to taste.

To make enchiladas:

Preheat oven to 375 degrees F.

In a shallow casserole dish, place one layer of four tortillas to cover the bottom. Spread one-half of the chicken meat and one-half of the crushed tomatoes over the tortillas, and then add another layer of tortillas and the remainder of the chicken and tomatoes. Add the final top layer of tortillas. Pour on enough red chile sauce to cover the top. Bake covered for about 20 minutes. Then pour each of the raw eggs on top, evenly spaced so one yolk tops each tortilla. Bake uncovered for 10 more minutes or until eggs are cooked to taste and sauce is bubbly.

Note: The same recipe can be made with chopped green chile instead of red chile sauce. Red chile enchiladas are traditional, but green chile enchiladas are more popular these days. Surprisingly, enchiladas were traditionally made without cheese. If you prefer to top them with cheese, use queso ranchero (available in Mexican grocery stores) or Monterey Jack. Yellow cheeses such as cheddar and Colby were not traditionally used in New Mexico cooking.

Enchiladas Durango Style

Over the centuries, many other styles of enchiladas have been brought up the Camino Real to New Mexico from various parts of Mexico. This unusual version originates in the state of Durango and likely came here during late colonial times, when the churches in Santa Fe were under the jurisdiction of the Archdiocese of Durango and many people migrated from that area.

Serves 6

½ cup dried and crushed red chile
1 cup hot water
1 clove garlic
Pinch of cumin
Pinch of salt
1 bar (about 1.4 ounces) dark chocolate
1 cup grated ranch cheese or Monterey Jack cheese *
¾ onion, chopped
2 tablespoons butter
12 corn tortillas

To make the enchilada sauce, soak the crushed chile in hot water for five minutes. Place it (including the water) in a blender along with the garlic, cumin, salt, and chocolate. Purée, pour into a saucepan, and place on the stove over low heat until thickened. Mix the cheese and the onion together.

Pour a portion of the enchilada sauce onto a plate. Melt a portion of the butter in a skillet, and then heat a tortilla for 15 seconds on each side, until soft. Immediately drag the tortilla through the enchilada sauce to coat one side. Place the tortilla on a plate, chile side up, fill it with the cheese and onion (or other stuffing) mixture, roll it, and set it aside on another plate.

When all 12 enchiladas are rolled, smother them with the remainder of the enchilada sauce and top with grated cheese. Serve with beans, rice, and lettuce on the side.

*These enchiladas can also be stuffed with shredded chicken or ground beef.

Chiles Rellenos

Relleno means "refilled" or stuffed. This is the traditional New Mexican version of chiles rellenos, a popular dish that takes many different forms throughout Mexico.

Serves 4

8 whole green chiles, roasted and peeled
1 cup grated Monterey Jack cheese
3 raw eggs, yolks separated from the whites
Pinch of salt
Pinch of pepper
Olive oil
⅔ cup all-purpose flour
1 cup stewed and crushed tomatoes

Preheat oven to 350 degrees. Carefully slice each chile pod down one side. Remove the seeds, leaving the stem intact. Fill each chile with grated cheese, and then fold the sides of the chile together. Beat the egg yolks until smooth, adding the salt and pepper. Beat the egg whites until stiff and fold into the yolks.

Pour a shallow layer of olive oil in a skillet. While the oil is heating, spread the flour on a clean surface. Carefully drag each chile through the flour, and then sprinkle a little more flour on top. Holding the chile by the stem and the tip, dip it lightly into the egg batter. Immediately place it in the hot oiled skillet. Brown on both sides, and then place it on a paper towel to drain.

Put the breaded chiles into a baking dish or cake pan. Pour the stewed tomatoes over the top. Bake uncovered for 30 minutes.

EARTH

Passengers who look out jetliner windows while approaching or leaving the Albuquerque International Sunport, the state's only major commercial airport, will see vast expanses of harsh tan landscape sculpted by past flash floods into mazes of dry arroyos. From high above, it doesn't look as if anything could grow there, and in fact, in most places very little does. Cattle ranchers know that it takes forty acres of typical New Mexico ranchland to graze a single steer.

But in narrow corridors along the Rio Grande and the few other year-round rivers, greenery does grow, whether it's fruits and vegetables, dairy pasturage, hay and alfalfa, or just the wild salt cedar that invades riverbanks wherever they aren't being cultivated. The amount of irrigated land suitable for small farming is minuscule in the vast New Mexico landscape. In fact, it's about the same as the amount of farmland under cultivation in the tiny state of Vermont. Yet for many farmers, that's what makes it special.

Once in a decade or so, springtime in New Mexico brings a long spell of drenching rain. When it does, the results are spectacular—normally arid countryside is suddenly carpeted with brilliant yellow and purple flowers as far as the eye can see. According to farmers, this proves that the earth is rich in nutrients—if you can only develop it. Thus, for many, planting one cover crop after another is the essence of farming. Enriching the soil is like preparing a canvas for a masterpiece of what many farmers talk about as "the art of farming." At every small farming conference, vendors hawk bags of compost, jugs of compost tea, and cartons of live earthworms. Every produce farmer takes pride in his or her soil. When you visit a farm, they will insist that you feel the dirt, and they'll trickle it through their fingers searching for an earthworm to show you . . .

Daniel Carmona of Cerro Vista Farm north of Taos explains:

This was all in sagebrush. Since '97 we've cleared sagebrush and planted cover crops—buckwheat, winter peas, fava beans—in rotations, improving the soil, building up the organic matter. The soil tested at first to be excellent, except it needed organic matter and nitrogen. So cover crops are the way to get both. We try to have about half of our fields in cover crops. Then the next year we grow vegetables, and the year after that we grow cover crops again. That keeps weeds down while it puts organic matter and nitrogen in the soil.

Healthy soil is the most important thing you need for organic agriculture. You need microbes living on the organic matter in the soil. That's how you get healthy plants. It's pretty miraculous—the soil is just wonderful here. When

above: Heidi's Raspberry Farm

we plow down the cover crops and plant another cover crop and plow that down, we're getting more and more microbes and it just looks healthier. It's such a pleasure to work the soil. In fact, it's built into the rules for organic certification. You have to be doing soil improvement of some sort, because that's really the key to successful organics.

BACKCOUNTRY

Most of the farms covered in this book lie along the Rio Grande and its tributaries such as the Rio Chama. Most are located in the northern part of the state, where small farms have been under cultivation since Spanish colonial times or before, and where large-scale agriculture is unknown. Some are close to urban areas, including at least one farm within Albuquerque, New Mexico's largest city. Another is within easy walking distance of the town plaza in Socorro.

But others are in some of the most remote areas imaginable. For instance, Nancy Nathanya Coonridge grazes her goatherd on wild rangeland near the edge of the Acoma Indian Reservation. When I went to visit her, I turned off the interstate at the nearest small town and drove for an hour on a narrow strip of two-lane blacktop between a black, forbidding lava flow and sheer pink cliffs glowing in the dawn light, and then turned off onto a gravel road. Nancy's directions continue:

You are going across a prairie with the Sawtooth Mountains in front of you. In about ten miles (gee, don't go by mileage here but by the landmarks) you come to an orange 30-gallon drum turned on its side to use as a mailbox. Turn here. In four or so miles you reach some mailboxes. Please bring in the mail if we have any.

From the mailboxes, it takes at least one and a half hours on dry roads. Cross the cattle guard, continuing on the main road, keeping right. In .6 miles from the mailboxes the road splits. Go left with the main road. You will pass a couple more cattle guards. After a while you go up a steep hill. Near the top, don't go on the road to the left. Pass several roads, some even with names. Turn right, then right again, then left. The road goes downhill and the area opens up. You will see Bell and D-Cross Mountains ahead of you on the horizon. Drive through the green metal gate. As with all gates in cowboy country, leave them the way you find them—shut if they are shut, open if they are open. From the green gate to the next windmill is 1.7 miles. As you leave the green gate, you go downhill and cross a small dry creek bed. IMMEDIATELY TURN RIGHT up a long hill. This is where people go wrong and don't turn. Then as they follow the directions it still seems to make sense until they come to impassable places in the arroyo. (To repeat the directions: After the gate you drive only a little way, dropping into and across a small dry river bed and IMMEDIATELY turn right up a long hill.) There is an old faded pair of blue sweat pants in the tree right after you turn up the hill.

Stay on the main road, and after a while you will see the arroyo ahead of you. The road splits just before the arroyo. Use the right fork, which is the most well-traveled road. You will wind around and end up at a windmill. If the small arroyo you cross immediately after the split is full of water or mud, don't go that way, but at the split continue to the left and drop into the main arroyo and veer to the right going west. You will jump out to the RIGHT (do not jump out to the left!) and end up at a windmill. If you stay to the right at the split, you go more directly to the windmill. At the windmill there is a gate, usually open. Continue on straight through the gate. There is a sign here put up by our neighbor who was tired of people getting lost and ending up at his place. It is five miles to the dairy from this gate.

Keep going straight and you will drop into the main arroyo. Watch out for the boulders. You stay in the main arroyo and then follow the track out to the left. Tracks may go off to the right but will dead-end at a split rail fence. The track continues on top for a while and then goes back into the arroyo. You have one more small jump out and back in before the main exit, which is straight ahead up the left bank. It is now a 15- to 20-minute drive to the dairy.

Once you are in the big meadow, you may see the buildings on the hills on the west horizon.

EXPLORING NEW MEXICO'S FARM COUNTRY

Farms are tucked away in the most unlikely places around New Mexico. A thorough exploration of the state might take you to places like Portales, in the southeastern prairie, where local growers produce more Valencia peanuts than the rest of the United States combined and sell them to Sunland Inc., the local peanut

above: Martinez Orchards' wind machine

processing and marketing cooperative. Or to the extreme northwest corner of the state, where Navajo families raise sheep and tend small patches of corn and round, sweet watermelons not far from the Navajo Agricultural Products Industry's seventy thousand–acre tribal farm near Farmington. The NAPI farm holds the distinction of being the largest single recipient of federal farm subsidies and hasn't turned a profit since 1980. But for a close-up chance to experience what's special about small farming in New Mexico, try one of the following day trips along back roads through some of the most visited parts of the state.

A Northern New Mexico Day Trip

The easiest road trip through the heart of New Mexico's small farm country is also one of the most spectacular, winding through a striking diversity of ecosystems from rugged desert and cool mountain valleys to rich bottomland along the Rio Grande and the hotly contested "dry water" of the Rio Pojoaque. Diversity is reflected in the communities along the route, including centuries-old Spanish villages, Indian pueblos, and Anglo "back-to-the-land" organic farmsteads.

This 104-mile trip loops from the Indian pueblo of Pojoaque to the fruit farming villages of Dixon and Embudo and back again, following the High Road to Taos, one of northern New Mexico's most popular scenic drives, and the less-known River Road. It is easy to reach from Santa Fe (start at Pojoaque, twelve miles north of the capital city) or Taos (start at Embudo, fifteen miles south of town). Allow at least five hours for the drive.

The High Road: Coming from Santa Fe via US 84/285, start at **Pojoaque**, an ancient Towa pueblo with a very small tribal population. The large cultural center and museum, including a replica of the original pueblo, shares the highway side with a shopping center of non-Indian enterprises, such as a bank, a supermarket and a liquor store, which lease from the tribe and serve the residents of the Pojoaque Valley. The main sources of tribal income are the Cities of Gold Casino—one of the first Indian gambling casinos in the state, built in the pueblo's former high school building—and the lavish new Buffalo Thunder Resort, with its thirty-six-hole golf course.

A short distance past the Cities of Gold Casino, turn right on NM 503, which follows the Nambé River through a green valley that has traditionally been a dairy farming center. Along the way, you'll pass a turnoff on the right to **Nambé Pueblo**, one of several small, secluded Indian pueblos along the route, which has a public picnic area, waterfall, and fishing lake. Then the highway heads abruptly into arid foothill country at the base of the Sangre de Cristo Mountains.

Turn left onto NM 520 at the sign marking the way to Santuario. Here you'll make a steep descent into the large agricultural village of **Chimayó**. Originally an Indian pueblo, Chimayó's population declined following the Pueblo Revolt of 1680 and the Spanish Reconquest. Lacking enough able-bodied people to work the pueblo's rich cornfields, Chimayó became one of the few Indian communities to invite non-Indians to join them. In Spanish colonial times, it was common practice in Santa Fe to banish petty criminals, many of whom went to join the Chimayó people. As a result, Chimayó became a predominantly *meztizo* (mixed Spanish-Indian blood) community, one of the few in early New Mexico. Soon other Spanish settlers claimed farmsteads in nearby parts of the valley. The village is best known for the **Santuario de Chimayó**, one of the most picturesque eighteenth-century village churches along the High Road to Taos, which is worth visiting for its glimpse into the spirituality that is central to rural life in northern New Mexico. As the destination for thousands of Catholic pilgrims who walk there from all over the state to arrive on Good Friday, the Santuario contains a small room where visitors take holy dirt from a *pozo* (literally, a "well," though it contains no water). The pozo marks the spot where, according to legend, a Christ figure appeared in 1810. Dirt from it is said to have miraculous healing powers, as attested by the many crutches, baby shoes, handwritten prayers, and other artifacts that fill the adjoining vestibule. Nearby, another church, the Chapel of the Niño de Atocha, is dedicated to the child Jesus, who many believe roams the village after dark doing good deeds and looking out for the health of children. On the village plaza, one of the last surviving examples of a fortified plaza, with entrances too narrow to allow motor vehicles to enter, the **Chimayó Museum** traces the history of the village. Raising sheep and weaving blankets and garments with the wool in a distinctive Spanish colonial style that came up the Camino Real from Saltillo, Mexico, has been a traditional occupation in Chimayó for hundreds of years, and visitors to one of the several weaving shops in town can still watch old-timers plying their trade on handlooms. Chimayó is also the center of chile cultivation in northern New Mexico.

above: Coonridge goats

From Chimayó, proceed east (the opposite direction from Santa Cruz and Española) on NM 76, which climbs to an elevation of more than eight thousand feet at the base of Truchas Peak, the centerpiece of the vast, alpine Pecos Wilderness. Here, the village of **Truchas**, with its narrow streets, colorful cemetery, and verdant surrounding pasturelands, seems to have changed little over the years, though a closer look reveals that it is home to numerous artists' studios and even a rural bed-and-breakfast inn—a big change from just a generation ago, when Anglo outsiders were not welcome in this and other mountain villages. As always, the main occupations in town are raising sheep and a few cattle, which typically graze on national forest allotments in the summer months and are relocated to lower ground in the winter, and cutting firewood and roof beams in the forest. A few organic farms such as Gemini Farm have sprung up here in recent years, though because of the short growing season most of the produce consists of root vegetables such as radishes and parsnips. Truchas was selected by filmmaker Robert Redford as the shooting location for the 1986 film *The Milagro Beanfield War*, based on Taos author John Nichols' novel about small farmers' struggle for acequia water rights.

Like Truchas, **Las Trampas** is set along a year-round stream that flows from the high Sangre de Cristos to irrigate small vegetable plots and lush pastures. The village is the site of the **Misión de San José de Gracia church**, the most picturesque of the village churches along the route. It has been in use since 1776. Las Trampas is one of several traditional communities around northern New Mexico that is battling to recover village *ejidos* (community grazing and farming land) that was deeded to their ancestors by the U.S. Congress pursuant to the 1848 treaty ending the Mexican War but later appropriated by the federal General Land Office, real estate swindlers of the notorious "Santa Fe Ring," and an Albuquerque-based lumber company. The land at issue amounts to about forty-six thousand acres, or almost a thousand acres for every man, woman, and child in the village.

Las Trampas is the gateway to the Rio Embudo watershed, where dozens of creeks flow from the snowcapped mountains into narrow, green pastoral valleys sheltered between dry ridgelines covered with piñon pines. From the highway, unpaved side roads meander off to tiny villages lost in time—El Valle, Vallecito, Rodarte, Llano, and half a dozen others, all clustered within an area of about twenty square miles. Here, the highway ends in a T-intersection. Turn left—west—on NM 75. (If you were following the entire High Road to Taos scenic route, you would go right on NM 73 through Peñasco instead and then drive through the national forest, but for this farmlands tour you'll want to turn left.)

NM 75 will bring you to the turnoff on your right to **Picurís Pueblo**, the smallest of the nineteen Indian pueblos in New Mexico, with a present-day population of about 330. It has occupied the same secluded location, far removed from the other northern pueblos, for nearly eight centuries. Visitors to the pueblo will find a museum displaying, among other artifacts, the bronze-looking micaceous pottery for which the pueblo is known. There is also a restaurant serving Pueblo Indian fare made from produce grown locally in the area. The Misión de San Lorenzo church, built in 1776 and abandoned a century later, has been restored by pueblo craftsmen using materials found during excavation of the site and original building methods. Although the pueblo does not grow much in the way of food or vegetables, it has its own tribal bison herd, which produces meat used to feed schoolchildren and the elderly and is also sold at Santa Fe and other regional farmers markets.

From Picurís Pueblo, NM 75 descends alongside the Rio Embudo, bringing you to **Dixon** on a side road off to the right. Sheltered between high hills at 6,000 feet elevation, irrigated by 200-year-old acequias that divert river water, this mixed Spanish and Anglo village of about 1,500 people has been a productive farming area for centuries. Dixon has the largest concentration of certified organic farms in New Mexico. The Dixon Cooperative Market, a member-owned grocery store, sells food from area growers to co-op members around the Embudo Valley (membership is also open to visitors for $25 a year, and the market says it will have an online Internet store some day soon to serve nonlocals [www.dixonmarket.com]). The co-op also sponsors the lively **Dixon Farmers' Market** on Wednesday afternoons from July through the end of October. Today the main crops are apples and grapes. In the village, the small family-owned **La Chiripada Winery** [www.lachiripada.com] has regularly won awards at the New Mexico State Fair Wine Competition, the Southwest Wine Competition, and other independent winery competitions around the country, with varied offerings ranging from dry barrel-fermented whites to cellar-quality reds and intriguingly fruity picnic wines. The Johnson family, who built the adobe winery by hand in 1981, works in cooperation with their neighbors, the Tuckers, to produce an annual crop of twenty to thirty tons of grapes; open for free tasting seven days a week; 505-579-4437. Just down the road, at the intersection of NM 75 and NM 68, **Vivac Winery** [www.vivacwinery.com] is the labor of love of two brothers, Dixon natives Jesse and Chris Padberg, and their wives, who make quality cabernet sauvignon, merlot, and zinfandel as well as a proprietary "Fire Vineyard" blend with lingering notes of smoke, ripe peaches, and green chile; open for free tasting seven days a week; 505-579-4441.

This brings you to the intersection with NM 68, the main highway from Santa Fe to Taos, and concludes the High Road portion of the journey. (If you're taking this drive from Taos, you'll start at this point and return via the High Road.)

The River Road: You are now at the confluence of the Rio Embudo and the Rio Grande, just below the long grade where NM 68 descends nearly two thousand feet from the plateau where Taos is situated. From NM 75, turn left—south—on NM

facing: Matt Romero farm

68. A drive of about a mile will bring you to **Embudo**, a valley community of fruit orchards and traditional small farms, where chemical-free growing has always been the norm. Representative of the local farmers who grow a phenomenal range of crops on small plots of land is **Comida de Campos**, where Ermita and Margaret Campos, with their multigenerational family, grow apples, blackberries, blueberries, cherries, currants, nectarines, peaches, pears, plums, quince, raspberries, and strawberries, as well as artichokes, asparagus, basil, beans, bell peppers, broccoli, brussels sprouts, cabbage, cauliflower, celery, chile, corn, cucumbers, eggplant, endive, horseradish, onions, and tomatoes.

The Campos family uses most of their produce in their on-site cooking school, where they and guest chefs offer classes in Native Feasts, Farm Cooking, and Farm Cooking for Kids during the summer months. They sell their excess crops from a fruit stand on the main highway and at the Taos and Santa Fe farmers markets; 505-852-0017 or 877-552-4452. Another notable grower in the area, Johnny McMullin of **Embudo Valley Organics**, raises two thousand free-range turkeys each year on a twenty-five-acre farm fenced into one-acre pastures planted with alfalfa, clover, chicory, rye, and fescue; he moves the birds from one pasture to another every few weeks. McMullin sells all his turkeys through supermarkets, natural food markets, and food co-ops in Albuquerque, Santa Fe, Los Alamos, and Taos. He also sells turkey eggs to Taos Pueblo for ceremonial purposes.

Continuing south for about three miles, you'll see a turnoff on your right to **Velarde**, another pastoral fruit orchard village that dates back to early Spanish colonial times. It was originally called La Joya, a Spanish word meaning "jewel," which was used to denote the best farmlands in Nuevo Mexico; it was later renamed for one of the oldest families of Spanish settlers in the area, whose descendants continue to farm in Velarde. From the turnoff, a maze of winding farm roads heads south along the river. (Actually, there are two river roads, one on each bank of the Rio Grande, but the route along the east bank is greener and more varied, offering glimpses of many traditional multicrop fields. Follow the narrow paved road, County Road 41, which eventually becomes NM 389. Near Velarde at 1508 Highway 68, you'll find **Black Mesa Winery**, where former Coloradoans Jerry and Lynda Burd make twenty-three different varietal wines ranging from local reds such as cabernet sauvignon and Sangiovese to a champagne-process sparkling white wine. Their grapes—seventy tons per year—come from the couple's four vineyards in Velarde as well as from other growers around the state. The tasting room on the main highway is open seven days a week and charges a nominal fee; 505-852-2820 or 800-852-6372; [www.blackmesawinery.com].

Several miles down the River Road, on your right, is **Los Luceros**, a territorial-era ranching compound listed on the National Register of Historic Places. Anthropologist-philanthropist Mary Cabot Wheelwright, an heiress of Boston's prominent Cabot family who is most remembered for establishing the Wheelwright Museum of the American Indian in Santa Fe, bought the hacienda and 140 acres of pastureland, fruit orchards, and cottonwood bosque in 1923 and made it her home for the next thirty-five years. Recently restored by a Cabot family nonprofit foundation, Los Luceros features formal flower gardens and an art gallery, as well as a working farm area with apple trees, alfalfa fields, and a few horses, cows, and sheep. The Sangre de Cristo Audubon Society supervises the restoration of the forest areas along the Rio Grande and monitors the bird life there. Open to the public daily from April through October; 505-852-3245. Next door, at the **Los Luceros Winery**, Bruce and Sue Noel grow cold-weather grapes from Canada and England to produce their unusual seyval blanc, vidal blanc, cayuga, and baco noir wines. Their tasting room is open weekend and holiday afternoons and by appointment at other times; 505-852-1085; [www. nmwine.com].

A short distance south of Los Luceros, the village of **Alcalde** is home to the **Alcalde Sustainable Agriculture Science Center**, a research and outreach facility operated by New Mexico State University for the benefit of fruit growers in northern New Mexico. The problem of late freezes makes farm profits uncertain for the more than 350 small growers in the area, so the center experiments with late-planting and short-season cultivars of berries, grapes, apples, and peaches, which it tests in 2.5-acre organic plots and recommends to local farmers. Tours are available by appointment; 505-852-2668.

The River Road ends at NM 74 just west of Ohkay Owingeh (San Juan) Pueblo. To continue your rural road trip and avoid most of the traffic congestion in the city of Española, turn right (west) on NM 74 and cross the Rio Grande. After about a mile, just past the village of **Chamita**, turn left on the first paved road, crossing the Rio Chama, and then turn left again onto US 84/285 at the village of **Hernandez**. This highway will bring you in to the south end of Española. Do not

follow the main highway back across the Rio Grande. Instead, turn right just before the bridge onto NM 30. This back route takes you past **Santa Clara Pueblo** and the imposing **Black Mesa**, a steep lava formation that towers over **San Ildefonso Pueblo**. Off-limits to non-Indians, the mesa top holds the ruins of an ancestral pueblo that remains an important ceremonial site. This traditional pueblo is famed for its black-on-black pottery and has a small museum; visitors must check in at the tribal offices before entering the pedestrians-only central plaza area. Where NM 30 meets NM 502 in a complex interchange designed to accommodate Los Alamos commuter traffic, keep to the left (east). After crossing the Otowi Bridge over the Rio Grande, turn left at the main paved road into San Ildefonso Pueblo and then immediately turn right onto County Road 285/84. This narrow road follows the Rio Pojoaque among long, narrow farm plots—Spanish colonial land grants that have been subdivided by inheritance over more than a dozen generations, always keeping frontage on the usually dry riverbed to preserve water rights. The result is long, narrow farms where small corn milpas and alfalfa fields press up against sheep and llama pens, artists' studios, and hidden, sometimes opulent estates. County Road 84 provides a close-up look at the rural villages of **El Rancho, Jacona, and Jaconita** along its eight-mile route to the main Santa Fe–Taos highway. Water rights along County Road 84, from San Ildefonso Pueblo to Pojoaque, are the subject of the astoundingly complicated Aamodt litigation, which was filed in 1966 and is now the longest-running court case in U.S. history. At Pojoaque, the county road joins busy four-lane divided US 84/285 for the quick last leg of the drive back to Santa Fe.

The Upper Rio Grande

Motorists who drive north from Taos on NM 522, following the Rio Grande toward its headwaters, enter a land almost unknown to Puebloans and early Spanish colonists. This was the *comanchería*, the domain of the nomadic Comanche raiding parties that became notorious for attacking farms from Texas to Kansas and southern Colorado. They sometimes preyed on outlying Indian pueblos until 1779, when they reached an uneasy truce with Spanish traders who bartered tools, cloth, and food with them for bison hides and Plains Indian slaves and agreed not to settle in Comanche territory. Soon after the region became U.S. territory in 1848, smallpox and cholera epidemics wiped out most of the Comanches in the area, and ten years later Fort Garland was established in the center of southern Colorado's San Luis Valley to protect new farming settlements north of Taos.

In the decades that followed, New Mexican Hispanics moved north to start new farming villages such as **Costilla, New Mexico**, and nearby **San Luis, Colorado**. Minority groups, including Scandinavians, Japanese, and Mormons, also established small, remote potato-farming communities, several of which still survive, hidden at the ends of long, unpaved back roads.

The area saw another wave of would-be settlers in the late 1960s and early '70s, when it became the center of a counterculture "back to the land" movement. Hippies disenchanted by urban problems dropped out and moved to the mesas around **Arroyo Hondo**, north of Taos, to start communes such as Morningstar New Mexico, the Hog Farm, and New Buffalo, which was glorified in the 1969

above: Black Mesa, San Ildefonso Pueblo

film *Easy Rider*. (Members of New Buffalo voted against allowing photography there, so the commune was re-created as a movie set on Mulholland Drive near Los Angeles.) The movie inspired a wave of newcomers—musicians, artists, poets, and idealists, but, unfortunately, few farmers—which overwhelmed some of these utopian compounds. Inexperience combined with the hardships of farming the poor, arid sagebrush country spelled the end for most of the hippie communes. The nearly abandoned New Buffalo underwent a renovation in the early 1990s to become a nostalgic bed-and-breakfast. The intentional spiritual community of **Lama** lasted for thirty years before being all but destroyed by a fast-moving forest fire in 1996, and rebuilding efforts are proceeding slowly. **New Buffalo** opened its doors to provide shelter for the refugees from the Lama fire and never reopened as a B and B. The Hog Farm relocated to a two hundred-acre ranch in Laytonville, California, where leader Hugh "Wavy Gravy" Romney operates a performing arts camp for kids called Camp Winnarainbow. Though the old hippie communes may be gone, their influence on northern New Mexico farm culture lives on. Hundreds of baby-boomer veterans of the hippie era continue to live on small farmsteads scattered through the region and have played a key role in the organic and sustainable agriculture movement in the state. Cultural tensions that arose between counterculture Anglos and traditional Hispanic farmers in northern New Mexico also persist today, and many old-timers still apply the epithet "hippie" to all Anglo farmers.

Taking NM 522 north from Taos (it becomes CO 159 when it enters Colorado) for about two hours and turning west at Blanca on US 160 will bring you to one of the region's most spectacular natural areas, Great Sand Dunes National Park. The park adjoins the Nature Conservancy's Medano-Zapata Ranch, home to a herd of more than two thousand bison.

The Rio Chama: From Española (midway between Santa Fe and Taos) where US 84/285 meets NM 68, turn west and follow US 84 up the Rio Chama, past old Spanish farming villages such as **Mendenales** and **Tierra Azul**. About twenty-three miles from Española, the little town of **Abiquiú** is the main population center in the area, with a country store, a gas station, and a motel. Abiquiú was founded in 1754 as a pueblo of genízaros—Hispanicized Indians without tribal affiliation—who were given land here to establish a buffer community between the Spanish and Pueblo settlements along the Rio Grande and the Navajo and Apache lands to the west. In the early twentieth century, Abiquiú residents voted to be a village under state jurisdiction, rejecting the option to declare themselves an independent Indian pueblo. Beginning in the 1930s, the village's most prominent resident, painter Georgia O'Keeffe, put Abiquiú on the map with her paintings of the area's colorful, surrealistic rock formations. In recent years, other celebrities have made their homes in the Abiquiú area.

As you approach Abiquiú, you'll see a sign on your left marking the parking area for the archaeological site of **Poshuouinge**. A rocky half-mile trail climbs two hundred feet to a hilltop overlooking the 750-year-old pueblo ruin, the most accessible of several sites where the Indians of the Chama Valley developed an unusual method of dry-land farming that used wafflelike grid plots and volcanic ash mulch to capture rainwater and snowmelt. Nearby, on the other side of the highway, stand the burned-out ruins of a *morada*, or **penitente chapel**, once used by the Hermanos de la Luz, a secretive lay religious sect that became widespread in northern New Mexico with the weakening of the Catholic church presence in the area after Mexican independence. There are still many penitentes around Abiquiú.

Another unusual religious presence in Abiquiú is **Dar al-Islam**, an intentional community founded in 1979 by American Muslim converts with the help of a princess of the Saudi royal family, who donated funds to buy the 8,500-acre ranch, and an Egyptian architect who oversaw the construction of an adobe mosque, school, and homes. Closed to visitors except by appointment since the September 11, 2001, terrorist attacks, the community now leases most of its irrigated land along the river to local farmers but has long-term plans for an herb farm, a tree nursery, a fish hatchery, a cattle feedlot, and an Arabian horse ranch. The **"White Place,"** a canyon on the Dar al-Islam property that was immortalized in several Georgia O'Keeffe paintings, remains open to hikers. To get there, watch for the turnoff from County Road 155, which turns off to the left west of Abiquiú and runs east along the opposite bank of the Rio Chama. This road also takes you past farms and estates belonging to celebrities such as film stars Marsha Mason and Shirley MacLaine and bestselling self-help authors Harville Hendrix and Helen Hunt.

A jewel among the numerous small farms whose access roads leave the main highway around Abiquiú, **Harmony Farms** occupies thirty acres on the first acequia below Abiquiú Dam. This classical European-style organic farm produces an array of vegetables and herbs, including onions, spinach, green beans, zucchini, broccoli, amaranth, lettuce, basil, dill, cilantro, and several varieties of tomatoes, which they sell at Santa Fe Farmers Market and several other farmers markets in the region, as well as at their own farm stand, which operates in Abiquiú on Wednesday afternoons during the season. Visitors to the farm, which is open to the public during the annual Santa Fe Farmers Market Farm Tour and the Abiquiú Studio Tour, as well as by appointment (505-685-0724), will find long, narrow plots of vegetables and herbs bordered by head-high stands of bright yellow mountain sunflowers and a profusion of other blossoms in white, orange, and magenta hues. The flowers attract bees, ladybugs, and other beneficial insects. There is no bare ground anywhere in sight. "If you leave one bare patch of ground showing," farmers Richard and Nora explain, "insects will take over and eat everything. When a plot is not in use for vegetables or herbs, it is always growing a cover crop to add organic matter to the soil, loading it with nutrients that will be released into future crops. "While alfalfa is the preferred cover crop because it adds nitrogen to the soil, almost any plant will work. "If you let weeds grow, they make a good cover crop," Richard says. They usually try to plow under two consecutive cover crops before planting a vegetable or herb crop. They've been doing it for eight years and take justifiable pride in the rich, soft, wormy earth. The future is uncertain, however. The owners of the land were in the process of selling it as this book was being written, and the farmers had no idea whether the next owners would let them keep farming or if they would have to seek new acreage and start from scratch—a common source of uncertainty for tenant farmers.

Adventuresome travelers may wish to continue up US 84 beyond Abiquiú for forty-five miles to **Tierra Amarilla**. For most of the way, the Rio Chama is out of sight several miles to the west, where it flows through the roadless Chama Wilderness and is itself a federally designated wild river, without agricultural usage except for the gardens tended by the monks at the well-hidden **Christ in the Desert Monastery**. Tierra Amarilla, a Shangri-La sheep-herding village in a broad, green, idyllic valley, is best known as the scene of an armed conflict between the local Alianza Federal de Mercedes (Federal Land Grant Alliance) and government officials in 1967. The group sought the return of community *ejido* land that had originally been part of the village's Spanish land grant but had been seized by the federal government and made part of Carson National Forest. Under the slogan "Justice is our creed and the land is our heritage," activist Reies Tijerina led an armed raid on the Río Arriba County Courthouse. The district attorney, whom Tijerina had planned to arrest for violating alliance members' civil rights, was not there, but in the ensuing gunfight a prison guard and a sheriff's deputy were shot. National media coverage rallied public support, and a sympathetic jury acquitted Tijerina of charges stemming from the courthouse raid. The following year, Tijerina was elected to lead the Hispanic contingent of the Poor People's Campaign march on Washington D.C., under the leadership of Martin Luther King, Jr., who was assassinated less than a month before the march. Around the same time, Tijerinas's house was firebombed. Soon after, Tijerinas was prosecuted on federal charges arising from the Tierra Amarilla courthouse raid, even though he had been acquitted in state court. He was sentenced to two years in federal prison, where his cellmate was notorious Mafia informant Joseph Valachi. After his release, the former activist moved to Mexico, where he lives today, but the dispute over communal village land in Tierra Amarilla continues to this day and has spread to other villages in northern New Mexico. The Rio Arriba courts were moved to a new courthouse in the city of Española.

El Camino Real

El Camino Real de Tierra Adentro ("the King's Highway to the Interior"), which connected Nuevo Mexico's capital at Santa Fe with Mexico City, 1,500 miles to the south throughout the Spanish colonial era, followed the Rio Grande through central and southern New Mexico. The historic route has been replaced by Interstate 25, which runs through open desert several miles west of the river, but travelers who have plenty of time can still explore several stretches of the original Camino Real route which survive as farm-to-market roads. It's 285 miles one-way from

facing: Harmony Farm

harmony
TOUR
2006
Harmony Farm
TOUR
Greenmarket
Healthy • Fresh •
RUSSIAN BANANA
FINGERLING
YuKon

Santa Fe to Las Cruces, the terminus of this tour. Allow at least eight hours for the back-road trip; a return to Santa Fe on the interstate will take about four hours.

The original Camino Real came into Santa Fe as what is now Agua Fria Street, which still has some farms along it just a few blocks from one of the busiest streets in the city. This is especially true in the village of **Agua Fria**, a designated "traditional historic district" along the normally dry Santa Fe River. Although the village is virtually surrounded by the city, its special status makes it immune from annexation. The centerpiece of the village, **San Isidro Church** dates back to 1835 and is still in use. The church is named for the patron saint of farmers and protector of crops. On May 15, the Fiesta de San Isidro (also known as "His Day of Goodwill"), the people of San Isidro and many other New Mexico farming villages hold processions during which priests bless the fields.

Agua Fria Street ends at Airport Road, where a left turn soon brings motorists to Cerrillos Road, the city's congested commercial strip. Turn right on Cerrillos Road to reach Interstate 25, and take the interstate south for two miles to exit 276 by the now-abandoned Santa Fe Downs horse racetrack. Following County Road 54 for several miles through the horsey rural suburb of La Cienega, encouraged by occasional signs that say "Museum" or "Las Golondrinas," will bring you to **El Rancho de las Golondrinas** ("the Ranch of the Swallows"), New Mexico's finest open-air historical museum. The ranch was originally built around 1710 as a *paraje* (country inn) to accommodate travelers on the Camino Real. The two hundred-acre property is situated in a bowl-shaped valley from which no trace of the modern world is visible. The original fortresslike inn has been restored; other historic buildings, including a penitente morada and a one-classroom schoolhouse, have been brought from other parts of the state, and a few period buildings such as a waterwheel-powered flour mill have been reconstructed. Visitors will find a barnyard with burro corrals, sheep pens, a chicken coop, and a goat barn, as well as fields of blue corn, wheat, lavender, chile, pumpkins, squash, and other crops. The old ranch comes alive on weekends, especially Spring Festival in early June, Summer Festival in early August, and Harvest Festival in early October coinciding with the Albuquerque Balloon Fiesta. During the festivals, scores of volunteers in eighteenth-century period costume demonstrate traditional farm skills such as shearing sheep, spinning and dying wool, stringing chile ristras, extracting molasses from sorghum stalks, and making wine from grapes grown on the property. During the summer, at other times of the week, visitors can stroll around the ranch and find themselves completely alone except for a few farm workers (505-471-2261; www.golondrinas.org).

Returning to Interstate 25 at exit 271, you'll soon find yourself driving down a long, steep hill called **La Bajada** (the Descent), which drops seven hundred feet in elevation to the level of the Rio Grande. The steep grade was the biggest obstacle on the entire Camino Real. After coming all the way from Mexico City, wagons had to stop at the foot of La Bajada, unload their wagons, carry their cargo uphill on burros, haul the wagons up empty, and reload them at the top. La Bajada was such a significant landmark in Spanish colonial times that the land below it became known as Rio Abajo (Lower River) and above it, Rio Arriba (Upper River).

At the foot of La Bajada, the interstate enters the **Santo Domingo Reservation**, site of the largest present-day Indian pueblo in the state. It is one of seven adjoining reservations—Cochiti, Santo Domingo, San Felipe, Santa Ana, Zia, Jemez, and Sandia—that together occupy a vast expanse of central New Mexico. If you leave the interstate at exit 259, turning left and continuing through the pueblo,

above: Lawrence G. Marken is a volunteer at El Rancho de las Golondrinas
facing: Golondrinas wheat mill

you'll find a partially paved back road along the Rio Grande, Tribal Road 84, which borders the remaining communal farming fields of the Santo Domingo and San Felipe people. As it leaves Indian land, the road becomes NM 313, taking you through the village of **Algodones** and past **Coronado State Monument**—the ruins of a large pueblo called Kuaua that reluctantly fed and sheltered conquistador Francisco Vásquez de Coronado's expedition in 1540—and enter **Bernalillo**, a sizable farming town that is now partially gentrified thanks to its proximity to Albuquerque. For a look at what local farmers claim is the best farmland in the state, turn right (northwest) on US 550, cross the river, turn left on Rio Rancho Boulevard (NM 528) and, after several miles, turn left again on **Corrales Road** (NM 448), a beautiful scenic drive that takes you through a historic agricultural village where cornfields, old adobes, and acequias are found side-by-side with modern multimillion-dollar mansions. Although the village is less than ten miles as the crow flies from downtown Albuquerque, it has been protected from suburban tract development because there is no bridge across the river near Corrales. The river marks the boundary of the Sandia Reservation, which has refused to allow a bridge to be built. As a result, it's a long drive from the city.

Eventually, Corrales Road will bring you into the city at Alameda Boulevard near the intersection with Coors Boulevard, the main thoroughfare through the city's west side. After crossing Interstate 40 and Central Avenue West, a left turn on Bridge Boulevard (also known as Calle César Chávez) will lead you into the **South Valley**, an area on the outskirts of Albuquerque that has traditionally been agricultural land. Like Corrales, the South Valley is sheltered from suburbanization by the lack of bridges over the river. Although large-scale agribusiness took over parts of the valley in the 1950s by offering large sums to poor Hispanics for their ancestral farmlands, the area remains beautiful, largely rural, deeply traditional, and the poorest neighborhood in Albuquerque.

Rio Bravo Boulevard crosses the river and brings you back to Interstate 25 just south of the Albuquerque International Sunport. Head south on the interstate for five miles to exit 215, the turnoff for the Isleta Gaming Palace. From here, NM 47 follows the old Camino Real route down the east bank of the river through **Isleta Pueblo**, where the graceful white church of **San Augustin** (circa 1613) is one of the oldest mission churches in the United States, and continues into farm country. Some of the communities along the way, including the pastorally named Bosque Farms, have become suburban bedroom communities of Albuquerque. **Los Lunas**, a former Spanish land grant and one of the largest towns on the route, was home to Solomon Luna (1858–1912), a churro sheep baron and son-in-law of a territorial governor, who served as president of the New Mexico Sheep Growers' Association. Widely known as "the one who remained clean among corruption," he was offered a candidacy to the U.S. Senate and later invited to become the first state governor, but he declined both positions. He drowned in a sheep-dipping vat under suspicious circumstances a year after New Mexico became a state. The elegant (and, some say, haunted) **Luna Mansion** in Los Lunas is not only a historic landmark and museum but also a fine and surprisingly affordable steak and seafood restaurant (505-865-7333).

South of Los Lunas, NM 47 heads into almost timeless farm country where most of the fields produce alfalfa and hay to supply nearby ranches. Motorists will find colorful cemeteries and photogenic village churches along the roadside. At the bridge across the river to **Belen**, cross to the west side of the river and continue south on winding NM 109 for the best back road look at the local farms. The road eventually crosses the river again and joins NM 304, the east bank farm-to-market road, which eventually intersects US 60. Take the main highway across the bridge to get back onto Interstate 25. The next twenty-five miles are barren desert without roads or settlements along the river until you reach the vicinity of **Socorro**, where many farm fields are sandwiched between the river and the town's main street. Continue south on the interstate to exit 139 and go east a short distance to the village of **San Antonio**, where one of the main buildings at the central crossroads is **Sichler Farms Produce**, a large family-owned stand where Chris and Paula Sichler sell chile and other vegetables and fruits under a sign declaring, "Food Grows Where Water Flows." The Sichler family also owns other produce stands and farm acreages in Albuquerque's South Valley in the town of Peña Blanca near Cochiti Pueblo and elsewhere. Open August through October; 505-838-2839.

Turning south at San Antonio on NM 1, you'll find one of the most striking examples of farming in harmony with wildlife around, **Bosque del Apache National Wildlife Refuge**. This famous birdwatching area is flooded in the cold months to provide habitat for migratory birds, including forty to fifty thousand snow geese, fifty thousand or more ducks, and up to fourteen thousand sandhill cranes. (The refuge got its start because it was the wintering ground of a small flock of endangered whooping cranes. Although the number of whoopers has doubled in the past decade or so—320 in the world at last count—those that used to come to Bosque del Apache have recently joined another flock that winters along the Texas Gulf Coast.) Water from the Rio Grande is diverted into dammed marshes in the refuge during the cold months to provide habitat for the geese, ducks, and other waterfowl, while in the summer it is channeled to acequias that serve the surrounding private lands, where farmers grow corn and alfalfa. Under a cooperative agreement with the government, the alfalfa is harvested for sale to livestock ranchers, but the corn is left in the fields to provide food for the cranes and other migratory birds.

NM 1 continues along the old Camino Real route, in close proximity to the interstate, for twenty-four miles to the Fort Craig Rest Area, where a road turns

above: cotton and pecans, Hatch area

off toward the river and the new **El Camino Real Heritage Center**. The interpretive center tells the story of the Camino Real's four hundred-year history and of trade and cultural exchange between New Mexico and Mexico, Spain, and Asia. It's possible to follow the back roads through the desert, paralleling the interstate all the way to Las Cruces, except for three miles between exit 92, where NM 1 ends, and exit 89, where NM 181 starts. Roads skirt two large Rio Grande reservoirs, **Elephant Butte Lake** and **Caballo Lake**, and loop through **Truth or Consequences**, a town of retirees and artists famed for its mineral hot springs. The most picturesque segment of the drive leaves the interstate at exit 59 by Caballo Dam. From there, NM 185 winds its way through the little towns of Arrey, Derry, Garfield, and Salem on its way to **Hatch**, which is known for its chile crop. More than a hundred family farms along this road grow about one-third of all chile produced in New Mexico, though most of it is sold not directly to consumers but to a few large processing and wholesaling conglomerates. The first weekend in September, the peak of the green chile harvest season, the annual Hatch Chile Festival draws more than thirty thousand visitors with its community celebration, which includes a parade, the coronation of a Chile Queen, a "Biggest Chile Pod" contest, a fiddling contest, and other events. (Most visitors stay in Truth or Consequences or Las Cruces, since the Hatch area has only two small mom-and-pop motels.)

Continuing along NM 185 will take you about thirty-five miles more into the city of **Las Cruces**. Along the way you'll see plenty of examples of other large-scale farming operations besides chile that help make Las Cruces the agribusiness center of the state, especially cotton fields and pecan orchards. (Although the Indians brought cotton to New Mexico in pre-Hispanic times, pecans are not native to the area and did not arrive until the early twentieth century, when they were introduced as an experimental crop by Fabián García, the famed New Mexico State University horticulturist. Today the nearly thirty thousand acres of pecan orchards around Las Cruces produce over fifty million pounds of nuts annually. The Hatch and Mesilla valleys have also become a major onion growing area since the 1990s and now produce more onions during the summer months than any other state in the U.S. The local onion variety, New Mexico Early Grano, was developed by Fabián García and has been hybridized with other types to create prized sweet onions such as Vidalia and Maui Sweet.

Las Cruces is the home of the Agricultural College at New Mexico State University. For visitors interested in farming, though, the best ending for this tour is the state-run **New Mexico Farm and Ranch Heritage Museum**. To get there, follow Interstate 25 to exit 1, the last exit before it merges into Interstate 10. Head east on Dripping Springs Road, toward the dramatic rock spires of the Organ Mountains, and you'll see the museum's driveway on your left after about two miles. Driving into the parking lot, you're likely to see Texas longhorn cattle grazing close to the fence. Outdoors, you can stroll past corrals, gardens, and a collection of antique farm machinery and watch cows being milked in the dairy barn. The indoor galleries contain historic photos and artifacts that tell the story of farming and ranching in New Mexico, spanning three thousand years. There are also long-term temporary exhibits such as the present gallery about saddlemakers of the Southwest (4100 Dripping Springs Road; 505-522-4100; www.frhm.org).

WILD THINGS

In New Mexico, wildlife is never far away. Even in major cities such as Albuquerque, black bears often wander into residential neighborhoods to scrounge garbage during dry summers when their preferred food, wild raspberries, is scarce in the mountains. In Santa Fe, mountain lions have occasionally been spotted leaping between rooftops near the downtown plaza, to the amazement of tourists and locals alike.

So it's not surprising that wildlife poses special challenges to small farmers. The National Organic Standards Program, which spells out federal requirements for organic farm certification in the United States, contains a rule that requires

above: farming and ranching museum, Las Cruces

"the conservation of biodiversity, and the maintenance or improvement of natural resources, including wetlands, woodlands, and wildlife." Until recently, this vague guideline was undefined. But as corporate agribusiness has moved into the organic foods market, interpretations of the roles of biodiversity and natural resources have become skewed to accommodate practices that look suspiciously like conventional single-crop megafarming. To clarify the biodiversity rule, the National Organic Standards Board worked with the Wild Farm Alliance and the National Center for Appropriate Technology to develop specific standards, which became official in August 2005.

To study strategies for farming in harmony with nature, the Wild Farm Alliance—a diverse group of farmers, ranchers, researchers, agroecologists, conservationists, and grassroots organizers—visited small farm practices in several states, including New Mexico, where they worked with Seeds of Change, Heidi's Raspberry Farm, and No Cattle Company. Doug Findley of Heidi's Raspberry Farm has been growing berries on his four-acre plot in Corrales since 2001. He claims the riverfront farmland around Corrales is "the best growing land in the state." While the area has been cultivated by Spanish colonists and, before that, Pueblo Indians since ancient times, parts of his land have never been brought into agriculture. Findley, whose father was a biologist, grew up enjoying nature, and he operates his farm with special attention to biodiversity. He has removed invasive tree species—tamarisk, Russian olives, Chinese elms—from the riparian part of the farm to allow space and water for the cottonwoods, willows, and other natural vegetation along the river to return to its natural state. He insists that the Mexican seasonal workers who help with the berry harvest refrain from killing toads and snakes. "The main thing is," says Findley, "are you fighting Mother Nature to do your farming, or are you allowing native animals and vegetation to grow on your property—everything from worms to buzzards?" Visitors to the farm are likely to encounter some of the twenty-five to thirty wild turkeys that live on the property, attracted by the safe haven the natural areas provide. Findley voices personal pride about having been used as a "guinea pig" by the Wild Farm Alliance. As for the new federal biodiversity standards, though, he rolls his eyes and says the main result has been "much more paperwork."

In the Mimbres Valley of southwestern New Mexico, the No Cattle Company holds the distinction of having been the first organic farm ever certified in the state. Growers Michael Alexander and Sharlene Grunerud have been growing apples, vegetables, grains, and flowers here since the mid-1990s. Wildlife is a constant presence because the farm is immediately downriver from a Nature Conservancy reserve. Bears, peccaries, deer, ring-tailed cats, bobcats, mountain lions, and tree-climbing gray foxes are frequent visitors, and rabbits, gophers, lizards, snakes, and other animals live on the property, along with quail, flycatchers, ravens, and rare Mexican black hawks. Alexander and Grunerud have also erected bat boxes to attract free-tail and brown bats, which feed on the codling moths, cucumber beetles, and corn earworms that pose the most serious insect threats. Bears and coyotes are seen as beneficial to the orchards because they eat fallen apples, which often contain codling moth larvae. The coyotes, as well as the ravens and hawks, suppress the population of pocket gophers. The only destructive wild animals that are not kept in check by predators are deer, which are particularly fond of chile peppers. Oddly enough, the most effective repellent Alexander and Grunerud have found to keep the deer away from the plants is a natural hot pepper mixture they spray on the chile plants.

Predators are a serious concern for Nancy Coonridge. Her goat dairy is located in one of the most remote areas of New Mexico, where her herd of seventy to eighty Alpine, Nubian, La Mancha, and Oberhasli goats ranges free in a rugged, unfenced landscape of arroyos and hills covered with creosote, mountain mahogany, and saltbush. The area is home to coyotes, bears, mountain lions, and wolves. No human goatherds accompany the goats. They are released into the wild after morning milking, and their homing instinct brings them back by dark. The best solution Nancy has found for the threat of predators is guardian dogs. She has been using dogs to protect the herds since 1984, trying purebred and mixed Australian shepherds and Pyrenees mountain dogs. In 1996, following the appearance in the area of endangered Mexican gray wolves reintroduced under the Albuquerque Zoo's captive breeding program, Coonridge turned to a rare breed of guardian dogs

above: wild turkeys, Heidi's Raspberry Farm

called maremmas. These tall, shaggy white dogs have lively, intelligent expressions, cheerful dispositions, and massive bearlike jaws similar in appearance to Pyrenees dogs, but they are of ancient origin and genetically distinct from any other modern dogs—an "heirloom" breed, you might say. They are said to have been Julius Caesar's favorite dogs more than two thousand years ago and have traditionally been used in the Italian Alps to protect sheep flocks and goatherds from wolves. The dogs are placed with the herd at the age of six months and, from then on, live with the goats, not the human family. The maremmas stay with the main herd to protect them and do not round up strays the way some other sheepdog breeds will. Stray goats are at the greatest risk, not only from large predators but also from rattlesnake bites and from breaking legs on the rough rocky slopes. Coonridge uses radio collars to help locate and rescue any stragglers that don't come home. In recent years, the dogs have assumed the role of alerting humans when a goat is missing and leading them to it.

Bears used to be a major problem for beekeeper Les Crowder, who has 150 beehives on his Sparrowhawk Farm near Belen. He produces 600 gallons (7,200 pounds) of honey in a good year and also depends for his livelihood on the lucrative side business of driving his hives out to the almond groves of California, where they are rented as pollinators because most California bees have been killed by overuse of pesticides.

A marauding bear can destroy dozens of beehives in a single night. The usual reaction in New Mexico has been to kill bears that tamper with hives, which is under the authority of a unique state law known as the Jennings Amendment that lets landowners shoot wild animals that destroy crops, kill livestock, or compete with domestic animals for forage.

While traveling in Canada, Crowder found that beekeepers there use solar-powered electric fences to ward off bears, so he tried one of the devices at his farm, and it worked. But when he introduced his discovery at a meeting of the New Mexico Beekeepers Association, it was not enthusiastically received. "Some people just like to shoot bears," Crowder says, shaking his head. "Instead, the chargers for my electric fences started disappearing. So I attached them to the hives with barbed wire, where they couldn't be removed without disturbing the bees. Then at the next meeting, I told people about it and said, 'If another of my chargers disappears, I'll know that it was taken by somebody in this room.' I haven't lost a charger since."

Now, besides being organic, natural, and chemical-free, Sparrowhawk Farm can claim proudly that it is "bear-friendly."

above left: Heidi's beehives
above right: farmers market herbs

THE FARMLAND PARADOX

The current state of small farming in New Mexico reveals a puzzling phenomenon. Most traditional farmers, whose families have tended the same plots of ground for centuries, share a common worry that their children will not carry on their land-based way of life but will move away to the city instead, leaving no one to care for the ancestral farms.

On the other hand, many young aspiring farmers, who have become interested in growing crops and raising livestock because of college classes or internship programs such as Willing Workers on Organic Farms, dream of starting their own acreages.

Too often, cultural conflicts between older Hispanics and young Anglos interfere with any possibility of their working together to keep New Mexico's small farms alive. Yet there have been some rays of hope.

In farming areas close to Albuquerque and other large cities, skyrocketing acreage prices have inspired owners to hold on to agricultural land for investment purposes even though they have no interest in farming it themselves. It is important that they keep the land under cultivation because it holds property taxes lower and makes some costs related to the land deductible from income taxes. Recently implemented federal programs offer additional benefits. For instance, under a new law, landowners can deduct up to 30 percent of their annual income by donating a conservation easement—an arrangement similar to the wild farm initiatives mentioned earlier in this chapter to set aside parts of a working farm or ranch for wildlife habitat—and farmers and ranchers can deduct up to 100 percent. This only applies to easements donated in 2006 and 2007 (unless Congress makes the now-temporary legislation permanent), but low-income farmers can spread the deductions offer up to sixteen years. Local groups such as the Taos Land Trust (505-751-3138; www.taoslandtrust.org) are actively involved in helping farmers take advantage of these programs.

Investment and tax incentives to keep land under cultivation mean that many landowners are open to the idea of tenant farmers working their acreage for them. In Corrales, for instance, according to Heidi's Raspberry farmer Doug Findley, would-be farmers who search hard enough can find plenty of vacant plots waiting for them, and lease payments are often minimal—sometimes a mere token payment of $25 per acre per year. One Corrales tenant farmer, he says, grows corn and other crops on twenty separate pieces of ground in the community. Findley tells a story of standing in a checkout line in the local supermarket, talking about affordable farming opportunities, when a woman in line overheard them and offered to lease them her vacant farmland on the spot.

But let's face it—borrowing land is not the same as owning it. Some northern New Mexico organic farmers say they have been displaced from their rented land and forced to seek other acreages, occasionally (though not often) in the middle of growing season, as many as five to seven times in the span of a decade. More often than not, this involves moving to a different community.

One approach that seeks to make it possible for "young, beginning, and small" farmers to buy their own land has been developed by Ag New Mexico, with offices in Clovis, Belen, and Roswell, and Albuquerque-based Farm Credit of New Mexico, specializing in loans to these categories of farmers. The combined total of "YBS" loans the two companies make amounts to nearly $160 million a year. They also offer financial training and management education classes to YBS borrowers.

The qualification for a "young" farmer is under thirty-five years old. A "beginning" farmer is one who has been in business ten years or less. A "small" farmer is one whose gross agricultural sales are $250,000 a year or less. (This is the generally accepted nationwide definition of "small" farmers; but in New Mexico the Department of Agriculture classifies a "small" farmer as one with $50,000 or less in gross sales, and three-fourths of the state's small farmers bring in less than $10,000 a year.)

Programs like Ag New Mexico and Farm Credit do hold out hope for some young, beginning, and small farmers who yearn to own their own land. For others, though, loans like this are viewed with deep distrust. Very low incomes combined with the risks of weather-related disasters raise well-founded fears that small farmers who go into debt could lose everything. Young people who have studied the recent history of family farming in America are keenly aware that easy credit for farm loans in the 1970s and '80s was soon followed by foreclosures and bankruptcies.

Yet there can be little doubt that public and private programs for young, beginning, and small farmers will continue to grow and evolve. In a time when more young people want to be farmers and more land is lying fallow awaiting somebody to cultivate it, great opportunities lie in bringing the two together.

SALSAS AND MOLES

Salsas and moles are essential to Mexican cuisine. Both date back at least to Aztec times. (*Salsa* means "sauce" in Spanish, while *mole*, pronounced "MO-lay," comes from the Nahuatl, or Aztec, word for "sauce." The two words have distinct meanings in modern Mexico, though.) In New Mexico, traditional sauces are green chile, red chile, homestyle salsa, and *pico de gallo*. A huge influx of Mexican emigrants in recent years has introduced new sauces such as various moles and fruit salsas to New Mexico.

Salsa Casera (Homestyle Salsa)

Also called salsa mexicana, *this is the familiar salsa commonly served with* totopos *(tortilla chips) in Mexican restaurants and at parties and receptions.*

5 or 6 vine-ripened tomatoes
1 medium sweet onion
6 serrano chiles
6 sprigs fresh cilantro, finely chopped
2 teaspoons apple cider vinegar
(lime juice can be substituted)
2 teaspoons olive oil
2 teaspoons sea salt

Cut the tomatoes and onion into chunks. Chop them lightly in a hand chopper or food processor. Save the tomato juice to add to the salsa. Slice the chiles lengthwise; remove the stems, seeds (which contain most of the hotness of these chiles), and light-colored cores; and then slice the chiles lengthwise to make eight strips per chile and slice crosswise until finely chopped. Combine all ingredients and mix well. Let stand 1 hour before serving.

Variations: For a festive *De Colores Salsa*, add ¾ cup diced green, yellow, and orange bell peppers to the salsa casera, along with an extra teaspoon of olive oil.

Pico de Gallo ("rooster's peck") is the same as salsa casera, except that it is made with jalapeños or chipotles (smoked ripe jalapenos) instead of serranos.

Salsa de Fruta

Fruit salsas, sometimes known as fuego y hielo *("fire and ice"), are still relatively unknown in the United States, where most people are unaccustomed to the idea of mixing hot chile with sweet ingredients. Try it and find out what you've been missing.*

Salsa Sandia is the same as salsa casera with 3 cups of chopped seedless watermelon substituted in place of the tomatoes. Lime juice, not vinegar, should be used. Refrigerate for 1 hour before serving. Place 1 cup sour cream in serving bowl and top with 1 cup salsa sandia; serve with totopos.

Delicious fruit salsas can also be made with cantaloupe, peaches, mangos, papayas, or pineapple.

Salsa Verde

1 cup roasted, peeled, and chopped green chile, mild or hot
1 large tomato, chopped
1 small onion, chopped
1 or 2 cloves garlic, peeled and chopped
½ teaspoon sea salt

Combine all ingredients in a mixing bowl and let stand for at least ½ hour.

Variation: For Mexican-style salsa verde, substitute 4 chopped green tomatillos in place of the tomato.

Totopos Azul (Blue Corn Tortilla Chips)

Totopos are the triangular corn tortilla chips served in Mexican restaurants and at parties and receptions. They originated in Mexico as a way of using leftover day-old tortillas. In New Mexico, blue corn tortilla chips are preferred. You can buy tortilla chips in any New Mexican supermarket or natural foods store, but once you try making them at home and discover how simple it is and how much better they taste, you may never go back to store-bought chips.

12 (6-inch) blue corn tortillas* (or more if you're planning a party)
½ cup vegetable oil
Sea salt, to taste

Slice each tortilla into three strips, and then slice each strip crosswise diagonally to make triangles. Heat oil in a large skillet over medium high heat. Carefully place a batch of tortilla triangles in the hot oil and fry until crisp, flipping once. Remove and drain on a paper towel. Season lightly with salt. Continue cooking the rest of the triangles.

*Use tortillas made by a New Mexican tortilla factory—it's hard to roll homemade tortillas thin yet strong enough to make good chips.

Chile Verde

Unlike salsa verde, which is served with totopos as a dip, chile verde is the green chile sauce served over enchiladas, eggs, and other entrées in New Mexico.

Makes 2 cups

1 tablespoon vegetable shortening
½ cup chopped onion
2 tablespoons flour
1 cup roasted, peeled, and chopped green chile
1 cup chicken or vegetable broth
1 clove garlic, peeled and crushed
¾ teaspoon sea salt

Heat the shortening in a skillet over medium heat. Sauté the onion in the shortening. Stir in the flour and cook for 1 minute. Add remaining ingredients and simmer for 20 minutes.

Chile Colorado

Chile colorado is the red chile sauce served over eggs, enchiladas, and other entrées in New Mexico.

Makes 2 cups

2 tablespoons vegetable shortening
2 tablespoons flour
½ cup finely ground red chile
2 cups cold water
¾ teaspoon sea salt
1 or 2 cloves garlic, peeled and crushed
½ teaspoons oregano
½ teaspoons ground cumin seed

Heat the shortening in a saucepan over medium heat. Stir the flour in and cook for 1 minute. Add the ground red chile and cook for 1 minute more. Gradually add the water, stirring constantly so lumps do not form. Add remaining ingredients and stir. Reduce heat and simmer for 10 to 15 minutes.

Adobo

Adobo means "marinade" in Spanish. Though adobos differ in various parts of the world, New Mexican adobo is very similar to chile colorado but is used differently.

5 cups water
20 pods dried red chile
2 cloves garlic, peeled and crushed
1½ teaspoons chopped fresh oregano
1½ teaspoons chopped fresh rosemary
1½ teaspoons sugar
½ teaspoon sea salt

In a large saucepan, bring the water to a boil. Break up the chile pods and remove the stems and most of the seeds. (The more seeds you leave in, the hotter it will be.) Boil over low heat for 15 minutes. Put some of the softened chile in a blender along with about a cup of the water it was cooked in. Blend until smooth and pour into a mixing bowl or other container. Repeat with the next batch of chile and continue until all have been blended.

Stir in remaining ingredients. Return the mixture to the saucepan and simmer for 15 to 30 minutes, stirring occasionally.

Adobo is used to make carne adovada (marinated pork) or pollo adovado (marinated chicken). For either, cut or tear about 3 pounds of meat into chunks, put it in a large bowl or cook pot and smother it with the adobo. Cover it tightly and refrigerate for 24 hours. When fully marinated, simmer the meat and sauce in a stockpot over low heat for 8 to 12 hours, stirring occasionally. Skim off and discard any froth or fat that forms on the surface.

Variation: Although it is nontraditional, carne adovada or pollo adovado with the excess liquid poured off is excellent when stir-fried with fresh vegetables.

Mole Poblano

This complex sweet-and-spicy Mexican sauce is the mole that is most familiar to norteamericanos. *It is usually used in both the United States and Mexico for pollo en mole (chicken stewed in mole poblano). It is also delicious when served over enchiladas filled with fried bananas or apple pie filling, and can even be used as a topping for ice cream.*

The mole mixture can be made ahead of time and diluted with chicken broth at the time of cooking. It can also be frozen for later use.

Makes enough for 2 chickens

4 chiles guajillos (dried)
8 chiles poblanos (fresh) or chiles anchos (dried)
4 tablespoons garenburros (wild currants), currants, or raisins
½ cup almonds
6 tablespoons raw sesame seeds
¼ cup raw pumpkin seeds
1 slice farm bread
1 corn tortilla
1½ teaspoons ground cinnamon
6 whole cloves
½ teaspoon anise seeds
1 teaspoon black peppercorns
1½ teaspoons dried oregano
3 ounces dark chocolate
1 tablespoon sugar

Wash the dried chiles in cold running water. Remove the stems, veins, and most of the seeds. Toast the dried chiles lightly in batches on a griddle or in a large skillet until they just start to brown. Then place them in a large bowl and cover with boiling water. Steep for 30 minutes. Add the currants or raisins to the water so they rehydrate.

Place the almonds, sesame seeds, and pumpkin seeds in separate pie tins. Roast them in a 350 degree F oven, stirring frequently until they begin to turn golden (about 10 minutes). Toast the tortilla and the bread slice in the same oven.

Grind the cinnamon, cloves, anise, and peppercorns with a mortar and pestle, a spice grinder, or a clean coffee grinder. Break up the chocolate into small pieces. Tear up the tortilla and the bread slice.

Combine the chiles, almonds, sesame seeds, and pumpkin seeds, and divide them into at least three separate batches. Place each batch in the blender and purée, adding water a little at a time to bring the mixture to the consistency of gravy. Pour it into a bowl and repeat with the next batch.

Gradually add the currants or raisins, ground spices, oregano, bread slice, tortilla, sugar, and chocolate into the last batch while pouring the previously puréed batches back into the mix.

Variation: For a uniquely New Mexican mole, substitute ½ cup shelled, roasted piñon nuts in place of the almonds.

Pollo en Mole

While mole poblano is traditionally used to make pollo en mole, there are several different ways of making this popular dish.

Serves 4 to 6

4 cloves garlic, peeled
½ medium onion, peeled
2 teaspoons olive oil
3 large tomatoes
2 cups mole poblano mixture
1½ cups chicken broth
Chicken, cut in half or in pieces

Preheat oven to 375 degrees F.

Drizzle the garlic and onion with olive oil, wrap in foil, and roast for 45 minutes. During the last 20 minutes, roast the tomatoes in an ovenproof container to retain juice. Purée the garlic, onion, and tomatoes in a blender. Combine the purée with the mole mixture and chicken broth in a cooking pot. Place chicken in the pot and stew for 1 to 1½ hours. (Some people precook the chicken and tear it into chunks for stewing.) Serve hot with corn tortillas and rice.

BELL PEPPERS
$3.00 per lb.
Carrots
$2.00 / pound

ECONOMY

Small-scale farming is not a line of work people go into to make big money. Unless they are clandestinely growing a high-profit, high-risk contraband recreational herb, the majority of small farmers in New Mexico earn less than convenience store employees. Taking up farming is a profound philosophical and, yes, political choice, and with it often comes a commitment to shun material luxuries and lead a life of voluntary simplicity.

In today's cash economy, it is virtually impossible for small farmers to compete successfully in the same arena with big agribusiness. Retailers, wholesalers, trucking companies, and other middlemen take up more than two-thirds of the price consumers pay for produce in supermarkets, so big farms must sell large quantities of a single crop to make a profit. This in turn usually means a big investment in heavy equipment and warehouse space. The inability of small operators to compete in conventional mass markets was one factor that drove a large part of America's population from farms to cities a century ago.

The desire to farm has inspired young growers and those seeking to keep their old family farmsteads alive to devise ingenious new marketing methods, as well as unusual crops rarely found in supermarkets. The objective in the case of specialty gourmet produce is to command higher prices. (Today, prices for standard produce at farmers markets tend to be higher than for conventionally grown supermarket produce but lower than organic supermarket produce.) The key secret to making farming profitable, however, is for farmers to eliminate middlemen and deal directly with consumers. According to many farmers, talking face-to-face with the people who will eat their food is also one of the greatest pleasures of their profession.

The foremost method of selling small farm produce and meat is the weekly farmers market. Usually open-air, these markets have been proliferating in the past few years. According to the U.S. Department of Agriculture, the number of farmers markets in America has increased by 150 percent in the past decade to a current total of 4,385; the number increased by 18 percent from 2005 to 2006. The picture is even brighter in New Mexico, which has 67 percent more farmers markets per capita than the national average.

Other ways of earning money as a farmer also depend on participation in farmers markets. Most members of Community Supported Agriculture groups (CSAs) are recruited at farmers market stalls. Customers who buy processed farm products over the Internet typically try them for the first time at farmers markets and reorder them with Web site information on the product labels. Overall, the health and prosperity of independent farming in New Mexico—and

facing: Willa and Cari Edwards shopping at Santa Fe Farmers Market

everywhere in the United States—is intertwined with the success of farmers markets.

FARMERS MARKETS

Miley Gonzalez, New Mexico's secretary of agriculture, who is also a tenured professor at New Mexico State University, chair of the Agriculture Biotechnology Task Force of the National Association of State Directors of Agriculture and, according to *Hispanic Business* magazine, one of the one hundred most influential Hispanics in the United States, recently talked with us in Santa Fe about New Mexico's farmers markets.

> *Santa Fe Farmers Market is one of the premier markets nationally. It's in the top two or three. Farmers markets nationally continue to grow. Here in New Mexico, last year we had thirty-seven and this year we're up to forty-five. It's an opportunity for people to come and buy fresh, locally grown product. We also support direct marketing, where people are selling maybe by the roadside or directly through the Internet, so a lot of things happen not only because of the New Mexico Department of Agriculture but also because USDA helps to sponsor.*
>
> *Part of the overall process is to make sure people understand that we have a variety of products that are locally grown, that they're fresh. When we begin to look at the health benefits of eating fresh fruits and vegetables, we're going to go to the grocery store anyway to get those, so why not support local producers, knowing that that product is coming direct from our neighbors? Whether it's herbs or spices, wonderful fresh fruit, peaches, apples—I was up here last month when we were harvesting cherries—I think the consumers know that we're there week in and week out and that the product is great. It's fresh, it's locally grown, it's healthy; that's what we need to concentrate on.*

THE DIFFERENCE BETWEEN ORGANIC AND SUSTAINABLE

Since 2002, when the USDA organic food regulations were adopted, New Mexico has been a leader in organic farming. The rules require that every organic farm be inspected and certified

above: Gilbert and Isabel M. Naranjo selling produce at Santa Fe Farmers Market

annually. New Mexico was quick to establish its Organic Commodities Commission, providing certification to the state's farmers at a reasonable fee. It also offers certification in other states, such as neighboring Arizona, that do not have organic commodity boards or inspectors—at a much higher fee.

Some, though not all, farmers markets in New Mexico have rules that only organic foods can be sold there. This may help ensure the continued growth of small farming and farmers markets because there is a phenomenally fast-growing trend among consumers toward purchasing organic groceries. In food marketing today, few buzzwords are as powerful as "organic."

Organic foods now account for only 3 percent of the $380 billion grocery industry in America, but according to Ronnie Cummins, director of the nonprofit Organic Consumers Association, most food in U.S. grocery stores will be organic by 2020. The reasons for the change, he says, will be concerns about health and food safety in a time when genetic modification, radiation, neurotoxins, pesticides, herbicides, chemical fertilizers, hormones, and steroids have become so much the norm in American agriculture that nations around the world have banned many food product imports from the United States.

But many observers believe that the rising popularity of organic foods will mean that organic farming will no longer be sustainable farming. Large corporations like Earthbound Farms (which started in 1984 as a two-acre farm in California's Carmel Valley and has grown to become North America's largest producer of organic produce) ship to about three-fourths of all U.S. supermarket chains. Wal-Mart, with locations in most towns across the continent, has also jumped into the business of marketing organic foods. According to Washington-based Worldwatch Institute, food in America travels 1,500 miles from farm to table, accounting for an astonishing amount of petroleum consumption and air pollution as well as delays of a week or more from the time produce is picked until it finds its way onto store shelves. The solution may lay less in compliance with organic farming regulations than in developing a radically different farming infrastructure that is locally grown and freshly picked.

As organic foods become commonplace, moreover, many growers believe it may dull the competitive edge that sustainable farmers enjoy. A look at the shelves in any large natural foods market reveals that quite a few large farming corporations have already taken the plunge into the organic market. Some small farmers also believe that large-scale organic agribusiness, with its powerful lobbies and political clout, may persuade the U.S. Department of Agriculture and Congress to lower the rigid requirements for organic products, making the "organic" label less meaningful. The rules already contain a few loopholes, such as one that allows for products to be labeled "Made with Organic Ingredients," a term that is easily confused with "Certified Organic" but merely means that 70 percent of the ingredients are organic.

One problem that could force changes in regulations is that soil used for growing organic produce must be pesticide and waste free. If consumer demand causes a widespread shift to organic fruits and vegetables, it could be difficult to find enough qualifying farmland in major breadbasket regions such as California's chemical-drenched Imperial Valley.

As the word "organic" loses its luster, many small farmers opt for the word "sustainable" instead, referring to agriculture and lifestyle that do not deplete natural resources or permanently damage the earth. This allows them to assure customers that their produce is chemical-free while avoiding the paperwork and inspection procedures that can easily overwhelm small-time family farmers. Others emphasize such qualities as "fresh," "locally grown," "heirloom," and "artisanal." Some longtime sustainable farming advocates have simply forsaken the "organic" label altogether—which also eliminates massive, meticulous, and detailed state and federal paperwork requirements. Others are keeping their organic certifications but quietly surpassing the government requirements. This has complicated the food-labeling maze with newly coined terms like "superorganic" and "beyond organic."

WHY FARMERS MARKETS?

The Busker

"Every bite of food that goes into our mouth is a vote."

Michael Combs

Michael Combs, a street musician by trade who has also served as a manager of the Santa Fe Farmers Market, loves to expound his outspoken views about the recent history of American agriculture and the emerging role of farmers markets.

Little by little our locally grown agriculture is coming back. Before World War II we ate almost nothing but locally grown organic produce, but nobody thought it was organic. We just didn't have this huge agrichemical industry. But after the war they didn't gear down. They said, "Well, let's find new things to do with all these poisons we've developed for warfare." So they waged war on our soil.

Over the next thirty years, the average mouthful of food that we ate began to travel from farther and farther away. Our little towns used to be ringed with small dairies. Santa Fe had five or six of them, and Albuquerque had fifteen or twenty. Now our milk travels hundreds of miles.

You get a head of lettuce from the Imperial Valley of California, it costs ten thousand calories of energy by the time you've shipped it through the wholesaler, the distributor, the retailer. When it gets to the kitchen table, you get a hundred calories out of it. So that's not sustainable.

It's easy to feel so disempowered politically and economically today, but you have to realize that every bite of food that goes into our mouth is a vote.

You have to become informed about "Where was this egg before it got to me? Was it living in a concentration camp?" That's where most of our eggs, dairy, beef, poultry, and pork come from. The atmosphere inside those buildings is so bad, with ammonia and methane, that all the animals have respiratory infections, so they have to keep them on heavy doses of antibiotics, which go straight through us into our water, so our streams now are just loaded with these toxins, producing superviruses that are not treatable with antibiotics.

We didn't always have this incredibly dysfunctional system of producing food. So you can vote for a better world every time you put food in your mouth. Back in, let's say, 1900, probably 90 percent of the food we ate was what all mammals eat—regional, seasonal foods. These foods—here in New Mexico, like through the winter, winter squashes, apples, dried red chiles, piñon nuts, corn, beans—put our bodies in harmony with the external environment.

When we're eating wheat grown in Kansas and pineapple from Hawaii, it's also destroying our rural farm communities. Back to the '30s and '40s, our rural communities were thriving more because they had access to the markets. Our sawmills made lumber out of local timber. Our coal was being produced here in New Mexico. We were a wheat-exporting state. We were the pinto bean capital of the United States. Even when you went to buy food at the store, you would be buying string beans, onions, and other foods that the store manager was contracting with the local farmers. Only a small amount of our food was coming from somewhere else, and almost all of it was grown organically. But in the late '40s, the '50s, and the '60s, the agro-industrial empire moved in.

Now it's turned around and it's starting to go back in the other direction. If you look at our farmers market today, you will find breads baked from grains that were grown here in our region from the wheat cooperative up in Costilla. You can buy cheeses made from goats and even sheep that were grazing right here in our region, converting grasses into foods for us.

Our farmers have learned about row covers, grow holes, greenhouses, and cold-hardy species; it used to be we had to wait until around April to get green food, and we'd be craving it. Now farmers have learned that chard and kale and salad greens will grow and survive a freeze. Here in New Mexico we're the Saudi Arabia of solar energy, so our greenhouses are kicking butt. Last week, a week before the spring equinox, we were already swamped. We had so much food here that the farmers had to take stuff home.

People say, "Well, it's expensive." It apparently looks *more expensive, but you may be able to skip the chemotherapy you might have needed from eating toxic foods that were grown far away and long ago. Once you get used to eating locally grown foods that were harvested yesterday, you don't want to go back.*

Other people in the world spend 30 to 90 percent of their income on food. Back in the '50s, Americans spent 25 percent of their household income on food, and now that's been cut in half. We spend 12.5 percent of our income on food. So the truth is, we can easily afford it. We shell out four bucks for a quart of ice cream, four bucks for a latte drink, we'll go to a movie for ten bucks, but when it comes to our food, we go, "Oh, look at that cardboard box of stuff for 39 cents. I'll take it home and try to make nourishment out of it." Eating locally grown food is a really good thing for your health.

And it's so enjoyable to come meet the growers. You don't have to rely on a label that says "organic." If you have any questions about how your food was grown, you ask the farmer. It's beginning to restore that link of market towns. Every little town around here—Española, Taos, Las Vegas—used to be a market town that supported thriving rural farm families. They could come in and sell their milk, beef, lamb, wheat, beans, and buy or trade for the fruit that they weren't producing.

Then there used to be the chileros, *the guys who would go around in their trucks to the different households in the '50s, '60s, and even into the '70s—a lot of us can remember these guys—and they would bring the surplus production—squashes, carrots, chile, piñon nuts, apples—and go house to house. But as more and more women went into the work force, there was no one at home to buy this stuff. And with the crime fear from television, people didn't want strangers driving up into their yards any more, honking and selling. So that's when the farmers markets here in New Mexico started to begin getting going in the late '60s, as a way to help the vegetable growers and fruit producers connect with customers for their produce. It's a great thing to participate in.*

In Europe, even working-class people won't eat sewage. They insist on food. *They know that this guy who grows their olives or that guy who grows their radishes, their grandfather purchased from his grandfather. When you get that connection, and you're putting food on your table to share with your friends, you can tell the stories behind these foods.*

A lot of farmers have a day or two a year when you can go out and see how they're farming. And then there are CSAs—you can sign up with a farmer and help support their farming by giving them a check at the start of the season when their expenses are high and their output is low. Then all through the season you can get boxes of vegetables that vary. It's so fabulous to start adapting your cooking habits to what's available at that time of year.

Go ahead and wait for the asparagus until it shows up, wait for the apples, wait for the green chile. You can eat red chile all through the winter and spring, so when our first local green chile gets here, it just means so much more. It's so empowering that once you start eating locally grown fresh delicious food, you will realize how cheap it really is and you'll never go back.

CUCUMBERS
$1.50/ pound

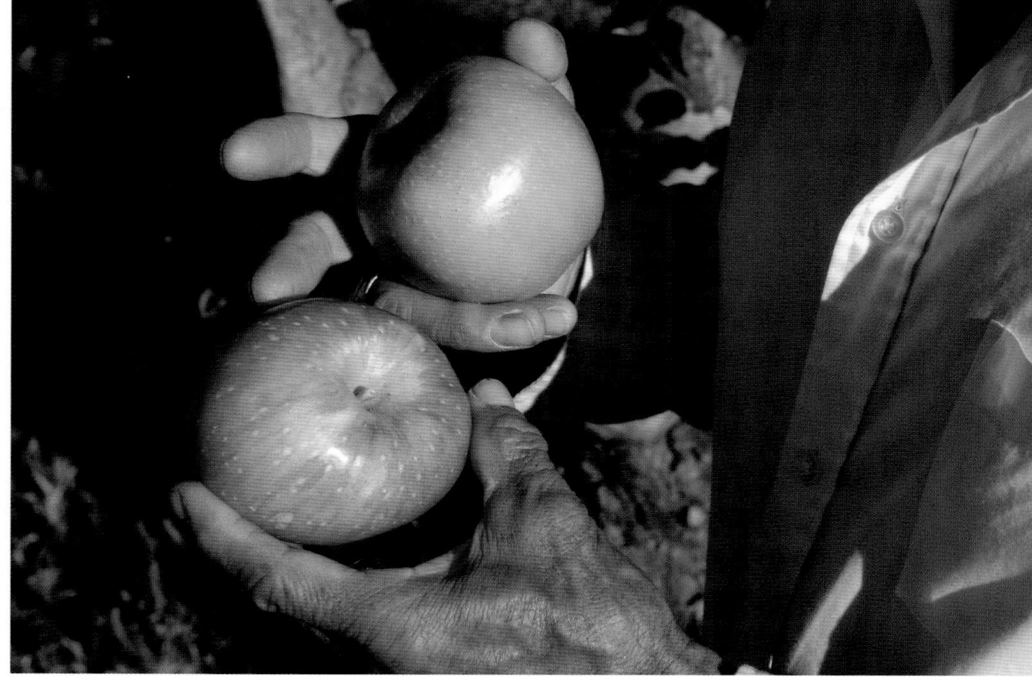

SANTA FE FARMERS MARKET

The granddaddy of farmers markets in New Mexico, the Santa Fe Farmers Market has been operating continuously since the late 1960s, when it started as an informal gathering of counterculture "back-to-the-land" growers who joined with traditional local farmers, chile roasters, and woodcutters selling from the tailgates of pickup trucks along the roadside. With help from organizations including Concerned Action, Inc., the League of Women Voters, and the County Extension Office, the group became a nonprofit corporation in 1971 and established a permanent weekly location in the parking lot of St. Anne's Church on the edge of the Santa Fe *barrio*. Over the next fifteen years, it moved to several different locations in the same part of town before settling at last in the Santa Fe Railyard. It has occupied one area or another of the railyard ever since.

The Santa Fe Farmers Market is the largest farmers market in the state. (The Las Cruces Farmers and Crafts Market has a few more vendors—but not many of them are farmers.) An estimated six thousand to eight thousand people come to the market every week during peak season, and in a year one hundred eighty thousand people come, generating $2 million in sales. For every dollar that is spent at the farmers market, two to three dollars gets spent in the surrounding community, so the market has become an influence in the economic and cultural development of Santa Fe. It has become a community space where people come to hang out, meet their friends, and listen to free music. In summer, about a third of the market's patrons are tourists, and the rest are local food lovers who want to buy fresh produce direct from the grower. Known for its fine restaurants, Santa Fe is a community that values the culinary arts, where over the years competition from the abundance of natural, gourmet, and specialty food markets has driven all but eight conventional chain supermarkets out of business. The farmers market is the leading venue for buying produce because even natural foods retailers cannot rival its food for freshness.

The market operates on Tuesday mornings in summer and Saturday mornings year-round. During the cold months, roughly from Thanksgiving to Earth Day, it moves indoors to El Museo Cultural de Santa Fe, which is also located in the railyard. In 2007 the farmers market will move temporarily to a parking lot at De Vargas Mall to make way for the redevelopment of the railyard as a park.

The Santa Fe Farmers Market Institute, the market's charitable sister organization that is eligible for grant funding, has signed an eighty-year lease that requires construction of a building to house the vendors in the new commercial development zone of the railyard. When completed, the new farmers market will accommodate fifty indoor and one hundred outdoor vendors, surpassing the ninety to one hundred vendor spaces in its last location. In the winter its fifty indoor spaces will replace those at El Museo Cultural, which provides space for an average of thirty-six vendors. Besides the indoor Market Hall, which will serve as a community event

center on days when the farmers market is not open, the building will contain farmers market and institute offices and a 6,500-square-foot space for a natural foods restaurant.

MORE FARMERS MARKETS

Overall, with a few exceptions, the state's most active and well-established farmers markets are in the upper Río Grande region.

Like Santa Fe's market, the **Española Farmers Market** also received funds from the state legislature to acquire one of the last pieces of agricultural land within Española city limits and move there from its longtime location in the parking lot of Northern New Mexico College's Commercial Kitchen, where local farmers can process "value-added" products such as salsas and jams. It operates from mid-June to the end of October, on Monday, with unusually long hours—from 9:00 a.m. to dusk.

The **Los Alamos Farmers Market** is thriving. Although it is not in the midst of farm country as Española is, Los Alamos is the highest-income community in New Mexico and has only one supermarket and no natural foods store. It is held on a different day from other markets in the area, so vendors who sell at Santa Fe, Taos, Española, and Dixon often sell in Los Alamos too. The market operates on Thursday mornings from May through October.

The **Pojoaque Farmers Market**, located at a small Indian pueblo at the intersection between the highway from Santa Fe to Española and the highway to Los Alamos, is one of New Mexico's newest markets, established in 2006 and operated by the same management as the Los Alamos Farmers Market. Most vendors here are regulars at the Los Alamos market. At this writing, Pojoaque had only about ten vendors, but the market also has a cooperative "community table" where produce is sold for growers who can't attend personally. The market operates on Wednesday afternoons and Saturday mornings from May through October.

Jean Treadway, the new market manager for **Dixon Farmers Market**, says,

> *Our market this year [2006] has been really up and down. We've had some great days with the customers—lots of customers and poor sales, which is surprising, but I think they're coming for a community event, to talk and that sort of thing. Then another day we'll have few customers but very good sales. We haven't hit anywhere near our peak of farmers. We have nine, ten, maybe eleven farmers coming in, and last year they were having as many as twenty-five by this time. Partially it's related to the co-op [the Dixon Cooperative Market], which has been operating for a year now and has brisk sales. Our farmers sell there, so our customers know they can go on Tuesday or they can go on Saturday. But we have a good market with extraordinary food. The vegetables being sold are just so beautiful.*

above left: Trent Edwards fieldlifting a raspberry

The Dixon Farmers Market, which is operated by the Dixon Cooperative Market, takes place on Wednesday afternoons from June through October.

The **Taos County Farmers Market** is a continuation, in spirit at least, of a tradition that dates back many centuries. Taos Pueblo was the main center in New Mexico for trade between the Pueblo people and the Plains Indian tribes, and when the Spaniards arrived, the town plaza became northern New Mexico's key marketplace for everything from food and household goods to slaves. The present-day market is held in a grassy space adjacent to the Taos town hall, bustling with vendors, shoppers, and good music. The prepared foods stall, Johnny Ds, sells a range of breakfasts as well as burritos and stews. The market is held on Saturday mornings from May through October. Says Eytan Salinger, the market manager,

> *This is for me a dream place to be on a Saturday morning and to have this opportunity to be amongst farmers and to be part of this production here. It's very easy for me to be motivated to do this because it's a very special and privileged place to be at the center of a local farming community that has so much to offer. The town of Taos is so enthusiastic about having this here because they see how important it is as a support for the local and traditional farming community across cultures. It's got very deep roots. Because it has such deep meaning for me and for everyone who's here, it's a must for me as long as I'm in Taos to be part of it. We also have tourists come in from all across the country and internationally as well; we've had Dutch and German people, English people, people from Ireland.*

New in 2006, the **Questa Farmers Market** is sponsored by the Questa Chamber of Commerce. Spearheaded by Daniel Carmona, who also operates Cerro Vista Farms and CSA, the market has received an enthusiastic response from local produce vendors. It also includes crafts vendors every third or fourth week. Located in the Questa supermarket parking lot, the market is open Sundays from 11:00 a.m. to 2:00 p.m., June through September.

Other farmers markets around New Mexico include:

- **Alamogordo Farmers Market**, County Fairgrounds, Saturday mornings, mid-June through mid-October.
- **Albuquerque:**
  - **Albuquerque Downtown Market**, Robinson Park (Eighth & Central), Saturday mornings, July through late October.
  - **Caravan East**, 7605 East Central, Tuesday and Saturday mornings, July through mid-November.
  - **South Valley Growers Association**, Cristo Del Valle Presbyterian Church (3907 Isleta SW), Saturday mornings, mid-May through mid-October.
  - **Village of Los Ranchos Growers Market**, Los Ranchos City Hall, (6718 Rio Grande NW), Saturday mornings, mid-May through October.
- **Aztec Farmers Market**, Westside Plaza, Wednesday afternoons, mid-July through October.
- **Belen/Valencia County Growers Market**, Anna Becker Park, Friday afternoons, late July through October.
- **Bloomfield Farmers Market**, Highway 550 at Route 64, Thursday late afternoons, mid-July through October.
- **Bernalillo: High Desert Farmers Market**, 282 Camino del Pueblo, Friday afternoons, July through October.
- **Carlsbad-Eddy County Growers Market**, San Jose Plaza, Wednesday and Saturday mornings, late June through October.
- **Cedar Crest Farmers and Arts Market**, Cedar Crest Center, Sunday mornings, seasonal.
- **Chaparral Farmers Market**, 101 County Line, Saturday mornings, May through October.
- **Clayton-Five State Producer Growers Market**, Highway 87 at First Street, Wednesdays and Saturdays, 11 a.m–1 p.m., mid-July through October.
- **Clovis Farmers Market, North Plains Mall**, Tuesday mornings and Saturday afternoons, mid-May through October.
- **Corrales Growers Market**, Wednesdays at Corrales Recreation Center and Sunday mornings at the Village Center across from the post office, late April through third week in November.
- **Elephant Butte: Sierra County Farmers Market**, Route 195, Saturday mornings, third week in July through October.
- **Farmington: San Juan County Farmers Market**, Animas Park, Tuesday afternoons and Saturday mornings, mid-July through October.
- **Gallup Farmers Market**, Downtown Walkway, Saturday mornings, August through October.
- **Grants Growers Market**, City Hall, Saturday mornings, early August through October.
- **Las Cruces Farmers & Crafts Market**, Downtown mall, Wednesday and Saturday mornings, year-round.
- **Las Vegas: Tri-County Farmers Market**, old Safeway parking lot, Douglas at Seventh, Wednesday and Saturday mornings, late June through October.

SHOPPING TIPS

To get the most out of your visit to the farmers market!

- *For the best selection of produce and meats, go to the market early.*
- *Walk around the market and see what's available first, so that you can compare prices, products, and quality.*
- *Try a new vegetable. If you don't know what an item is, ask the farmer.*
- *Farmers can share great suggestions about how to prepare different foods.*
- *Ask for samples. Most vendors will be glad to let you taste their products.*
- *Bring change and bills of smaller denominations to make shopping fast and easy.*
- *When you go to the market, bring an ice chest to keep your perishable purchases fresh until you get home.*
- *Bring your own basket or canvas shopping bag, or buy one from the farmers market booth.*
- *Stroll and socialize. Farmers markets are a great public gathering and people-watching place.*

above: Suzi Q. Kriger shopping at Santa Fe Farmers Market

- **Mesilla: Mercado on the Plaza**, Mesilla Plaza, Thursdays and Sunday afternoons, 10 a.m.–2 p.m., year-round.
- **Moriarty Farmers Market**, Broome's Feed Store, Friday afternoons, June through October.
- **Portales Farmers Market**, West First at Avenue B, Monday late afternoon and Thursday late afternoon, late June through first hard freeze.
- **Ramah Area Farmers/Arts & Crafts Market**, Ramah Cafe parking area, Saturdays, 10 a.m.–1 p.m., July through October.
- **Roswell: Pecos Valley Farmers & Gardeners Market**, Courthouse lawn, Tuesday and Saturday mornings, mid-July to first frost.
- **San Felipe Farmers Market**, Casino Hollywood grounds, San Felipe Reservation, Wednesday late afternoons, late June through mid-October.
- **Silver City Farmers Market**, Seventh at Bullard, Saturday mornings and Gough Park, Tuesday evenings, mid-May through late October.
- **Socorro Farmers Market**, Socorro Plaza, Tuesday mornings and Saturday evenings, July through October.
- **Sunland Perk Farmers Market**, Ardovino's Desert Crossing, Friday mornings, May through October.
- **Tierra Amarilla: Jardines del Norte Farmers Market**, Community Bank parking lot, Saturday mornings, mid-July through September.
- **Tucumcari Farmers Market**, K-Mart parking lot, Tuesday late afternoons and Saturday mornings, mid-July through mid-October.
- **Tularosa Farmers Market**, James Vigil Park, Saturday mornings, May through October.

WHAT MAKES A SUSTAINABLE FARMERS MARKET?

In New Mexico, most farmers markets are operated by nonprofit organizations, though a few, such as some Albuquerque-area markets, are owned by private entrepreneurs and operated for profit. A few small-town markets eschew legal entities completely and just "get together," though this means they can't hire paid employees or carry insurance. New Mexico's farmers markets differ from those in some other parts of the country, such as the South, where most farmers markets are owned by the state and organized for large-scale food wholesaling as well as sales to individual consumers, and parts of the Northeast, where independent grocery stores are often called "farmers markets" even though there's not a farmer in sight. And unlike some states such as Maine and California, New Mexico has no state laws defining or regulating farmers markets. As different as they may be in some ways, a survey of New Mexico farmers markets reveals some qualities that spell success or failure.

Most New Mexico farmers markets limit participation to local vendors from surrounding counties. This promotes one of the basic principles of sustainability by keeping money within the local community. Such restrictions are sometimes modified for special situations. At the Santa Fe market, a farmer from another part of New Mexico can sell there if no vendor from the eligible counties is selling the same product. For instance, Tom Delehanty of Pollo Royal drives 270 miles round-trip from Socorro every week to sell his Label Rouge chicken at the Santa Fe Farmers Market because no other vendor there sells chicken; but paradoxically, Delehanty can't sell the eggs that his chickens lay because he would compete with a local egg vendor. Taos is within the eligible area for the Santa Fe market, and both of them operate on Saturdays, so many Taos area farmers prefer to go to Santa Fe, where there are more customers. Accordingly, many sellers at the Taos market come down from southern Colorado.

In some areas of New Mexico, traditional farmers all grow the same crops and may all have only one crop available for sale at a given time. If the market only carries carrots one week and garlic another, it not only diminishes public interest but also drives prices down. So, many farmers market directors, when deciding whether to accept a new vendor, strive for as diverse a selection of products as possible. This policy also has the advantage of encouraging farmers to raise rare, unusual, and heirloom crops that nobody else in the area is growing.

Almost all New Mexico farmers markets preserve their integrity by requiring that vendors sell only products grown or raised on farmland owned or leased by them. This rule keeps out peddlers who buy their products at wholesale, a practice that can quickly dilute the market's overall reputation for quality and give consumers less reason to buy there instead of at the supermarket. But it also keeps farmers from pooling their resources cooperatively, using a single vehicle to drive their produce to town, and sharing the expense of a vendor space.

Many markets, especially those that operate in the morning, find that offering ready-to-eat food such as freshly made pastries or breakfast burritos, as well as beverages, boosts attendance significantly. In particular, fresh-brewed coffee is essential at larger markets, even though no coffee beans are grown in New Mexico. Some market boards rationalize their way around the "keep it local" rule by only selling coffee that is locally roasted.

All farmers markets come up against the question of whether to allow canned or jarred foods like jams, salsas, goat cheese, herbed mustards, garlic oil, and salad dressings. Such items can boost sales because they make good gifts and tourist souvenirs. They also provide small growers with a continuing source of income beyond the growing season. But they may raise tricky questions about reselling, since such common ingredients as sugar are not produced in New Mexico and some local food processors use ingredients raised by other farmers in the area. Decisions generally must be made on a case-by-case basis, and many markets have rules about what percentage of the ingredients must be locally grown.

Almost all farmers markets have a few vendors who sell nonfood items—goat milk soaps, lavender sachets, cornhusk dolls, and the like. They are generally juried in on a case-by-case basis and should have some relationship to ingredients that the farmers have grown and raised themselves. But nonfood items are by far the biggest pitfall for any farmers market. Many markets, when they are just getting started or trying to expand, have trouble attracting enough farmer-vendors to cover their operating expenses. The seemingly simple solution is to invite artists and craftspeople, who are ubiquitous throughout New Mexico, to participate. But the more the market takes on the appearance of a weekly arts-and-crafts fair, the fewer customers buy food there. Discouraged by low sales, farmers drop out of the market, sending it into a downward spiral until there are no farmers left. The most striking example is the Las Cruces Farmers and Crafts Market, held on summer Saturdays in the city's underutilized four-block-long pedestrian mall. The market is large—perhaps the largest in the state—and so popular that it's often hard to find a parking space within walking distance. But on a typical Saturday, among the painters, jewelers, and T-shirt hucksters, there are fewer than a dozen produce vendors to be found, even though Las Cruces is the hub of one of New Mexico's biggest farming areas and the home of the state agricultural college. Many farmers voice similar complaints about some of Albuquerque's several farmers markets. To steer clear of this pitfall, most northern New Mexico markets disallow vendors whose products have no direct connection with food. Santa Fe has had a separate artists market at the same time as the farmers market but in a different part of the railyard. Still, a vicious battle of words raged before the city council over whether arts and crafts sellers could sell their wares in front of the new farmers market building when it was completed; at the end of the day, the farmers won.

ENTERTAINMENT AND SPECIAL EVENTS

To boost attendance, a good farmers market will foster a lively atmosphere and enhance its role as a community meeting place by presenting music and hosting special events. The free entertainment possibilities are limited only by the management's imagination.

In Santa Fe, there is always music at the farmers market, sometimes several musicians or groups performing in different areas of the market at the same time. It started with "buskers"—street musicians—who were banned from the downtown plaza by city ordinance and found the farmers market to be the most high-traffic venue available. Today, musicians at the market also include traditional *norteño* musicians from nearby rural villages, mariachi groups, and even a class of Suzuki-method

violin students. In addition, the market sponsors such events as children's Carnival Days, a Tomato Festival, a Lavender Festival, and a Fall Festival with pumpkin carving demonstrations. It also hosts a series of "Shop with the Chef" programs, in which chefs from local restaurants guide visitors on a produce-buying spree through the market and then cook their purchases on the spot, sharing samples with participants and passers-by. The Taos Farmers Market also has live music every weekend.

The Española Farmers Market sponsors a vegetable contest in which ribbons are awarded for the largest vegetables and the most unusual vegetables. They also hold a Chile Roasting Day, a Horno Cooking Demonstration Day, and a Children's Poetry Contest, in which kids submit poems related to food that the market manager then publishes as a chapbook.

The new, small Pojoaque Farmers Market's first special events were related to wildlife—a demonstration featuring hawks and eagles from the Santa Fe Raptor Center and a presentation by a local naturalist featuring about forty snakes that was designed to convince people that most of them are safe to be around and to show how to move them and whom to call to remove venomous rattlesnakes.

Taos Farmers Market has folksingers or local *norteño* musicians weekly, as well as puppeteers and clowns. There is even a resident practitioner of "hand counseling" (palm reading).

Several markets also hold fundraising raffles for prizes ranging from bags of produce, baked goods, and jams to a drawing in which prizes include a side of grass-fed beef and a freezer to keep it in.

OTHER SOURCES OF FARM INCOME

Community-Supported Agriculture

According to the U.S. Department of Agriculture, a CSA—an increasingly popular method of selling produce and meat—consists of "a community of individuals who pledge support to farm operations so that the farmland becomes, either legally or spiritually, the community's farm, with the growers and consumers providing mutual support and sharing the risks and benefits of food production." This kind of prepaid purchase arrangement provides farmers with much-needed working capital at the beginning of the season, when money is in short supply.

In successful CSAs, the members' investment also goes to pay the farmer a salary during the growing months. The members become an integral part of the small farming operation and can share vicariously in the farmer's spiritual connection to the land. In some cases, members even have the option of paying for a portion of their membership by working on the farm a few days a week.

In a true CSA, where each member receives an identical share of each week's harvest, members reap the benefits of a bountiful season with larger portions of food. Members typically pick up their boxes of produce weekly at a central distribution point, often the local farmers market. Members also share such risks as unseasonable freezes, floods, hail, drought, pest invasions, and other events that can diminish or destroy crops.

Not all CSAs in New Mexico work the same way. In some cases, instead of receiving a pro rata share of each week's production, members get a credit in the amount of their payment and can spend it at any time on anything the farmer is selling at the local farmers market, receiving a discount from the prices paid by the general public.

New Mexico's oldest CSA, and one of the most unusual, is Beneficial Farm, located on Glorieta Mesa, a vast, almost inaccessible "island in the sky" of nearly level grasslands bordered by 500-foot cliffs overlooking the Pecos River Valley. The farm was founded in 1994 in connection with the Santa Fe Waldorf School. Rudolf Steiner, the European visionary who founded the international Waldorf School movement and the belief system called Anthroposophy in the early twentieth century, also devised a method and philosophy of agriculture that he termed Biodynamics. It incorporated many of the principles of organic and sustainable farming, which were not heard of at the time. Steiner opposed the growing use of chemical farming, which, he contended, degraded the quality of produce by destroying the spirit of fruits and vegetables. His biodynamic growing method included some odd practices, such as burying cow horns filled with manure and powdered quarts in the fields to decompose and digging them up months later to spray on crops. He also developed elaborate compost recipes using such herbs as chamomile, dandelion, valerian, and yarrow, fermented into deer bladders and later used in homeopathic amounts to fertilize crops. The Biodynamic Farming and Gardening Association, founded in 1938, boasts more than four hundred members throughout the United States.

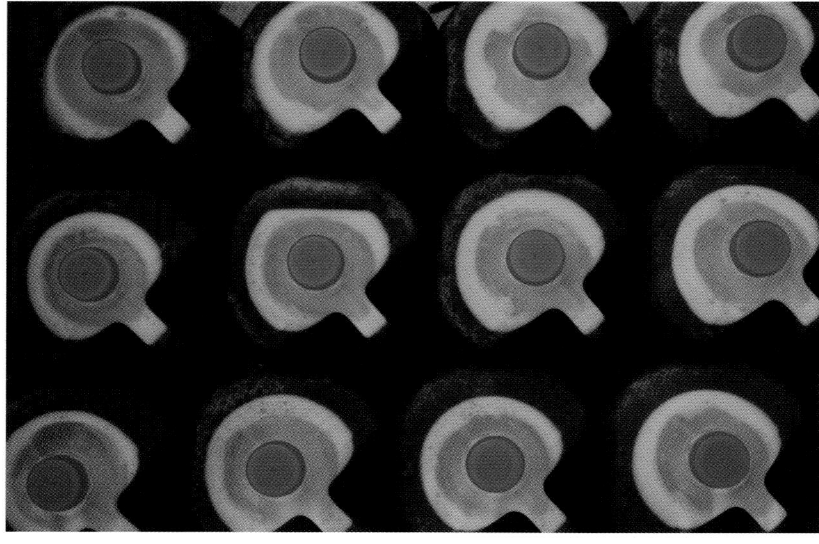

While Beneficial Farm started as a CSA serving families of Waldorf School students, it has since been opened to the general public. In 2006, the farm's CSA joined with eight other farms and ranches in New Mexico and Colorado and three retail outlets to form the Beneficial Farm and Ranch Cooperative. This merger makes a greater variety of produce available to members and reduces the risk of local crop failures, while helping the participating farms compete more effectively with large corporate organic growers.

CSAs come in many sizes. An example of a small-scale CSA is operated by Gail Minton, who runs the petite Squash Blossom Farm in Taos. Minton says,

> *I have been involved in farming and gardening since I was a child. I learned from my parents in Vermont and began doing gardening more actively in 1999 with a CSA that I started in New Hampshire. Then I left it to move here to Taos in 2001. The CSA there is thriving and has over sixty-five members and a full-time farmer that they pay. That was very satisfying, and it was quite an education about groups, trying to convince the members that the important thing was to provide a livable wage for that farmer. They got that message and were able to raise enough money on shares and some grants from statewide organizations to support that farm and get it on good financial footing. When I came to Taos we acquired 2.2 acres of land on the Acequia del Monte del Rio Chiquito in south Taos. We have one and a half acres in alfalfa and probably about a quarter of an acre in vegetables, fruit trees, and flowers. I've been running the farm since 2001 and began my CSA here in 2003.*

Retailing at the Farm

Roadside produce stands used to be common along New Mexico's highways, and several of them still operate in August, September, and October along the main route between Santa Fe and Taos, which is heavily traveled by tourists. The stands were often managed by elderly members of farm families who were no longer able to work in the fields. A good example is Sopyn's Fruit Stand, located on the edge of a peach orchard near the village of Velarde. At this picturesque old stand, with its sagging red roof, you can buy peaches and cherries fresh off the trees, often picked earlier the same day, as well as red chile ristras. Produce stands have become fewer, though, as many farmers have switched to selling at farmers markets, where they get more customers in a shorter time.

A striking example of selling direct from the farm is Dixon Apples, which is located not at the village of Dixon but in an isolated canyon near Cochiti Pueblo. The fifty-acre orchard has been in operation for more than sixty years and is now operated by the granddaughter of the original founder, who developed two unique, prizewinning strains, Champagne apples and Burgundy apples, that are widely considered—at least in New Mexico—to be the world's best apples.

Dixon's does not sell through wholesale distributors, farmers markets, a roadside stand, or the Internet, nor do they advertise. Instead, their reputation has grown by word-of-mouth over the years; now, a visit to their orchards during the late September–early October harvest has become a much-anticipated event for residents of Albuquerque and Santa Fe. On a weekend day during the harvest, it is not unusual to find cars parked along the dirt road into the farm for as much as two miles. By the end of the last harvest weekend, all the apples are sold.

Value-Added Products

The concept of "value-added" farm products—fruits and vegetables that have been processed and packaged—is enthusiastically promoted at organic and small

above: Dixon's apple cider jugs

farm conferences as well as by the New Mexico Department of Agriculture. Part of a broader effort to promote New Mexican food products nationwide, value-added products sold at farmers markets include a variety of salsas, pickled chile peppers, candied chiles, goat cheese, herbed mustards, garlic oil, vinegar flavored with edible flowers, salad dressings, cookies, tortillas, fruit or chile jams and jellies, herbal cosmetics and remedies, beeswax candles, and many others.

One of the most original value-added product lines is Southwest Chutney, an enterprise by Lisa Fox, one of the writers of this book. The spicy chutneys, which can be used in many ways—as a marinade for meat or fish, a filling for pastries or empanadas or a topping for eggs or pate or hors d'oeuvres—is made with organic and heirloom produce from various farmers in the greater Taos and Questa area, include Juniper Red (tomatoes, green apples, raisins, red chile, and secret spices), Taos Christmas (red and green chile, apples, raisins, roasted piñon nuts, and garlic), Calabacita Red (summer squash, tomatillos, piñons, and red chile), Sweet Onion (onions, orange zest, golden balsamic, and wine) and Peachy Green (green chile, peaches, cherries, lemons, and ginger). She sells through several farmers markets and her café in Costilla and plans to begin offering the products through a Web site in 2007.

Value-added products help the farmer generate more income from a limited quantity of crops. More important, they extend the selling season, especially for vendors at year-round markets like Santa Fe and Las Cruces.

The biggest challenge in getting into value-added production is kitchen certification. Anyone who sells processed foods to the public must make them in a commercial kitchen certified by the New Mexico Environment Department. Making a kitchen ready for certification can be prohibitively expensive for start-up businesses—often $6,000 or more. Some processors start out renting kitchen space in a local restaurant during closed hours. Others use a "food incubator," a community commercial kitchen that several processors can share. Users are usually expected to leave the incubators and get their own commercial kitchens certified when their businesses get on their feet. There are presently five such incubator kitchens in New Mexico—in Los Ojos, Española, Questa, Albuquerque, and Taos. One can only hope that more such kitchens will spring up around the state, since processing capacity is a primary element that holds many of New Mexico's small farmers back from realizing their full potential.

Agricultural Tourism

The idea of agricultural tourism, or agritourism, seems perfect for New Mexico, where travel and tourism accounts for nearly one-fifth of the state's total economy. Yet aside from farmers markets, farm-related tourist enterprises have been slow to catch on.

Rural Economic Development Through Tourism (REDTT), a program sponsored by New Mexico State University, actively tries to encourage agritourism with conferences for farmers and ranchers as well as grants. Since the REDTT program started in 1992, it has awarded about $400,000 to local tourism councils to identify and develop potential tourist attractions. The lion's share of this money has been to dude ranches, wildlife safaris, fee hunting, and fishing resorts—enterprises that are not in keeping with the sustainable farming philosophy of working in harmony with nature. But that may be starting to change.

Community agricultural festivals—such as the Hatch Chile Festival, the Abiquiú Farm Festival, and the Lavender Festival, sponsored by the Santa Fe Farmers Market—have proven their potential to attract tourists. Markets have also promoted farm tours (days when participating farms open their gates to visitors) and have had some success. Vista Hermosa Llama Farm in Corrales doubles as a sort of petting zoo, inviting the public to play with the llamas and see their corn and soybean fields. Several pecan and pistachio farmers, such as Nutcracker Suite Pecan Farms in Anthony, Crackin' Fresh Pecan in Roswell, Stahmann's Farms in San Miguel, and Pistachio Tree Ranch in Alamogordo, are also open to visitors, as are berry farms including Robinson's Raspberries in Apache Creek and San Patricio Berry Farm in San Patricio. Most of New Mexico's wineries have tasting rooms, and many depend on them for a large part of their income.

During the month of October, corn mazes, made by trampling paths through the dry cornstalks after the harvest, have also proven popular daytrip destinations for families. Some of the larger ones have grown to include other tourist attractions. New Mexico's first corn maze, started in 1999 in Las Cruces, features not only a nine-acre maze but also a hayride to a pick-your-own pumpkin patch, an underground "black hole" slide, and a tricycle trail. McCall's Pumpkin Patch and Corn Maze in Moriarty has a petting zoo, a cow train, pedal karts, a giant slide, and a pumpkin cannon that can fire pumpkins for up to a quarter of a mile, as well as a thirteen-acre maze. The farm also hosts nondenominational church services on Sunday mornings.

The most ambitious agritourism operations are farm bed-and-breakfast inns such as the Ellis Country Inn in Lincoln, Crystal Mesa Farm near Santa Fe, and Magdalena Ranch near Magdalena. A standout in this genre is Los Poblanos Organics in Los Ranchos, a village in Albuquerque's North Valley.

Los Poblanos supplements its farming income by operating a bed-and-breakfast inn. On the farm property is a nineteenth-century ranch house that was remodeled in 1934 by John Gaw Meem, one of New Mexico's leading architects, who originated "Santa Fe style." In the 1990s, the historic house was again renovated and turned into an inn with nine individually decorated luxury rooms and suites, where rates are about the same as for a room in a downtown Albuquerque hotel. Guests are free to roam the farm's vegetable, fruit, and lavender fields and savor the views of the surrounding mountains. The inn managers also offer cooking classes.

Los Poblanos grows a diverse array of herbs, vegetables, flowers, and fruit, including apples, melons, grapes, and even citrus fruits like navel oranges and tangerines. There's also lettuce, chard, garlic, rainbow carrots, LPO popcorn, romanesco broccoli, sweet peppers, carrots, corn, green beans, potatoes, onions, heirloom tomatoes, and various unusual varieties of chiles, including the farm's namesake, poblano chiles, also known as Mexican chiles. These are the most popular chiles south of the border and make wonderful chiles rellenos, often stuffed with a mixture of ground meat, diced fruit, and chopped nuts. The farm also grows fields of lavender, and in July the air all over the farm is redolent with the flowers' soothing fragrance. At a lower elevation than most other lavender farms in New Mexico, Los Poblanos was one of the few farms whose plants survived the early freeze of 2005, which created a scarcity of lavender in the 2006 season.

Monte Skarsgard, who prefers to be called "Farmer Monte," reports that, thanks to the rapid growth of the local market for organics, his gross sales have grown by 300 percent between 2003, when he started operating the farm, and 2006; he expects sales to double again in 2007—all from a farm only twelve acres in size. He also raises free-range chickens for their eggs, and he bottles the organic fertilizer used on the farm for sale to home gardeners. He sells most of his produce through the Los Poblanos CSA, which makes weekly home deliveries to members in Albuquerque, Santa Fe, and Placitas. All in all, Los Poblanos epitomizes what can be done to combine farming and tourism—even though it has no corn maze.

COOK WITH THE CHEF

Brad Kraus, a guest chef in the Santa Fe Farmers Market's Shop with the Chef program, offers these recipes for dishes he has cooked at the market. Kraus was the master brewer at the now-defunct Wolf Canyon Brewing Company, which was a gourmet restaurant as well as a microbrewery. He now heads up the Abbey Beverage Company, a joint venture with the Christ in the Desert Monastery near Abiquiú that will produce Monk's Ale in the tradition of ales brewed by Trappist and Benedictine monks in Belgium since the seventh century.

above: a migrant worker harvesting fruit at Dixon Apple Orchards

Buffalo Tenderloin with Oyster Mushrooms in Stout Sauce

Serves 4

1½ cups sweet stout or milk stout, divided
2 ounces dried oyster mushrooms
or 8 ounces fresh
3 shallots or 1 small onion, diced
8 (4- to 5-inch) buffalo tenderloin medallions
Sea salt
Black pepper
4 tablespoons butter, divided
3 teaspoons cornstarch

Heat ¾ cup of the beer in a small saucepan to simmer. Remove from heat, add the dried mushrooms, and cover. Allow to soak for 20 minutes.

While the mushrooms are soaking, dice the shallots or onion and season the steaks with sea salt and black pepper. Melt two tablespoons of the butter in a sauté pan large enough to hold the buffalo medallions without crowding. Sauté the medallions over medium heat until done to taste, and then remove them to a platter and cover with foil.

Sauté the mushrooms and the shallots or onions. Mix them into the cornstarch and an ounce or two of the remaining beer. Deglaze the sauté pan with the mushrooms soaked in beer and the rest of the beer. Do not reduce the beer or you will concentrate the bitterness. Reduce the heat to simmer and add the cornstarch mixture, stirring constantly until the sauce thickens.

The steaks can be returned to the pan to warm. Then dress each steak or the entire platter with the sauce. Accompany with roast potatoes or root vegetables.

Tart à la Bière

Serves 6 to 8

½ cup butter, divided
2 cups sifted pastry flour
1 tablespoon sugar
Pinch of salt
Ice water

⅔ cup (7 ounces) turbinado or
soft brown sugar, packed
2 large eggs
¾ cup (6 ounces) Belgian Trippel or
light wheat beer

Cut two-thirds of the butter into the flour with the sugar and salt. Add enough ice water to make the pastry dough hold together. Wrap in plastic wrap and chill for 30 minutes.

Heat the oven to 425 degrees F. Roll the pastry dough out on a floured surface and line a 9-inch tart pan. Sprinkle the turbinado sugar over the pastry in the very bottom of the pan.

Beat the eggs in a bowl, and then beat in the beer. Pour the mixture into the tart pan, directly onto the sugar. Cut the remaining butter into small pieces and dot the surface of the tart with them.

Bake for about 35 minutes, until the filling is set. It should be just firm to the touch. Allow to rest for at least 10 minutes before serving warm, or cool completely and serve cold. Garnish with a dollop of whipped cream.

A cornucopia of foods finds its way from New Mexico growers to consumers, mostly through farmers markets, where about three-fourths of all small farm produce is sold. Many of the vegetables offered at farmers markets are exotics and heirlooms; many of the fruits are unusual varieties uniquely adapted to the erratic New Mexico climate. And many of the meats and animal products are unlike anything you'll find in your local supermarket.

There are also other distinctively New Mexican farm products, such as plum wine and lavender. The array of recipes included in this chapter, some drawn from traditional regional recipes, others from professional chefs and amateur gourmet cooks, are designed to offer quick and easy solutions to the kind of questions that often occur to shoppers at farmers markets, such as, "What can you make with Swiss chard and rhubarb?"

VEGETABLES

As consumers who make regular weekly stops at their local farmers market quickly discover, part of the pleasure is watching how the harvest changes from week to week, constantly presenting new challenges in cookery.

At the few markets that are open in early spring, shoppers will find plenty of root vegetables such as carrots, garlic, shallots, and potatoes, as well as greens like Swiss chard, spinach, arugula, mustard greens, salad greens, and Chinese greens, which are often grown in greenhouses. As the end of spring approaches and a hot climate replaces the intermittent freezes of March and April, other vegetables appear, especially asparagus, which grows in amazing abundance in the Velarde and Embudo area, but only for a brief time. There are also red and golden beets, cauliflower and broccoli, and kale and young peas. By July, when all farmers markets are open, vegetables appear in the greatest profusion and include cucumbers, summer squash, garlic, beans (green, purple, and yellow), eggplant, and tomatoes, as well as sweet peppers and corn. The pungent smell of roasting green chile calls to shoppers during the fall harvest, when the farmers markets also offer up such exotica as edamame, daikon, kohlrabi, and leeks, as well as unbelievably large cabbages.

Vegetable farmers you may meet at New Mexico's farmers markets are as diverse as the bounty of their fields.

Matt Romero, an Española native, left his profession at age forty-two as chef at the Ohkay Owingeh casino to take over operation of a ten-acre Velarde farm belonging to his wife Emily's grandmother. Although Matt's mother had also grown up on a northern New Mexico farm, she had hated it and passed her distaste along

facing: blessing of the crops, Las Golondrinas

to Matt at an early age. "I couldn't even grow a garden," he recalls in a recent *Santa Fe New Mexican* article posted in his farmers market booth alongside his favorite recipes. When he returned to farming under the tutelage of his uncle, a traditional farmer in Alcalde, Matt focused on hard-to-find gourmet and specialty vegetables such as sweet Italian peppers, hot yellow Bolivian purira chiles, Japanese eggplants, and bok choy. In a relatively few years, his niche marketing strategy has made him the top-selling vendor at the Santa Fe Farmers Market and enabled him and Emily to buy their own farm in Dixon. He now serves as president of the Santa Fe Farmers Market Institute and conducts Shop with the Chef programs at the market.

Brothers **Teague and Kosma Channing**, lifelong Santa Fe residents, with their lanky, bearded appearance, suspendered baggy trousers, and floppy broad-brimmed hats, might have stepped right out of nineteenth-century rural America. They took an interest in agriculture after visiting their mother's relatives in the farm country of rural Poland, and then spent time in Mexico becoming fluent in Spanish, an essential survival skill in the villages of northern New Mexico. In 1993, at the respective ages of twenty-four and twenty, the Channing brothers started Gemini Farms in Truchas with three acres of fallow land and a small herd of goats; they built a house and barn from salvaged materials and locally cut roof timbers. The human population of their farm has been rather fluid, with a changing cast of friends and interns from Teague's alma mater, Tufts University, and the University of California–Santa Cruz. The third permanent member of the group, Ann Lefevre, an experienced northern New Mexico farmer, fell in love with Teague and moved to Gemini Farms to care for the goats, milk them, and make cheese. Today they maintain a double-sized booth at the Santa Fe Farmers Market, where they sell a wide range of vegetables, including garlic, spring greens, potatoes, tomatoes, carrots, chile, basil, corn, squash, beets, beans, and parsnips. While they make a small profit at the market, much of their produce goes to feeding themselves and their friends, making Gemini primarily a subsistence farm. Despite the great amount of work it took to put the farm in shape, the land is leased, and the brothers do not expect to ever own it. Their experience with the realities of farming has left them as idealistic as ever. Their ambition is to someday move to a larger place of their own where they can grow wheat, pasture horses, and irrigate more sustainably with gravity-fed acequias instead of pumps, moving away from any kind of reliance on fossil fuels. Then they hope to form a community-supported agriculture group that will furnish food for the whole village.

above: Matt Romero farm

The Channing brothers are by no means the youngest growers at the area's farmers markets. That honor goes to the students of **Camino de Paz Montessori Middle School and Farm** near Santa Cruz, New Mexico. Parents who have looked into alternative education for their children are usually familiar with Montessori schools, where children are taught in three-year age groups in a child-size environment with small-scale furniture, and are encouraged to make decisions for themselves and to achieve competence over their environment. Many know that Maria Montessori (a contemporary of Rudolf Steiner, who founded the Waldorf schools around the world) was Italy's first female physician as well as one of World War I–era Europe's leading scientists, philosophers, humanitarians, peace advocates, and feminists. But few realize that she, like Steiner, also originated the concept of *Erkinder*, "earth schools" where children live close to nature, eat fresh farm produce, and perform chores related to growing and marketing food while doing classroom studies according to their interests, without pressure from teachers. Camino de Paz ("Road of Peace"), one of the few active Montessori Erkinders in the United States, is a working organic farm where young teens merge their practical experiences with outdoor education, arts, and music, as well as academic studies. Half of the students, who come from around the United States and from other places as diverse as Europe, South America, and New Zealand, are boarders at Camino de Paz or neighboring farms, while the other half are locals who live with their families in the predominantly Hispanic villages nearby. Using a team of Belgian draft horses instead of motorized equipment, the Montessori students grow about thirty different vegetables. They also raise sheep, goats, and free-range chickens, turkeys, and ducks. In the school's commercial kitchen, students ages fourteen and up make processed products such as goat cheese, apple butter, herb pestos, fruit chutneys, hot salsas, chile caponata, and eggplant tapenade. Students sell these products, as well as the farm's surplus vegetables, at the Santa Fe Farmers Market and through the farm's community-supported agriculture group made up of about thirty families in the area.

While many of these farmers raise as wide an assortment of crops as possible, others become fascinated by particular vegetables. For instance, while **Daniel Carmona** of Cerro Vista Farm north of Taos grows a variety of produce—carrots, onions, beets, leeks, peas, kale, and lettuce—for his farmers market booth and CSA, his real passion is onions. Carmona says,

> *It's really cold in Cerros, so the crops that do best here are crops that can take some frost. We're not challenging the elements when we grow them. We do particularly well with onions, so I'm considering onions as a stand-alone crop. This year I've got an eighth of an acre of experimental varieties. They do extremely well here, and I might be able to make some money with them in the winter, when I'm not doing the CSA or the farmer's market, because they store. After this year I'll know what kind of onions grow and if I can make any money selling them in the winter. The farming season here is only about four months long, so we need to learn how to extend it.*

Stanley Crawford is author of two books about his and his wife Rosemary's lives at El Bosque Garlic Farm in Dixon—*Mayordomo: Chronicle of an Acequia in Northern New Mexico* (1988) and *A Garlic Testament: Seasons on a Small New Mexico Farm* (1992). Interviewed at the Santa Fe Farmers Market, where he stood behind a table heaped high with garlic fresh from the earth, Crawford filled me in on what he has been doing in the years since he wrote those books.

> *I've been growing garlic from the mid-'70s on, although it took us a few years to figure it out. We had about a five- or seven-year break in the farmers market—we stopped selling in 1997 or '98 because I was working full-time for the Farmers Market Institute—but I kept coming to the market on Saturdays to help educate people about the permanent site. I stopped doing that in 2000, and then we didn't farm for about four years. We went back to it last year on a small scale, and this year it's a little bit bigger. The land was in pretty good shape because we only had gardens and the rest was in cover crops.*

Crawford says of garlic:

> *I like the plant. I like planting it, cultivating it, harvesting it, processing it, all of that, but I'm not a gourmet garlic person. Rosemary feeds it to me*

raw when I have a cold or something like that.

You can plant garlic any time from September on, but in September you're also in the same cycle as the annual and perennial grasses, so you're going to get a lot of grasses coming up. If you wait until October or even November, before the ground freezes, you're a little better off. The garlic will often not emerge at all until the spring, but it roots within a week of putting it in the ground even though it's quite cold. We don't mulch, we'll probably start next year because we've begun to use drip irrigation. You can't mulch with flood irrigation because the mulch blocks the rows. So we're going to try that next year.

We also have basil and other things. Cutting basil is always nice because it smells so beautiful, it's an incentive to keep going. When you get away from it for some years, it's interesting how you then work with a field. It becomes so much a part of you that you don't want to do anything else. Going to town means you're wasting time, not taking care of it, planting things, watching them come up, dealing with the weeds, irrigation and all that, so it becomes a very intense experience. I don't know that I like any part of it more than any other, it's a whole thing.

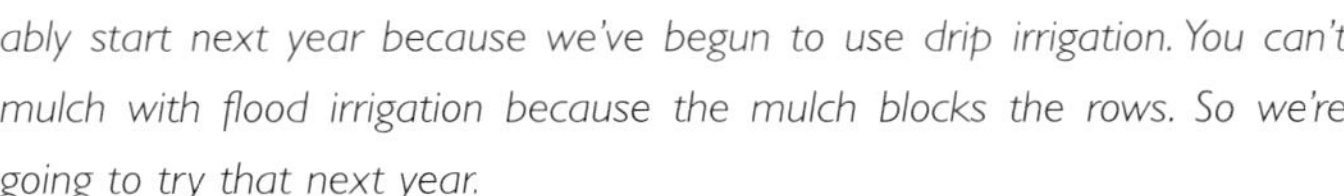

COOK LIKE A FARMER

Seeking recipes to help readers of this book prepare intriguing dishes from this kaleidoscopic array of fresh ingredients, we first thought to ask the farmers themselves. It seemed to make sense. After all, wasn't it Fannie Farmer who a century ago invented the modern recipe as we know it? Imagine our surprise when we learned that (1) Fannie Farmer never set foot on a farm, and (2) most farmers don't use recipes when they cook. Instead, they tend to adopt favorite cooking methods that can be applied to many different vegetables, such as stir frying, roasting, or steaming—and then let the crops speak for themselves.

Here are some cooking suggestions and observations about vegetables we received from farmers we interviewed at various farmers markets around New Mexico:

Aaron Greenwald, of the Greenwald Family Farm in Dixon, grows onions, beets, basil, lettuce, and Swiss chard. His parents were farmers in Dixon in the early '70s to mid-'80s, and Aaron moved back home from California about five years ago to continue farming the land his mother had bought in 1970. Aaron recommends a steamed mix of whatever vegetables are available. He starts out with "bottom of the pot" root vegetables that take a while to cook, such as sliced-up carrots, beets, and onions. On top of that, he piles Swiss chard, spicy greens, and beet greens, and then steams for an additional half hour, seasoning with soy sauce and butter. Served over a bed of rice, the vegetables have a great, fresh taste.

Patty Nelson of Brookwood Corner Farm in Dixon says,

We had to plow under all of our greens because of flea beetles [one of the more serious crop pests] this year. My poor customers have been just suffering. Grasshoppers haven't been bad—I've got my wonderful chickens out, and they get a lot of them. The only thing the chickens get is crickets and grasshoppers, they don't bother anybody else. We have grown some other vegetables this season like spectacular broccoli and kohlrabi. When it comes to cooking, there's just nothing as good as little, fresh potatoes roasted on the grill. You just can't go wrong with them. Other vegetables I stir-fry, roast them up, and put them in everything. You can do a zillion things with an overgrown zucchini. We had essentially a zucchini curry last night. It was excellent, and Lee didn't even know he was eating zucchini.

Emily Romero, wife of Alcalde farmer and Santa Fe Farmers Market Institute president Matt Romero, says,

When the tomatoes are ripe, my absolute favorite thing is to make tomato sauce for spaghetti. We have the garlic, we have fresh basil, we have fresh oregano, parsley, and thyme, and onions too. That makes the best tomato sauce ever. I chop up the tomatoes—sometimes I'll put them in the blender just to get them a little juicier—then sauté the onions and garlic in some olive oil, and then add herbs.

cally Grown
anically

Before tomatoes are ripe, I like to cook purple onions with everything, and I pretty much use carrots in every single stir-fry. The leeks, I'm not too good at cooking with leeks. My husband is, but we have a variety of lettuces, so it's like a salad at every meal.

Adam Mackie of Talon de Gato Farm (named for locust trees) in Dixon, sells a full range of vegetables at the Dixon and Santa Fe farmers markets, including cucumbers, sunburst squash, scallopini squash, green beans, rhubarb, leeks, and specialty peppers such as the padrón and shishito frying peppers that are becoming popular in northern New Mexico. His labor of love is French shallots, "a small bulbing onion with a lovely brown skin. You take the skin off, and it has a pale onion flesh striped with purple. Shallots have a lovely crisp texture, just right to chop one small shallot about the size of a head of garlic into a vinaigrette for your salad. French shallots are also a required ingredient for Béarnaise sauce, if you're making that."

Asked about his favorite way to cook harvest vegetables, Mackie says,

I was talking to one of the executive chefs from a restaurant in Santa Fe the other day. . . . He had been buying all my garlic scapes, which as you know is the shoot on top of garlic, and he was buying pounds and pounds of them every week, so I finally said to him, "What are you doing with these in your restaurant?" And he said, "Well, I just cook them and serve them. With good vegetables, you don't have to do anything." I thought about that, and, you know . . . I used to cook, but now I just fix the vegetables. Almost everything I grow is good if you just fix it with a little garlic and olive oil.

The leeks, for instance, I might cut them up and cook some pasta, and when the pasta is almost cooked, I'll throw the leeks in to cook with the pasta. Then when it's almost done I'll heat some olive oil and heat some garlic to soften it in the olive oil, drain the pasta and leeks, toss it with the olive oil and garlic, and you're away.

Then with my tomatoes, for instance, I will chop them to make a salsa crud. You need a savory tomato, a nice field-ripened tomato. You can't do this with store tomatoes. Just chop it up fairly small, chop up one of the French shallots with it, put some olive oil over it, and just let that sit while you cook the pasta. Drain the pasta, stir it in with the cold sauce, and serve it. You don't need a thick, hot steaming sauce in the summer. It's halfway between a salad and a cold pasta dish, and you get all the flavor of the tomatoes.

Padrón is a pepper about two inches long with a nice conical shape. It comes from Spain and is very popular there as a tapas pepper. You heat a good skillet with just a film of olive oil, pan fry them until they're just beginning to brown and wilt a little bit, put a little salt on them and drop them on a plate. Then sit down with a good friend and a cold beer and they'll be gone in no time. What's fun about them is that they're sort of like Russian roulette—every now and then one of them will be a little picoso. A jalapeño pepper is hot but it really doesn't have much flavor. These are long on flavor. People have been asking me for them at the market since April. We run out by nine o'clock. The shishito is a Japanese pepper—I don't know for sure, but I believe shishito means "wrinkled." It can be two to three inches long, cylindrical but deeply fluted like a saguaro cactus. They're milder, with just a little bit of heat, and they also have lots of flavor—just slightly different than the padrón and equally popular.

David and Loretta Fresquez's niece Brenda of Monte Vista Organic Farm in La Mesilla says,

Right now I'm cooking a lot of onions and zucchini sautéed in olive oil. I do the onions first, cook them down a little and then put in the diced zucchini. Some people like to put corn in it and call it calabacitas, *but I just like the zucchini and onions. I have it as a side dish, or sometimes I add a little cheese on top and it's my meal. And sometimes I'll put in a little dill for flavor, but you really don't need it. It's so fresh you don't need to season it with much other than salt and pepper.*

Funny Hendrie, co-manager of the Dixon Cooperative Market, calls her favorite dish East Meets West.

Take some zucchinis, one or two depending on how many people you want to feed, maybe three. Sauté some onions from the local growers along with a little garlic, cut your zucchini in slices an eighth of an inch thick, and throw them in. If you're not vegetarian, you can add some slices of ham or pork meat to the pot, and then you can get some yellow Thai curry paste—you only use about a teaspoon, and you must be careful not to add salt, because the curry paste already has salt. Let it all cook until the juices are mixed. It will all come together to make a delicious, exceptionally good zucchini dish.

Gail Minton, owner of the petite Squash Blossom Farm in Taos, has worked with nutrition teaching and counseling since 1970. She holds a master's in biology and nutrition and a PhD in environmental health science with a clinical nutrition component. She has been certified as a clinical nutritionist, and is now a clinical nutrition educator. Minton says,

We have a short growing season. Last week I had four strong frosts, but of course what was not lost was my kale, collard, or Swiss chard, or most of my perennial herbs, broccoli, and turnips. Those things will continue to grow all of October, and if the frosts aren't too hard and there isn't any heavy snow, they will grow well into the beginning of November. Then kale will just get brown and really die, chard a little earlier. In terms of nutrition, those crops happen to be probably the most nutritious things that all *people, of all biochemical individualities, all physiologies, can eat with huge benefit. They have protein, all the major minerals and trace minerals, certainly vitamin A and vitamin C.*

The other thing in the fall is if you can grow a good crop of winter squash, you'll have that until April, maybe even until July. And of course you have your own garlic all winter.

To get the benefit of Swiss chard, beet greens, and root vegetables, their nutrition is highest when they're fresh. If you have a way of storing things that is cool and dry—it could be fifty degrees or even forty, in your basement or a root cellar like the old-timers used—that's the best way to store things like carrots and turnips. Now, kale and chard and beet greens and collards need to be refrigerated. But they last. From your own garden they'll last two or three weeks, as long as they haven't gotten wet. You have to keep checking them to make sure they're not rotting.

To eat them, of course, there are a lot of ways. With root vegetables you can roast them. Cut them in small pieces, put them in a 425-degree oven and roast them with garlic and herbs and oil.

You can also pressure cook them. You can steam them. With the leafy greens, chard is the tenderest of the leafy greens besides spinach, so you can leave pretty big pieces. Kale, collard, and turnip greens are tougher, so I strip them off the stem and chop them very finely and have about a quarter of a cup of water in a pan and just let them steam and sort of braise in that. With garlic, I add stuff after—pesto that you've made, or oil, or tamari, or balsamic vinegar, whatever makes it more palatable for you.

Of course, these vegetables can be chopped and put in soups. I use a juicer, so I juice all the broccoli stems and other vegetables. Or I'll cut the stems very small and eat them. They can certainly go in soups that way.

I also do some freezing. You can freeze a number of things, depending on your freezer size. Do them just in a parboil so you break them down slightly and they don't have enzyme activity that will deteriorate so they spoil. Put them in

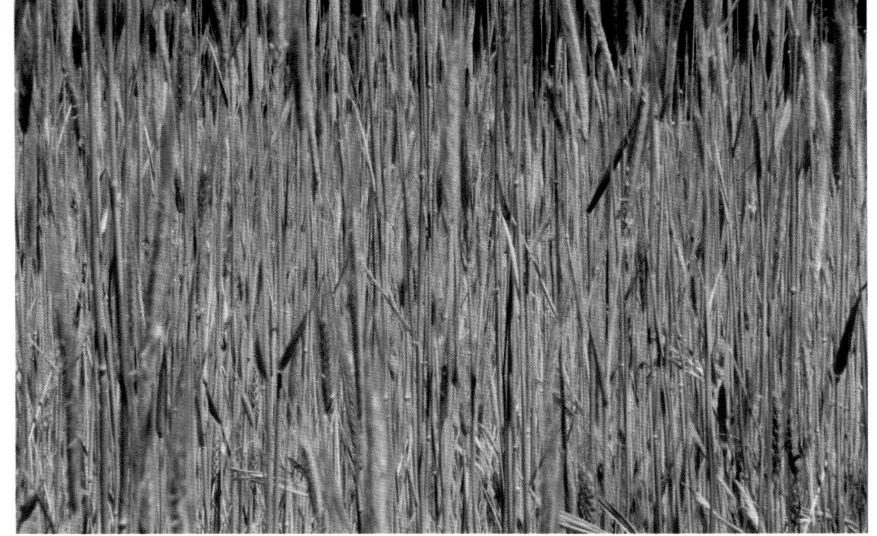

zipper-lock bags and freeze them. Sometimes they just don't taste like fresh, so at that point I'll start buying from California. You can still put them in frittatas or soups, but not salads.

Maria, with her partner Danny, operates Desert Funghi, a down-on-the-farm enterprise that grows several gourmet varieties and specializes in oyster mushrooms, which are native to New Mexico's Sangre de Cristo Mountains.

Besides oyster mushrooms, we also grow some other types—lion's mane, Stropharia, and wine cap, and we're attempting to grow shiitakes. We're also growing some medicinal mushrooms like rishi. [As for cooking she says,] I love to have mushrooms as an alternative to meat in a variety of dishes. They can have up to 30 percent protein, which is an excellent addition to any vegetarian meal. I love to just sauté them. That's the simplest, easiest way to cook them. You can add fresh goat cheese, fresh basil, or you can just sauté them and add some of your favorite flavoring, like garlic oil or sesame oil.

Tufik Hadad, a customer browsing at the Taos Farmers Market, says,

They grow leeks here, so I got leeks and made leek and potato soup, an old favorite of mine. First you have to clean the leeks, they're really sandy, so you've got to be real careful and peel them all back. I use a little bit of the greens because I like the color in the soup, but mostly you just clean them up and scald them. I don't use cream—I think that's traditional, to make it real rich, but I like it not so rich any more. I use olive oil in the bottom of the pan instead of butter, and a little salt and pepper—not too much stuff, though, because the flavor of the leeks really comes through. I parboil the potatoes first, and then sauté the leeks in oil, get them tender, and then simmer them together in water with a little dill, but not too much. I used to be real spicy, but now I'm more plain. I like to taste the vegetables.

THE ORGANIC WHEAT EXPERIMENT

When Don Juan de Oñate led the first expedition of Spanish settlers into New Mexico, he brought a full range of imported crops and seeds that had originated in Europe. They included cabbage, carrots, cucumbers, garlic, lettuce, onions, peas, radishes, and turnips—all vegetables that are commonly found in farmers markets across the state today. One Spanish import, however, was as significant to the Spanish settlers as corn had been to the Pueblo Indians. Wheat was more than a European staple food. It was *the* staple food of the Bible—and moreover, the stuff from which the Eucharistic host was made. It was essential to any communion. Along with grapes for sacramental wine and beeswax for candles, wheat was essential to Franciscan missionaries' efforts to Christianize the native tribes. Just as Spanish colonists shunned corn, using it as animal feed but considering it unfit for human consumption, the Pueblo people disliked wheat. In fact, even today, many traditional Indians avoid wheat products and only eat them on Christian religious holidays.

Centuries later, the U.S. federal government opened tracts of land in northeastern New Mexico to settlement under the Homestead Act of 1862. This law gave homesteaders 160 acres of land, to which they could gain legal title by living on it for five years and paying a nominal filing fee. In the 1880s, the railroad arrived in New Mexico, carrying unprecedented numbers of Anglo would-be settlers from the East and Midwest. They soon discovered that very little of the available land was suitable for dairies or field crops, but that much of the dry farmland could produce wheat. Within a few years, wheat became one of New Mexico's top agricultural products.

Statewide production reached more than eight million bushels of wheat. The heart of wheat growing was the Mora Valley, where more than two hundred varieties of wheat were grown and about three hundred flour mills were built to grind it. The high point in New Mexico's wheat-growing era came in 1933, when wheat from Mora was awarded Best of Show at the Chicago World's Fair. Around the same time, the collapse of wheat prices during the Great Depression spelled the end for most small wheat farms. All of the Mora mills closed down except one, the Cleveland Roller Mill, which has been preserved by the state as a museum. Only 1,400 families inhabit the 2,000 square miles of Mora County, and only three farms in the Mora Valley today grow any wheat at all.

Today wheat remains a major crop in New Mexico, though production has declined by nearly one-third in the past twenty-five years. Virtually all of it is grown on New Mexico's eastern prairies, using high-investment machinery and fields thousands of acres in size to produce homogenous white wheat that is shipped out of state to be milled into "Wonder Bread"–style flour.

A bold initiative to help small farmers came in 1995, when a marketing expert with the New Mexico Department of Agriculture accompanied the Taos County extension agent to visit farms of ten acres or less in the Costilla Valley, along the New Mexico–Colorado state line. Here he found about one hundred active farms and a local populace that was among the poorest in the state. This area, too, had been abundant wheat farming country at one time, but wheat no longer paid. At the prevailing market price of 3.3 cents a pound—a rate that hadn't changed much since the 1930s—wheat was a money-losing proposition for small farmers once wholesalers, processors, and other middlemen took their cuts.

The advantage the Costilla Valley farmers had was that most of their wheat farmland not only had never been treated with pesticides or other chemicals but had also lain fallow, often for generations. The water supply poured directly out of the mountains and was exceptionally free from pollution of any kind. So said Gonzalo "Go-Go" Gallegos, a local physical education teacher, football coach, and part-time meat cutter who was trying to promote the Sangre de Cristo Agricultural Producers Co-op, which he and other area farmland owners had incorporated two years earlier. The co-op was a ready-made vehicle for state agricultural grants.

But there was still a piece missing in the plan to revive small-scale wheat farming in New Mexico. There was no established market for the flour within the state, and shipping it to other states would raise expenses enough to make the flour unprofitable. The beginnings of an organic wheat market appeared thanks to Dutch baker Willem Malten, owner of Cloud Cliff Bakery and Artspace in Santa Fe. Before coming to New Mexico, Malten had lived at the Tassajara Zen Monastery, the oldest Zen training monastery in the United States and the largest outside Asia, located in the mountains outside Carmel-by-the-Sea, California. By the time Malten arrived there, the name Tassajara was widely identified with bread baking because of *The Tassajara Bread Book*, which was written by Edward Brown, a cook at the monastery, in 1969 and became one of the most popular cookbooks of recent times, still in print after more than three decades with nearly one million copies sold. Not surprisingly, when he came to Santa Fe, Malten brought with him a deep interest in the art, spirit, and business of bread baking.

While selling his baked goods at the Santa Fe Farmers Market, Malten was encouraged by author and fellow vendor Stanley Crawford (see interview on page 97) to explore possibilities for using locally grown flour in his products. Exploring the idea, Malten soon discovered that there was no such thing as "local" flour. Big farms in the eastern part of the state, where virtually all the wheat was grown, exported their crop to other states, where it was milled and commingled with flour from elsewhere, perhaps ultimately to be shipped back into New Mexico and sold to bakeries like Cloud Cliff.

Convinced that there was a market for fresh organic bread in Santa Fe, Malten approached the New Mexico Department of Agriculture to try to locate organic wheat flour, only to find that it was no longer grown in the region. There he was

above right: Roger Swanson, a volunteer, is the miller at El Rancho de las Golondrinas

referred to Gonzalo Gallegos's fledgling Sangre de Cristo Co-op. By agreeing to buy a substantial part of the co-op's flour production, Malten provided the beginnings of the market the co-op needed to make a business plan and grant applications for start-up funding. And so the Northern New Mexico Organic Wheat Project was born.

In its first year of wheat farming, the Sangre de Cristo Agricultural Producers' Co-op grew about sixty thousand pounds of wheat and sold virtually all of it to Cloud Cliff Bakery. The flour was used to make the bakery's organic Pan Nativo ("native bread"), which has become popular in local supermarkets and natural foods stores. Today, with 120 acres under wheat cultivation, the co-op produces more than two hundred thousand pounds of wheat. While more than half of their wheat is still used for Cloud Cliff's Pan Nativo, the co-op also supplies several cafés and pizzerias in Taos and sells five-, ten-, and fifty-pound bags of the flour to the public through natural foods markets in northern New Mexico.

But that's not the end of the story. Despite the co-op's apparent success in reintroducing small-scale wheat farming in New Mexico, it has only been able to survive its first decade thanks to agricultural grants. Besides the high but necessary cost of buying certified organic seed, the biggest reason until recently was that there were no operating flour mills left in New Mexico. All the co-op's wheat had to be trucked to a mill three hundred miles away in Dawn, Texas, and the cost of diesel fuel alone was more than one-third of the total market value of the flour.

That expense, along with much of the milling cost, was eliminated in 2006 when the co-op obtained a $13,000 grant from the New Mexico Department of Agriculture and bought a used flour mill, which it relocated to the Costilla Valley. The next step, Gallegos and other co-op members believe, is to develop their own brand of bread.

Willem Malten seems not at all dismayed by the prospect that his sole supplier of organic wheat might some day become his competitor. He has proposed several other ways to get the co-op on a sound financial footing, such as selling organic wheat berries and growing rotational crops or other specialty grains such as amaranth and quinoa. Meanwhile, Gonzalo Gallegos is taking classes in business management and marketing to prepare for the co-op's future development and expansion. Both men agree that the demand for local organic wheat is growing fast.

FRUIT

When it comes to organic produce, there is more demand for fruit than vegetables because organic fruit is produced less, according to Ron Walser, the fruit specialist at New Mexico State University's Cooperative Extension in Alcalde. On the East Coast, particularly, diseases and pests make it almost impossible to grow organic peaches or other fruits. Most such infestations are not a problem in New Mexico, so fruit growers—whether certified or not—generally do not use pesticides as a matter of course. The main exception is young pear trees, which are susceptible to fire blight in northern New Mexico until they are about five years old, though they grow fine in the southern part of the state.

above left: Gonzalo "Go-Go" Gallegos; *above right:* wheat pearls at Go Go's

Raspberries grow wild throughout New Mexico's mountains, providing the main food for bears during the fattening-up time before hibernation. So it's only natural that more domesticated strains of the berries would make a good small-farm cash crop. For example, one of the most visible among New Mexico's organic fruit growers and farmers market vendors, former construction contractor Doug Findley of Heidi's Raspberry Farm grows four varieties of raspberries in his four acres of fields in Corrales. From this relatively small plot, he and his twenty-year-old son harvest an astonishing twenty thousand pounds of berries during a two- to three-month season. Of these, he sells five thousand pounds fresh, but most of the berries go into the value-added side of the business as his sister, Heidi Eleftheriou, processes them into three kinds of jam—original organic raspberry jam, raspberry red chile jam, and raspberry ginger jam—using her proprietary recipe. The jams are hot sellers at farmers markets in Corrales, Santa Fe, Los Alamos, and elsewhere. "My goal," Findley says with tongue in cheek, "is to employ my whole family." More seriously, he says that he hopes to promote the creation of new farms by demonstrating how it can be done and would like to see demonstration farms created around the state in connection with farmers markets.

Most fruits grown in New Mexico, however, are not native to the area but were brought from Europe by the Spanish. Some, like melons and peaches, were traded northward by Mexican Indians; others, such as plums and grapes, were brought by early Spanish colonists. Still others, such as apples, were brought westward by Anglo pioneers in the late nineteenth century or introduced by seed salesmen in the early twentieth century. As a drive through farm country in September will quickly reveal, many kinds of fruit thrive in the New Mexico sunshine—despite Mother Nature's risk factors.

The most serious problem with growing fruit in New Mexico is weather. Drought, flash floods, hailstorms, and early fall frost are among the factors that can spell disaster for orchard growers. In the northern half of the state, especially, by far the biggest risk is late spring freezes. It is almost inevitable that sometime in the middle of fruit blossom time, a surprise sleet storm will come along, dropping the temperature to 28 degrees and knocking all the flowers to the ground. Since different fruits bloom at slightly different times, the exact day when the freeze hits determines which crops survive and which don't. One year apricots may bloom before the freeze and grow in profusion, while the peach blossoms may be destroyed as soon as they open. The next year, the freeze may come on a different calendar date, and different fruits may survive. Pears are the least fortunate fruit trees in northern New Mexico because their blooming season is the most likely to coincide with a freeze.

At one time, growers in New Mexico were encouraged to give up their heirloom trees, which were well adapted to the climate, and change over to Macintosh apples, which were thought to be more commercially viable. But shipping costs and other factors made New Mexico apples uncompetitive on the national market. Today, a primary mission of the NMSU Extension in Alcalde is to identify little-known varieties of apples that are late blooming (giving the best chance to survive late freezes) and self-pollinating (because honey bees are lethargic in the coolness of early spring). Very late bloomers, on the other hand, may not have enough time to develop enough sugar for the best flavor in cold areas. "Diversification is the key," Walser says. "New Mexico growers can't compete with red delicious apples from Washington on the wholesale market. The solution is to grow specialty apples and sell them locally and regionally direct to the consumers." He also urges growers to produce unusual strains of apples and other fruits that qualify under a new federal program that provides grants for growing "specialty crops." While the center constantly tests new varieties, recently they have recommended little-known strains such as Honeycrisp and golden supreme apples, as well as the heirloom Arkansas black apples, which are rapidly growing in popularity. Other tree fruits the Alcalde center has found to be well suited to New Mexico's climate include BlazingStar and China pearl peaches, Harglow apricots, black gold sweet cherries, Balaton and Danube tart cherries from Hungary, and Castleton plums.

The research center at Alcalde also tests and recommends new strains of strawberries, raspberries, and other berries and grapes. "Blackberries," Walser says, "are a good source of antioxidants—even better than blueberries. There's a great market for frozen blackberries, too. Not like raspberries—there are plenty of frozen raspberries." Recent recommendations include Apache and Navajo blackberries, Polana and Caroline raspberries, Honeoye and Everest strawberries, and Himrod, Reliance, and Venus grapes.

The Old-Timer

"We lived good during the Depression . . . We ate good."

Carl Berghofer

Everybody in the fruit-growing business in northern New Mexico knows Carl Berghofer, longtime farmer, fisherman, and storyteller in the village of Rinconada on the Rio Grande. Berghofer's father was a gold miner in Cripple Creek, Colorado, before moving down to Taos Junction (once a major bean-growing area) when the government opened the area to homesteading after World War I. The family later moved to their father's farm in Rinconada, about two hundred yards from Carl's present home. He worked thirty-two years for the New Mexico Game and Fish Department, retired in 1975, and returned to Rinconada, where he has been farming ever since. Starting with bare ground, Berghofer developed orchards and picks a thousand boxes of apples a year and 2,800 pounds of sweet cherries, as well as peaches, plums, apricots, pears, nectarines, and some seedless grapes.

"The stores in Taos were requesting asparagus," Berghofer recalls. "So Dad got some stock and planted it, and we raised asparagus and raspberries. Then the birds would eat the seeds, and they'd park on the fence posts and drop the seeds, fully fertilized and ready to grow, so all this asparagus is some that we planted here that grows wild all over the valley, all the way to Velarde."

These days, Berghofer sells most of his produce to the local school system. He also sells cherries and peaches from a roadside stand. Recalling the Great Depression, he says,

> *We had an old Model A touring car, and two or three times a year we'd fill the back of that thing full of fruits and vegetables and make a trip to Tres Piedras. We'd visit this ranch and that ranch and another ranch and unload all that produce, and we'd make just about enough money out of the whole thing to buy gas to get home on—it was all rough dirt road in those days. Then in the fall of the year we'd hear one of the guys coming down in a pickup, we'd hear it rattling up the canyon, and he'd unload a half a beef or half a pig. Somebody else would bring us a hundred pounds or two hundred pounds of beans, and somebody else would bring potatoes, and we'd trade it out that way.*
>
> *We lived good during the Depression. We'd get an old car tire and make soles and nail them on our shoes, but we ate good. We'd sugar-cure and salt-cure meat. Of course, we didn't have refrigeration then, but we had an icebox on the north side of the house, and after the fifteenth of November food would keep all winter. Uncle Louis and I dug out a root cellar and we'd keep carrots and parsnips and turnips and cabbages and everything in that cellar for winter food. We also kept chickens and rabbits. We never missed a meal.*

The Fruit Tree Collector

"the beautiful apple has replaced the ugly, tasty one."

Gordon Tooley

Gordon Tooley, owner of Tooley's Trees near Truchas, collects cuttings from hundred-year-old apple, pear, plum, and cherry cuttings from old homesteads. He has eleven thousand drought-tolerant, heirloom, and rare varieties of fruit.

above: new wheat mill

Tooley recalls:

My current wife grew up in New England. I apprenticed on a farm out there for a year and then came back to Colorado and did various plant-related jobs and got interested in all aspects of propagation, field growing, orcharding, keeping bees and perennials, and the whole balance of everything. We came back out here in 1990, and I bought this farm in 1991. It had pretty much sat fallow for about ninety years.

It took me about five years to get it clear and into shape. At that time I'd wanted to graft my own stuff, so I hit the Old Santa Fe Trail and old homesteads. As people immigrated here, they brought with them all these varieties of fruits and left abandoned orchards, so I found out what I could from people in the proximity—if the fruit was pig feed or good eating. A lot of the apples didn't have names, or the name had been lost, and yet they were interesting apples. So I have quite a collection of stuff that I don't know what it is, and then I have about seventy different varieties of other apples that I know what I have. I like mid- to late-flowering varieties for early-frost reasons, and then I graft on to various root stocks that are good for our climate here—semi-dwarf, well anchored, high pH tolerant, and low fertility. A lot of times with trees that have been in decline and aren't putting on vigorous growth, it's kind of hard to find good wood, and you really have to hunt to find good buds.

I've just been out collecting. The cherries I grafted up came from near Hernandez, I've got an apricot I'm working on from Chimayó, I've got some apples from over in the Manzano Mountains, I did quite a few from around Taos, from an old homestead in the Ranchos area. When we dig into this pile of straw here we'll uncover a bunch of other obscure varieties that have disappeared from commerce but the trees are still around. It's a kind of genetic bank. The world has gone from about eight thousand varieties of apples to around eight hundred. About five hundred can be found in North America, yet most of those aren't found in the stores. The beautiful apple has replaced the ugly, tasty one.

I'm grafting heirloom varieties and getting them out to people in their own homes and orchards. If someone wants to get a braeburn or a cameo or a pink lady, they can go to most stores and get them, but here we offer good cider varieties or red fruit for red applesauce or coloring cider or pie apples, drying varieties, winter keepers that will keep seven to ten months and still remain fresh and not mealy. Some are good for frying with pork. Some others are not edible at all, they're strictly for cider making. Others are russeted, ugly apples that are not round at all and have tough, rough skin but are very flavorful inside and long lasting.

Looking Peachy

"I want to carry on the tradition of fruit growing in Dixon."

Fred Martinez

The largest commercial fruit growers in the village of Dixon, Fred Martinez and his wife Ruby have 3,500 trees on eighteen acres of family-owned land. When we visited him, his new crop of peaches was ripe to perfection.

> *Things are looking peachy, as they say. We've been fortunate. The weather's been hot and dry, and so far we've had enough irrigation water, but it's going down daily, so we hope we can squeak by again. On our farm, on the riverbank a lot of chokecherries grow wild, so Ruby went out and picked some last night, and she made jelly this morning, so it's fresh.*

Fred and Ruby Martinez took over the job of running the orchards from his octogenarian father, Delfin, in 1999. Delfin, in turn, had bought the orchards from his uncle in 1950 and planted ten varieties of fruit there, including Golden Delicious, Rome Beauty, Jonathan, Winesap, Granny Smith, Fuji, and Gala apples as well as a new proprietary strain of red delicious apple and another new variety—the unexpected result of grafting golden delicious apples onto an old heirloom apple tree—which they call Ruby's Gold and describe as "like an albino Golden Delicious with a subtle mouth-refreshing taste." The family has been growing fruit in the area for so long that the long-established ditch that has traditionally supplied water to upper Dixon farms is named the Martinez Acequia after them.

A retired Los Alamos National Laboratory employee, Fred was recently written up in the *New York Times* due to his participation in Albuquerque's innovative Farm

above: Fred Martinez of Dixon

to Cafeteria program, which lets the school districts buy food for school lunches directly from small New Mexico farmers. The program is viewed by state departments of agriculture as a pilot project that, if successful, could help support small family farms throughout the United States.

A conspicuous feature in the Martinez orchards is a gigantic fan. The orchards are at the mouth of the Embudo River Canyon, and when temperatures drop during a late frost, cold air sinks to the bottom of the canyon and flows down into the orchards. If the temperature drops dangerously low, a thermometer touches off an alarm in the Martinez house, and Fred leaps out of bed to go out and turn on the fan, which circulates the air enough to raise the temperature by several degrees. "I want to carry on the tradition of fruit growing in Dixon," Martinez says. "It's good to linger in the past. But being progressive is why we're successful."

The World's Best Apples

"My grandfather made it through drought, hail, and frost."

Becky Mullane

Fred and Faye Dixon started the orchards in 1943, converting a failed dude ranch into a working farm. They used a mule-drawn "stone boat" to clear the soil of tons of volcanic rocks, which became the landmark wall that marks the property boundaries today. The Dixons ran the orchards for forty-two years until Faye's death in 1985.

Becky, the Dixons' granddaughter, grew up in Minnesota. Her parents brought her to New Mexico to visit the farm each summer, and she dreamed of someday living there. Four months after Faye's death, while Becky was an eighteen-year-old student at Northwestern, she wrote and asked Fred if she could join him in New Mexico to learn the apple business. He agreed, and she spent the next eight years in that task. Then she and Jim took it over. At this writing, Fred Dixon is eighty-six years old and living in Idaho. He returns to the orchards during the growing season.

In mid-April 2006, icicles dripped from the lower branches of the blossoming trees at Dixon's Apples the morning we first visited the orchards to interview owners Becky and Jim Mullane. The irrigation spray had frozen during the night. "Apples are a risky business," Becky said while taking a break from homeschooling the couple's children, Luke, Cody, and Natalie Faye.

We finally put in deep-well drip irrigation this year when the creek that has watered the orchards for more than sixty years just dried up. Last year we lost fifteen acres of trees [about one-third of Dixon's Apples orchards]. We're planting new trees, and it will take seven years to get good production.

But my grandfather made it through drought, hail, and frost. They had to shoo off blossom-eating deer and gophers that burrowed around the trees and ate the feeder roots. Fred once shot a bear that had him pinned to the ground. In 1971, New Mexicans lost 70 percent of their apple trees because of −38 degree F temperatures. They were told they would have to pull everything out and start over, but they refused to believe it. The next spring, the air was filled with the sweet smell of apple blossoms again.

Dixon's is the home of New Mexico's most famous apples—Champagne apples and Sparkling Burgundys, both developed by Fred Dixon. The orchards are not located in the fruit-growing country around the northern village of Dixon, as you might expect, but are southwest of Santa Fe at the mouth of remote Cochiti Canyon, on an unpaved road beyond Cochiti Pueblo and the recreation community of Cochiti Lake.

The temperature only got down to 33 degrees that April morning. The chill factor of the wind blowing down Cochiti Canyon made the icicles but did not kill the apple blossoms. When we returned in September, Dixon's was harvesting a bumper crop, and buyers from Albuquerque and Santa Fe, as well as from other parts of the country and the world, were parked for more than a mile along the lava stone wall to get their share of Dixon's Champagne apples, which many connoisseurs have called "the world's best apple." With no middlemen and no marketing costs, merely a long-established reputation, Dixon's sells its apples on-site for $14 a half-bushel bag, or about 63 cents a pound, a fraction of what conventional apples sell for in supermarkets. They do not sell at farmers markets because, by the end of harvest weekend, no apples are left.

Wine

"My winemaking methods are a little bohemian."

Charlotte Slater

There are presently thirty-eight wineries in New Mexico. Although commercial winemaking is a relatively new phenomenon in New Mexico, four centuries ago

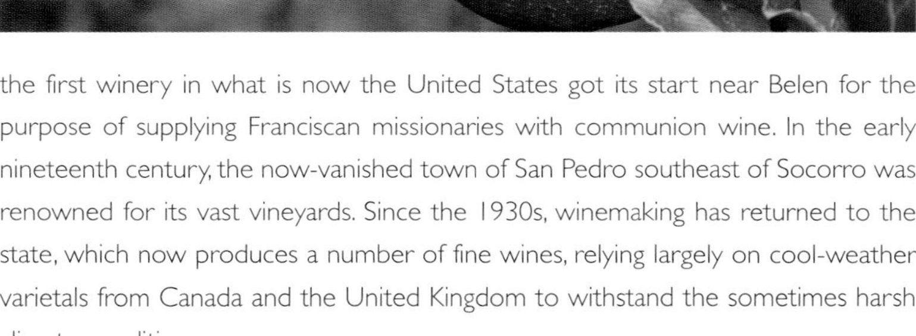

the first winery in what is now the United States got its start near Belen for the purpose of supplying Franciscan missionaries with communion wine. In the early nineteenth century, the now-vanished town of San Pedro southeast of Socorro was renowned for its vast vineyards. Since the 1930s, winemaking has returned to the state, which now produces a number of fine wines, relying largely on cool-weather varietals from Canada and the United Kingdom to withstand the sometimes harsh climate conditions.

The Ritchie-Slater Winery, though, is unique. Instead of using conventional grapes, Lan and Charlotte Slater handcraft their award-winning wines with a wide range of fruits from local farms, including chokecherries, wild plums, and raspberries.

High in the mountains in the Black Lake area southwest of Angel Fire on the road to Mora sits a beautifully restored log barn that now houses the winery's tasting room. The corrals have also been preserved to create outdoor patios, perfect for summer wine tasting. You can't help but take a deep breath and relax as you gaze toward the east. Pristine meadows slope downward to reveal Osha Pass rising on the horizon.

"The original barn here was built in the late 1880s as a dirt-floored log cow barn," Lan Slater says. "We spent about three years on the renovation of it. It was one of those projects that we would have been better off tearing it down and starting over, but it wouldn't have turned out with near the character that we ended up with. And we don't like to do anything the easy way anyway."

Before moving to their mountain home, the Slaters worked as electricians. Charlotte recalls:

> *For a while, we moved to Albuquerque because we were working down there. The home we bought in Albuquerque needed a lot of work. The landscaping was in bad disrepair, and we discovered an elderberry tree in the backyard. After a couple years of pruning and taking care of it, we started getting about two hundred pounds of elderberries off it every year, so we bought a freezer and filled it full of elderberries. We didn't know what we were going to do with them. Then one of my girlfriends was sitting on the patio with us one time and she said, "Well, they write songs about elderberry wine," and I just thought, "Well, duh . . ." so we went down to the local winemaking store and bought everything we needed to start making wine at home. I did that exclusively for four years. We'd get about two hundred bottles of wine a year off that tree. Kept the whole neighborhood in wine. Making wine just seemed to come naturally to me for some reason. I don't know, I can't explain it. I just threw it in the bucket and put a little yeast in it, and it turned out great.*

above right: strawberry field, Tesuque Pueblo

Lan continues:

All of Charlotte's friends and family told her how good this wine was, but she started to think that maybe your friends and family aren't always completely honest with you. So the first bottling of the first batch of wine Charlotte ever made, she entered in the state fair wine competition just to get a critique, and she won a bronze medal. That was how she figured out what she wanted to be when she grew up. Since then she's won a number of awards, including a gold medal Best of Show winner last year for a blend Charlotte's made that's been real popular that we call Moonlight. We're real proud of what she's done over the years.

Charlotte adds:

I've never made a grape wine. I started making wine in the backyard with fruit, that's all I know. My winemaking methods are a little bohemian. There's a lot of grape wine out there, and I don't have any interest in grape wine. But after we came home to Black Lake, we started looking around, and I'd find apricots and pears in Talpa and Rinconada, I get chokecherries from Taos and also from Mora and Guadalupita, I get plums from Ocate, and I get a lot of apples, pears, and things like that from Carl Berghofer in Rinconada. Just my personal preference, I prefer that the fruits are organic as much as possible, and as far as I know, all the local growers I use are organic growers. Most of them are certified, but a lot of things I get are just trees in people's backyards that one year they just go crazy and they have too much fruit, so as long as I can have 150 pounds of something, I'm good. There's really nothing that regulates me other than that the state strongly suggests you use 50 percent New Mexico product when available.

I went from five-gallon fermenters to thirty-gallon fermenters to fifty-five-gallon fermenters, and that's what I use now. The wines are not syrupy sweet wines, they're dry table wines. There's no residual sugar, just the full flavor of fruit without it being syrupy and sweet. That's sort of my signature, to not make a sweet wine. As soon as we get the fruit, if we have a wild plum, chokecherry, or something where you can't get the stones out of the fruit, I will very often ferment it with the stones in the fruit, and it gives kind of a nutty, earthy tone to it. We ferment everything—skins, meat, everything. I don't press anything.

Lan says:

We've been real lucky the last few years to be able to get local fruits from some of these smaller family-owned orchards where up until lately they just let the fruit fall to the ground. So we like to think that we're helping out the local fruit-growing community, so to speak, because they know we're always in the market for the local fruits, so they hopefully take care of the trees now.

The Ritchie-Slater Winery is open to the public for tastings from 12:00 to 7:00 p.m. Thursday through Saturday and 12:00 to 6:00 p.m. on Sundays.

LIVESTOCK

Bison

Near present-day Folsom, New Mexico, fossilized remains of twenty-three American bison were found along with points of arrows or spears used by paleolithic

above: washing, sorting, and pressing apples

Indians—the first scientific proof that Ice Age animals and human beings inhabited the Americas at the same time almost ten thousand years ago. Before Europeans arrived in North America, an estimated thirty to seventy million bison lived on the prairies that stretched from New Mexico to the Mississippi River and northward into Canada. By 1889, fewer than a thousand bison remained alive, preserved in captivity by the Bronx Zoo along with a handful of western ranchers who joined together to form the American Bison Society. So it is remarkable that these great beasts, the largest land mammals in North America, have not only been rescued from extinction but have grown in numbers to about four hundred thousand head in the United States, up from one hundred fifty thousand just ten years ago.

Media mogul Ted Turner, owner of nearly half the bison alive on earth today, is also the second-largest landowner in New Mexico. Yet even Turner, with his virtually unlimited resources, has been unable to solve the problem of marketing bison meat to supermarket customers. Large-scale bison-ranching operations like his are subsidized by the federal government, which buys surplus bison meat and distributes it free on America's poorest Indian reservations. Of the $6 million that the government spends on bison meat each year, more than $5 million goes to Turner. Though one might wonder whether a rancher as wealthy as Turner really needs taxpayer subsidies, it should be pointed out that the Turner Foundation donates a roughly equal amount to environmental causes each year. A more stinging criticism is the allegation by some Indian groups that Turner sells only low-quality meat for distribution to the Indians while diverting the prime cuts for his chain of forty-seven Montana Grill buffalo restaurants across the United States.

Yet there is little evidence that large-scale bison ranching can ever be a profitable enterprise without federal subsidy. Though wholesale bison meat prices have tripled in the past decade, a recent market study revealed that the average American eats sixty-three pounds of beef a year—and only about one *ounce* of bison.

Small-scale bison ranchers, who sell their meat through New Mexico's farmers markets, face no such problem. One of them, the Pueblo of Picurís Bison Project, was established in 2000 with a grant from the Los Alamos National Laboratory Foundation. Since then the pueblo's operation has grown from fifteen acres of pasturage to 113 acres and from one pregnant bison cow to seventy head. The project distributes meat to all Picurís households for feast days four times a year and provides meat to the pueblo's Senior Citizen Program and to the public schools in the nearby village of Penasco, where all students from the pueblo attend bilingual English-Tiwa classes. Danny Sam and his wife Joey, who manage the program, also sell bison meat at the Santa Fe and Los Alamos farmers markets and supply the restaurant at the tribally owned Hotel Santa Fe. They report that the demand for their bison meat, especially at the farmers market, consistently exceeds what they are able to supply. They hope to expand the Picurís bison operation to about two hundred head. Their biggest problem, like other small specialty-meat producers, is the lack of processing facilities, which requires them to ship their bison to Colorado for butchering.

Bison seem to be a lot like cattle. The cuts of bison meat are called by the same names as cuts of beef, which is why you can get a New York strip or sirloin buffalo steak, buffalo burgers or a buffalo tenderloin, but not buffalo chops or buffalo breasts. In reality, bison are only distantly related to either cattle or to Asian or African buffalo. Bison are part of a genus whose only other surviving relative is the larger, highly endangered European wisent. A nutritional comparison between bison meat and beef reveals vast differences.

Lana and Monte Fastnacht of LaMont's Wild West Buffalo in Bosque Farms, who also do a brisk business selling bison meat at the Santa Fe Farmers Market, point out that it is the only red meat cardiologists recommend to their patients. A recent study by Dr. M. Marchello at North Dakota State University has shown that bison meat contains more protein, as well as iron and essential fatty acids, than any other meat sold commercially. It also contains less cholesterol and fewer calories than beef, pork, chicken, or turkey. Most remarkable is its low fat content—about one-fourth the fat of beef or pork and one-third the fat of skinless chicken breast. Besides, as their customers attest, the texture and flavor of bison meat is so far superior to feedlot beef that it defies comparison.

With dietary advantages like that, it may seem amazing that bison hasn't completely replaced beef in the American diet. Yet few people have ever tasted it, few stores carry it, and it remains the secret of the Sams, the Fastnachts, and their steady farmers market customers. Why a secret? Because if word got out, you'd have to get up even earlier in the morning to make it down to the farmers market for your weekly supply of Lana and Monte's green chile buffalo sausage, beyond doubt the best (and healthiest) meat to be found on New Mexican breakfast tables.

Beef

By far the biggest farm and ranch industry in New Mexico is cattle grazing. About 1.5 million beef cattle graze on more than 40 million acres, accounting for more than 89 percent of all the agricultural land in the state. Of this, only an immeasurably small fraction is devoted to raising organic or grass-fed beef with an eye to sustainability. The Southwest Grassfed Livestock Alliance has only fifteen members in New Mexico, none of them with more than a hundred head of cattle.

The most visible of the grass-fed beef ranchers is Rick Kingsbury of Pecos Valley Grass-fed Beef, whose authentic cowboy garb and huge handlebar moustache are a familiar sight two or three days a week at regional farmers markets. "It's important to come to the markets," he says. "People want to talk to the person who's growing their food." Although he looks and sounds thoroughly western, he actually grew up on a dairy farm in New England and later moved to Virginia, where he started his own farm and family while still a teenager. Kingsbury and his wife, Sheila, moved to New Mexico in the mid-1980s.

The Kingsburys raise mostly purebred Scottish Hylanders, shaggy long-horned cattle that possess extraordinary strength and immunity to disease, making veterinary treatment with antibiotics unnecessary. "We don't use any hormones and give only the basic calf-hood vaccinations," Kingsbury says. Scottish Hylanders haven't been overbred, so they are intelligent animals with all their survival instincts intact. The beef they produce is rich, dark, and well marbled—"the best beef there is," Kingsbury says.

The Pecos Valley herd varies from a minimum of twenty or thirty head up to a hundred head of cattle, which live on natural grass and forage year-round, supplemented in winter with organic hay. "Most of our pastures are certified organic, and all of our rangeland has always been rangeland," he says. "We're working to certify some of our herd as organic for our consumers who require it, but we feel strongly that everything we do encompasses the meaning of organic."

Sound land stewardship is of paramount importance to Kingsbury; along with the land that is part of his own ranch property, he also leases neighbors' unused grazing land, with the understanding that he will reclaim and improve it. He uses cross-fencing or electric fencing to divide bottomland along the river into small pastures and rotates the cattle between them at intervals of several days to a week. The ranch also has access to mesa land where the cattle can be grazed for up to three or four months during the summer if there is enough moisture. Working with local environmentalists and the Southwest Grassfed Livestock Alliance, he avoids overgrazing and says that the way Pecos Valley Grassfed Beef grazes their cattle actually improves the land. "The corporate beef business is in trouble," Kingsbury says. "We need to be sustainable."

The biggest obstacle facing the grass-fed beef industry is that they have to travel so far to butcher the cattle. The closest USDA-certified slaughterhouses are in Colorado Springs and in various Texas cities. The cost of transporting cattle for such distances and then carrying the beef back pushes the price of quality grass-fed beef substantially higher than that of conventional feedlot-fattened beef raised with artificial growth hormones. Further, most processors aren't interested in single cattle or small numbers of cattle unless they can commingle them with larger herds. One of the goals of local grass-fed beef producers, Kingsbury says, is to get an organic-certified, USDA-certified meat-processing plant in northern New Mexico. But this is an ambitious objective. Such a plant would cost an estimated $2 million—far more than the total value of grass-fed beef raised in the state.

Sheep

Antonio Manzanares, of Shepherd's Lamb in Los Ojos, New Mexico, sells his organic lamb at the Santa Fe Farmers Market every Saturday. He says,

> *This has always been ranch country from the beginning. People used to come up from Abiquiú to graze their animals here in the summer; that's the first historical record of European people coming this way. They would come*

above: Rick Kingsbury

above: Pecos Valley Scottish Hylanders

up from the Abiquiú area for grazing, and then they would go back down there, because the winters were pretty harsh here, I guess. I don't know exactly why. And hostilities from the Utes at the time, I think.

As far as my experience in the ranch business, I grew up in a little village south of here. My grandfather used to own this place where we're sitting right now, and my dad had a real small place farther south, so I was never pushed into agriculture. I learned how to irrigate, how to garden, and how to take care of animals because it was sort of natural. That's what all of us knew how to do. Our families or friends worked other jobs and used the farm as a subsistence type thing, just to help out, to have a few cows, a few sheep, some horses. They didn't depend on it totally for their income like we do now. We're the first people in a couple of generations to try to make a living on the ranch. Molly comes from a traditional ranching family. Her dad has been in ranching all his life, and also worked for someone else until he decided to do it on his own, so she comes from a cow family, and I come from a mixed cow and sheep family. I did the farming, mostly raising hay, and had a few sheep and a few cows, not many. It didn't take much doing to do the livestock.

Anyway, after we got married, we had a few cows, and I already had a few sheep when we got married. It just worked out that we stuck more to the sheep than to the cows. In Spanish we have a saying, "Las borregas son mas agradacidas," *and in our case I think that has been true. The literal translation is, "Sheep are more grateful," meaning sheep will give you their wool, and the lamb, and even themselves after they get old. In our case, I really believe that,* Las borregas han sido mas agradacidas.

The importance of the farmers market is, I like the direct contact with the customer, and I think the customer likes that too. You know, the majority of the people in this country don't know where their food comes from, and they really enjoy meeting the person that grew their food, and they're willing to pay more for it because they know they're supporting that person, they get to know that person, they get to know him personally. They know us, we know them, we learn about each other. It's more human. It gives me a great satisfaction when people come say, "Your lamb is the best lamb we've ever had," and even those who say, "It's a bit chewy." Well, you know . . . it's good to know that we're providing something that's grown safely, and organically in our case, and in some cases you say "naturally"—not everybody is organic, and that's fine. A lot of people take a lot of pride in what they do, and we do too.

A Movable Slaughterhouse

In a region where most big agribusiness is cattle ranching, the main challenge facing small organic ranchers is the lack of processing facilities. As Bob Maldonado, secretary of the New Mexico Livestock Board, explains, "The only way local ranchers have got to sell their beef right now is by going to a feed lot or a sale barn or someplace like that. The only way you can sell meat in this state is to have it federally inspected. In New Mexico, there's only one meat plant that's federally inspected, down in Roswell, and it's more of a boning operation." (Removing meat from the bones, or "boning," is the final stage of meat processing after the animal has been slaughtered, skinned, eviscerated, trimmed, and washed.) Maldonado continues, "When you buy your meat over the counter, you don't know whether it's New Mexico meat or not, because there's about three major packing houses in the United States, and everything goes to them. In other words, the beef raised in New Mexico doesn't get consumed here. Ninety-five percent of the time it's got to go out of state to be slaughtered. If they bring it back at all, it's to sell over the counter in your big supermarkets."

above right: "Mobile Matanza"

Part of the solution to this problem is the state's first Mobile Livestock Slaughtering Unit, better known in Spanglish-speaking northern New Mexico as the "Mobile Matanza." It's basically a meat-processing plant in a stainless steel semi-trailer. Based in Taos and affiliated with the Taos Food Center, the *matanza* provides facilities for slaughtering beef, bison, lamb, and pork in Taos, Rio Arriba, and Mora counties, where it will serve about fifty small ranches. The truck driver, who is also the butcher, is accompanied by an on-site meat inspector. Taos County bought the unit with a $200,000 grant under the New Mexico Local Economic Development Act and unveiled it in September 2006.

Maldonado adds, "This is going to help the local rancher by cutting out the middleman. With this program, they can have it processed here and also get it marketed, which puts the dollar in their pocket. I see this mobile unit as a beginning. Every part of the state could use something like it. I see it as a pilot program for the rest of the state. As people see how this goes, there's going to be more and more of it."

Watching the *matanza* unveiling, organic sheep rancher Antonio Manzaneras of Tierra Amarilla nods and says, with that peculiarly *norteño* wait-and-see optimism, "I think it could benefit me if they will come over the mountains to do some lambs for me. But we still need the next step, which is the breaking facility, where you actually cut the meat. It's a proven system—it works somewhere else, but our conditions are a little different. In the wintertime it could be a little trickier because of the cold temperatures. The next step is putting small processing facilities around the state. And then of course there's marketing after that, and that's a challenge."

After slaughtering, ranchers have several weeks to get the meat to a processing facility, as long as the carcasses are hung in a cooler in the meantime. But the *matanza* has no storage facilities, so the individual rancher has to have his own.

Goats

It's hard to imagine a better place to raise goats than New Mexico. The first livestock on earth, goats were originally domesticated in the mountains of Iran about ten thousand years ago and soon spread throughout the Middle East, North Africa, and Spain, where much of the terrain and climate is similar to that of New Mexico. With their phenomenal digestive systems, enabling them to live on sparse, woody vegetation that is inedible to humans, goats are a near-ideal means of converting poor land into protein-rich meat, milk, and cheese, as well as hair and skin.

Although a species of large mountain goat is native to the Southwest, pre-Columbian Indians hunted them but made no attempt to domesticate them. Early Spanish settlers brought domesticated goats from Spain to Mexico and then New Mexico.

Oddly enough, goat meat is almost never found today in New Mexico supermarkets or even farmers markets. Though it can legally be sold in the state and can be found in Mexican food stores in the major cities, most goat meat comes from out of state. Goat ranching in New Mexico takes place mainly around Portales and other ranching areas near the border with Texas, where about 90 percent of goat auctions and goat meat-processing facilities are located. From there, it is wholesaled to other parts of the country, where it is eaten mainly within Mexican emigrants and Muslim communities. A recent marketing study found that Islamic Somali residents of Columbus, Ohio, buy more goat meat each year than the total number of meat goats raised in New Mexico. In past years, most of their meat came frozen from Australia and New Zealand, but the same study found that the Somalis prefer the taste of fresh free-range meat and can distinguish the difference between free-range and grain-fed goat meat by the way it smells while cooking. So meat from goats raised in New Mexico is almost never sold or eaten in New Mexico.

Small breeders in New Mexico find a better market with dairy goats instead of meat goats because of the higher profit potential of value-added products. Some, like Coonridge Goat Dairy in the wild hills north of Pietown, specialize in making gourmet goat cheese, sold wholesale to natural food stores and through their mail-order catalog and Web site. Because of the distance from markets, Coonridge does not sell at weekly farmers markets but does appear at various wine festivals around the state. Others, like Milk and Honey near Glorieta, make scented soaps and cosmetic lotions from goat milk and honey for sale at local farmers markets.

Nancy Nathanya Coonridge blends a pioneer way of life with modern technology at her goat dairy, which is so far off the grid in the central New Mexico backcountry that it is beyond the reach of public utilities. The propane camping lanterns that hang from the vigas in her house were once the only source of light after dark, before she installed solar-electric panels on the roof. The pasteurizing, cheese-making, and refrigeration equipment she bought from a cow dairy that was going out of business has been adapted to run on propane, too. All drinking water is rain and snowmelt that drains from the roofs of the buildings into cisterns. The most important function of the solar electricity is to power the computer in the living room, since e-mail is the most reliable mode of communication not only for her (the mailbox is fourteen miles away from the house) but also for the "Woofers"—interns from the international Willing Workers on Organic Farms program—who spend two weeks apiece working with her. She has had Woofer interns from many parts of the world, including France, Japan, Sweden, and Germany.

In her previous life, Coonridge worked as a truck driver in northern California and kept goats, selling condensed and powdered goat milk to the big Meyenberg Goat Milk Products corporation, which wholesales to 90 percent of American supermarkets. In 1981, when she decided to go into the goat dairy business full time, she searched the American West for a place that was not too cold, too hot, or too expensive, and chose the wilds of New Mexico.

Today, Coonridge maintains a herd of from fifty-five to ninety goats, depending on the range conditions. She has three kinds of goats in her herd—Oberhasli or alpine goats from Switzerland, identifiable because their ears stick straight up; Nubians, with long floppy ears and Roman noses; and La Manchas, an American-bred mutation that has no ears. She knows each of her goats by name; all registered dairy goats must have names, and all the goat kids born in the same year must have names that start with the same letter. The goats are raised in family groups and age groups. They stick together and, although they graze on unfenced open rangeland, they return home as a group at the end of the day. One advantage of having an organic goat dairy in such a remote location, she has discovered, is that she doesn't have to use antibiotics, hormones, or chemical wormers. The herd is isolated enough so that they are not exposed to diseases, and the goats graze on plants, such as wormwood, that kill parasites naturally.

Coonridge produces fifteen pounds of cheese a year in an assortment of organic herb flavors, including herb and garlic, herbs de provence, dillweed onion, curry, and green chile. Unlike most commercial goat cheese in the United States, which is made with a genetically modified rennet that can't be used in organic products, she imports a special vegetable rennet and imports all-natural cultures used in European villages. She uses a long-set cheese-making method, which takes much longer than commercial methods. Then she separates the protein and fat from the liquid and ages it for flavor. Coolness stops the aging process at the desired point, and the cheese is then jarred in organic sunflower seed oil to preserve it.

The cheese is Coonridge's only product. They do not slaughter goats for meat, though they do sell breeding stock to other dairies. She has also taught classes in underdeveloped African nations on traditional peasant methods of making goat cheese, which holds the potential to help reduce the malnutrition problems in such areas.

"When people eat my goat cheese," Coonridge says, "they may only know it just tastes good and has a great texture. Or they may know that goat cheese is a great source of conjugated linolaic acid (CLA), which lowers cancer risk and discourages body fat deposits. But I know they're really eating New Mexico sunshine and natural life. My greatest satisfaction comes from people appreciating my cheese on whatever level they can appreciate it."

Poultry

Until the mid-twentieth century, virtually all poultry was "free-range" by modern standards. Chickens had the run of wire-fenced chicken yards connected to chicken coops. Turkeys grazed in pastures and, especially in Texas hill country, were even herded like cattle in massive "turkey drives" to railheads for shipping.

But as American consumer tastes have drifted away from beef and other red meat in favor of white meat turkey and chicken, demand has skyrocketed, and the poultry industry has become shockingly industrialized. Today about 98 percent of all chickens raised in the United States spend their brief lives in corporate-owned "concentrated feeding facilities." Visitors unfortunate enough to tour one of these huge, noxious-smelling factories—let alone work in one—are likely to lose their appetite for poultry once and for all.

Factory-raised chickens spend their lives in less than half a square foot of space, and turkeys have less than three square feet. The birds themselves have been genetically altered to grow twice as fast and twice as large as their ancestors and to have abnormally large breasts. Because they are grossly overweight, they are prone to congestive heart failure and other diseases, including cancer. Turkeys now grow so large in the breast that they cannot mount to breed naturally, so all domestic turkeys now reproduce only through artificial insemination. Both chickens and turkeys have their beaks and toes cut off soon after hatching, supposedly to reduce fighting with birds in neighboring cages. As a result, they can only consume food that has been processed into pellets. Factory farmers defend the practice of keeping turkeys inside buildings full-time on the basis that if they were caught outside in the rain, lacking beaks, they would drown. And if all that weren't bad enough, today genetic programs are well underway to develop featherless chickens and turkeys that will make poultry factories more efficient by eliminating the need for plucking.

There are only a handful of organic free-range poultry growers in New Mexico, such as Pollo Real Chicken and Embudo Valley Organics free-range turkey

above: Nancy Coonridge

farm, but primarily through farmers markets, the public is being exposed to the unmistakably superior taste and texture of free-range fowl. A growing number of consumers is discovering that the higher cost of naturally grown poultry is well worth the price, and demand for locally grown organic chicken and turkey is growing faster than the farmers can keep up with it.

The Chicken Ranchers

"The smallest animals always bring the most money."

Free-range chicken farmer Tom Delehanty to a packed-house audience at the 2006 New Mexico Organic Farming Conference in Albuquerque

A sixth-generation farmer from Wisconsin, Tom Delehanty of Pollo Real moved to New Mexico in 1994 and soon became the state's leading free-range chicken producer. His small farm lies secluded on the bottomland along the Rio Grande within a few blocks of the Socorro town plaza. The farm's name carries a double meaning: it lies along the Spanish colonial Camino Real, the Royal Road that linked New Mexico with the capital in Mexico City; and it produces that rare commodity, real chicken.

The obvious question is, why would someone leave Wisconsin, America's agricultural heartland, to attempt farming in arid New Mexico? Delehanty explains that after he returned from wartime military service in Vietnam, he settled in southern California, where he sold electronic equipment—and met his wife, Tracey. Longing to return to the farming life and introduce Tracey to it, he persuaded her to move with him to far northern Wisconsin, where farms were cheap and he had old friends. But it wasn't long before he was reminded that Wisconsin gets too much snow. And there were other problems. Their farm was too far from a major population center, making it hard to deal directly with consumers. Then too, Wisconsin had strict regulations that would prevent them from setting up their own chicken-processing facility. When it came to raising chickens, they would be limited to buying chicks from a big company, feeding them for several months, and then selling them back to the company—a kind of modern-day servitude that rankled the Delehantys' independent spirit.

Tom and Tracey Delehanty chose to move to New Mexico because state regulations were permissive enough to allow small-poultry processing operations. He had been experimenting with "chicken tractors"—large, movable, wheeled wire enclosures that allowed chickens to range free over a limited area of pasturage and be relocated frequently to new areas of the pasture. He had invented a round version of chicken tractors called "chicken yurts" that have opaque coverings over the top, protecting the birds from inclement weather as well as hawks and other predators. The yurts are moved day-by-day across pastures of feed crops and weeds, leaving only trampled stalks in the chickens' wake like giant lawnmowers. The processing is done in a spotlessly clean, odor-free plant that Delehanty has set up in an old abandoned adobe farmhouse across the road from the mobile home where he and his family live. The plant is surrounded by broken-down trailers that house baby chicks until they are large enough to graze in the pastures. After the chickens have been slaughtered and processed, they are put into pickup-size refrigerated trucks and driven directly to the Santa Fe Farmers Market and other buyers.

above: Label Rouge chickens

After a decade in operation, his twelve-acre organic chicken farm processes from five hundred to a thousand chickens a day, making Pollo Real the largest pastured poultry operation in the United States. (To put this in perspective, Tyson Foods, the largest commercial chicken producer in the United States, processes more than sixty million chickens a day.) Delehanty plans to expand his chicken pasture to include twenty acres of unused land on a neighboring farm. But that's not the end of the story.

Unlike turkeys, "free-range" chickens aren't as free as one might think, though their treatment is vastly more humane than the conditions in the commercial "concentrated breeding facilities" operated by Tyson and others. Besides the need to contain the chickens and protect them from predators, Delehanty explains that the white meat birds that are virtually the only chickens available to farmers in the United States today will not graze in an open field. If food isn't conveniently close to them, they will simply lie in the shade until someone comes along to feed them.

In 2006, Delehanty discovered Label Rouge chickens. When customers taste one, they immediately understand that they are nothing like standard American chickens, and in fact, most people will never settle for supermarket chicken again. In France, Label Rouge started as a grassroots small-farming movement in the 1960s and has now grown to make up about one-third of the French poultry market, even though Label Rouge birds cost twice as much as conventionally raised chickens. Label Rouge has become a vital source of revenue for small farmers there. Label Rouge is not a breed of chicken but a set of protocols for raising and marketing them. Comprehensive standards govern genetics, maximum size and density of buildings, access to pastures, allowable feeds and medications, minimum weights and growing times, transportation and time elapsed between slaughter and sale. Like organic certification in the United States, France has third-party organizations that certify all Label Rouge farms, including bacteriology tests, processing inspections, and five taste tests a year. Label Rouge birds grow slowly, taking twelve weeks to reach marketable weight as compared to five or six weeks for conventional chickens. This slow growth is said to be the primary reason for the chickens' noticeably superior taste and texture.

In the United States, Label Rouge chickens or anything similar are a rarity. The University of Illinois studied the French chickens in 1999 but concluded that they were impractical for commercial production in the United States, mainly because of the relatively high cost of the end product. More recently, the National Center for Appropriate Technology sent representatives to France to gather technical information about the Label Rouge program and make it available to farmers and agricultural colleges in the United States. As in France forty years ago, the Label Rouge movement in the United States is spearheaded by a handful of innovative small farmers like Tom Delehanty.

The chickens themselves are hard to come by. Some original Label Rouge breeding stock has been imported (some might say smuggled) into the United States by way of Great Britain and Canada and is available to small farmers who are willing to commit to the program. At Pollo Real, Delehanty has been able to get four kinds of chickens—bronze rangers, grey rangers, poulet nous, and a few rare gourmet blacks. He says that an international texture and flavor rating system based on the French Label Rouge taste testing ranks the birds on a numerical scale as follows: American white meat chicken–5; bronze rangers, grey rangers, and poulet nous–7; and gourmet black–9.

Delehanty is now phasing out all his white meat chicken production in favor of Label Rouge birds. He finds that demand for them is strong, especially in Santa Fe. Since a whole chicken can sell for $15 or more, he finds it hard to sell them in Albuquerque, even though the city is twice as close to his farm; he says there is not much of a market for premium organic foods in Albuquerque—yet.

Pollo Real also operates a community-supported agriculture (CSA) group and expects to have 250 members by 2007. For an initial $300 buy-in, the members get what amounts to a prepaid open account for $300 worth of food at about a 15 percent discount from the market price. He can also offer CSA members organic eggs and vegetables, even though he can't sell them at the farmers market because of geographical restrictions.

Tom Delehanty, who also raises a few heritage turkeys and other poultry, operates spring through fall and, like most small poultry growers, vacations after Thanksgiving. A true artisan farmer, he considers producing premium food to be a fine art. He does not have any ambition to expand his operation beyond the limited scale of his Socorro farm but would like to find some young apprentices to whom he could pass on his skills. When asked what he finds to be the greatest satisfaction in farming, he says with a twinkle in his eye, "Leaving behind some improved soil—besides ourselves, that is."

HONEY

When it comes to raising animals, few people think of bees. Les Crowder, of Sparrowhawk Farm in Belen, thinks about them all the time. One of the Southwest's leading experts on beekeeping, he commutes to Santa Fe to teach a series of popular courses on the subject at the EcoVersity there, and he has come up with revolutionary innovations in beehives, bee immunology, and other related subjects.

Crowder's bees earn their freedom to frolic among the alfalfa and tamarisk blossoms along the Rio Grande all summer by journeying west in the early spring for pollination rentals, his family's biggest source of income. A recent study by Princeton University of large farms in and around California's Sacramento Valley confirmed that intensive farming has exterminated local honeybee populations by

eliminating natural habitats and poisoning the bees with pesticides—a process that has been going on since the 1950s. Large-scale monoculture farming also threatens the local bee population because it provides abundant pollen for a short time and then leaves the bees to starve. Agribusiness has killed off the bees that are essential to pollinate California's pear, cherry, apple, and almond orchards, as well as blueberries, cranberries, cucumbers, cantaloupe, watermelon, strawberries, avocados, tomatoes, lemons, alfalfa, onions, hay, and other crops. In fact, according to a recent study by the Department of Entomology at Oregon State University, 15 to 30 percent of the United States diet depends on the help of bees.

For this reason, beekeepers across America can charge top dollar for what is euphemistically termed "environmental services"—in other words, rental bees. To make up for the shortage of bees in farm country, California growers resort to temporarily importing bee colonies from all over the country, including New Mexico. These pollinator rentals make up about two-thirds of the average beekeeper's income for the year—twice as much as total sales of honey, beeswax, propolis ("bee glue"), bee pollen, royal jelly, and venom.

Even though 99 percent of bee colony rentals are by large commercial honey corporations, the other 1 percent includes virtually all small-scale beekeepers west of the Mississippi. Every February, for instance, Les Crowder loads up his truck with as many of his 150 beehives as it will carry and, with his wife, drives nonstop through the night to reach the California almond orchards where his insect swarms will spend the next several weeks.

The biggest risk factor in raising honey bees is parasites, and the annual coming together of bees from all parts of the country for the spring pollination season in California creates ideal conditions for epidemics such as the plague of nearly microscopic varroa destructor mites that decimated much of the U.S. honeybee population in the 1990s. Crowder recalls that one year he had a hundred hives going into the winter season, and at the end of winter only two survived.

None of the four thousand native North American species of bee produces honey. Only the European honeybee gathers pollen and nectar in sufficient quantities to pollinate crop fields and orchards on a large scale. European honeybees first came to New Mexico with Franciscan missionaries, who brought active, buzzing beehives across the Atlantic Ocean in the holds of wooden ships and then transported them a thousand miles up the Camino Real on the backs of donkeys. More than honey, the priests needed beeswax to make candles for religious use. Soon beekeeping became a standard part of colonial farming in New Mexico, as it was discovered that the presence of honeybees increased crop yields fantastically. Beekeeping expert Les Crowder says that feral Spanish bees were still common in New Mexico in the late nineteenth century, but they were apparently wiped out by the varroa destructor mite in the 1990s; he hasn't seen a single specimen for more than ten years.

Today, "environmental services" have become such a large part of the bee industry that many major producers have gotten out of the honey business completely and only keep their bee colonies alive for pollination rentals. The long chain of middlemen involved in processing, packaging, and marketing commercial honey—through two levels of brokerage and on to the packer, wholesaler, and retailer—leaves little or no profit margin for the honey producer.

Small beekeepers get around this problem by selling their honey by the jar directly to the public at farmers markets. This honey, direct from the farm to the buyer, may have several valuable health benefits. Medical and pharmacological studies have found that "raw," unfiltered honey has significant antibiotic properties. It has also been shown to prevent stomach ulcers and yeast infections, reduce the gastritis caused by too much alcohol, and promote faster healing of burns with less scarring. In Russia, it was even shown to slow the development of cataracts in the eye. Many people believe that hay-fever-type pollen allergies can be alleviated by eating honey containing the same kind of pollen. (Warning: Despite the health benefits, honey should never be given to infants under one year of age, since it can contain high concentrations of the spores that cause potentially deadly infant botulism.)

Honey's health benefits are strongest if it has not been heated to prevent crystallization or commercially filtered to make it look clearer. Heating destroys the antibiotic enzymes in honey, and extensive filtering removes the pollen that is thought to contain most of the health-promoting value.

An equally good reason to buy honey directly from local farmers is the same as for other small farm products: better taste. Never mind that store-bought honey is often diluted with sugar water during processing; big beekeeping companies feed their bees on the blossoms of white clover, an inexpensive cover crop producing a uniform honey that tastes the way you've learned to expect honey to taste. But honey can be produced from any flower.

Although almond honey sounds tempting, beekeepers who take their colonies out to the California almond orchards for pollination season report that they have to clean the hives thoroughly afterward to remove the tarlike, bad-tasting stuff. On the other hand, an imported ornamental bush called tamarisk or salt cedar has gone wild over the years and grows profusely along the banks of the Rio Grande, where it is generally viewed as a giant, virtually indestructible weed that consumes huge quantities of water, making life hard for other plants along the river. Yet many New Mexicans claim salt cedar honey is the best-tasting honey anywhere—deep amber and subtle with a distinct flavor of licorice. Other specialty honeys commonly found in New Mexico include mesquite, alfalfa, purple sage, and phacelia.

As soon as you enter the Crowder family's hand-built adobe home on the edge of the Rio Grande bosque south of Belen, you may suspect that they share a remarkable kinship with bees. Each room is six-sided, like the cells in a honeycomb, built around a hexagonal open courtyard in the center. Master beekeeper Les Crowder has 150 beehives on his farm and, in a good year, produces 600 gallons (7,200 pounds) of honey. "I don't want more bees," Crowder says. "I want to teach others to raise bees." Toward that end, he teaches natural beekeeping certification classes at Santa Fe's EcoVersity. The classes have proved surprisingly popular and are filled far in advance.

Raised in Albuquerque and Bernalillo, Crowder says he has always had a fascination with insects. "My mother tried keeping one beehive for a while," he recalls. "Later on, I was herding sheep on a ranch in Colorado for the summer. I was fifteen. When I came back to Bernalillo, my grandfather said, 'There's a swarm of bees out back. Let's put them in your mom's old hive.' " He adds, "My grandfather was an organic gardener before it became popular."

While tending to his single hive, the teenager started reading everything he could get his hands on about bees. "Then one day I was standing in a mint patch," he recalls, "when I had an epiphany. I suddenly saw the cycle from soil to plant to bee to me. Through the pleasure of taste, I became part of that system, connected to all of it."

From that moment, beekeeping became Crowder's path in life. In college at the University of New Mexico, he went to Ecuador on an exchange program and learned traditional beekeeping from villagers there. He then worked for a commercial beekeeper in Bosque Farms, where, he says, "I learned a lot of things I *didn't* want to do—like using antibiotics, repellents, comb fumigants, or mitacides. A lot of people say it's impossible to keep bees without using these chemicals, and I wanted to prove them wrong."

During the five years that he worked as a bee inspector for the state of New Mexico, Crowder began testing a theory that one of his UNM professors had developed. Bees, he reasoned, must be capable of developing resistance to disease. In ancient times, the Egyptians kept thousands of beehives on barges on the Nile without the aid of any antibiotics, and they survived. So if you could find where a specific disease originated, it stands to reason that native bees of that area would have a natural resistance to that disease. By "requeening" hives—replacing old queen bees with new ones of a more resistant strain—after several years he was losing hardly any bees to disease.

Another innovation Crowder has made is to replace conventional stacking box beehives with top bar hives of his own design. The bees build one hanging comb along the trough-shaped, four-foot-long bar across the top of each hive. Crowder's hives are cheap and simple to make, and because they do not distort the combs like standard box hives can, the bees are less susceptible to disease. But top bar hives require better bee management. Crowder likens it to fly-fishing—"You have to learn the technique."

LAVENDER

New Mexico has a long heritage of herb growing thanks largely to the presence of *curanderas,* or traditional healers. (In Mexico, most healers are men and are called *curanderos*, but in New Mexico they are almost always women and are referred to by the feminine form, curandera.) For centuries, rural Spanish families in New Mexico have grown medicinal herbs in their gardens for family use, and curanderas have passed knowledge of both home-grown and wild-crafted herbs from generation to generation. Among the most widely used medicinal herbs are *yerba buena* ("good herb" or peppermint), *manzanilla* (chamomile), *enebro* (juniper), *poleo* (Rocky Mountain brookmint), and *osha* (the root of a wild celery also known as Porter's lovage that grows wild in the New Mexico mountains and is widely considered by Hispanics, Anglos, and Indians alike to be the cure for the common cold). Today, the most popular medicinal herb crop is *alhucema*, or lavender. The story of lavender in New Mexico speaks to both the deep strains of tradition in the region's agriculture and its transitory, changeable nature.

Randy Murray, co-owner of For the Love of Lavender, not only grows lavender and produces a line of value-added products such as soaps, lotions, and essential oils but also offers consulting services for organic lavender growers and gardeners. Interviewed at the Third Annual Lavender Festival at the El Rancho de las Golondrinas open-air museum in August 2005, Murray said that before coming to New Mexico, he had been a corporate banker in the San Francisco financial district. One of his clients said he seemed "stressed to the max" and needed to find a hobby. He found it across the Golden Gate Bridge in Marin County at the Green Gulch Zen Center. The center supplied organic produce to a number of Bay Area restaurants, including Greens, where Deborah Madison—now a Galisteo, New Mexico, resident and one of America's leading authors on farmers markets and vegetarian cuisine—was working as a chef. "I could feel all the stress leave my body when I drove across the bridge on Saturday morning heading for the garden," says Murray. "Then it would all set back in on me when I returned to the city on Sunday night."

At the Zen center, Murray says, he did not take much interest in religion but became passionate about gardening. The center presented a class on lavender, during which they served lavender tea and lavender cookies. Murray found that he liked the look and smell of the plant. "I knew nothing about aromatherapy, but I knew that this was the plant for me. It worked directly on the nervous system as a calmative."

Randy Murray and his partner, Clint, moved to New Mexico in 1993 to start a store selling furniture, home decor, gardening supplies, and floral gifts. Within a few years, they veered into the business of lavender growing. They've been vendors at the Santa Fe Farmers Market for a decade and also show at other lavender festivals such as those held annually in Austin, Texas; Ojai, California; and Sequim, Washington.

The original variety of lavender, from which all of the two hundred or so other strains have been developed, is *Lavendula Angustifolia,* or common lavender. Usually, but inaccurately, called English lavender, common lavender is actually native to the hills of northern Spain. It was imported to Mexico as a medicinal herb and brought to New Mexico by Don Juan de Oñate's colonial expedition in 1598. It proved to be an ideal crop for New Mexico in most ways. It thrives in the dry, sandy soil of the high desert, and the angustifolia variety can grow in all agricultural climate zones of the state, tolerating winter temperatures down to zero Fahrenheit or below.

Before Murray arrived in New Mexico, lavender was a traditional garden herb in norteño villages but had not been raised as a cash crop in recent memory. Within a few years, it burst onto the scene as one of the most popular small-farm cash crops, filling fields throughout the region with colorful flowers and wonderful scents. Besides common lavender, other strains included Provence lavender, an ingredient of culinary *herbes de Provence*, and white lavender, often used for decorations and bouquets in Santa Fe and Taos weddings.

The lavender fields at Rancho de las Golondrinas were planted in 2000 by Murray and volunteers from Kitchen Angels, a nonprofit volunteer organization in Santa Fe that provides free meals for elderly, homebound people. Kitchen Angel Ted Orr, who has managed the Las Golondrinas fields since 2002, says he calls lavender a "peace plant" because he often saw groups of loud, uptight people whose behavior would change when they got around the lavender fields. "Whether because of the color or scent," he says, "they would mellow out."

In the summer of 2005, when we interviewed Murray and Orr, Rancho de las Golondrinas was in the throes of a grasshopper plague. "It's done some damage to the lavender," Orr said, "but not as much as we thought it would"—apparently proof of lavender's ability to survive New Mexico's unpredictable growing conditions.

But the three-foot woody plants must be deadheaded back in the fall, before the first hard freeze, and then pruned in the spring. In the first week of December 2005, an early hard freeze hit northern New Mexico while the lavender foliage was still green, killing the plants at Las Golondrinas and most other fields in the region. Lavender is a perennial plant, and it does not flower until the second year, so the following summer there was virtually no fresh lavender at New Mexico farms or farmers markets. Yet farmers were already planting anew, looking forward to a comeback the following year.

Lavender, like so many other New Mexican small farm crops, can weather the unpredictable climate, predators, and pests for centuries—and then suddenly vanish. But like all things New Mexican, lavender is part of a long tradition that does not die easily. Like bison, heirloom apples, and churro sheep, lavender is already on its way to returning to its rightful place in New Mexico's enchanted landscape.

Piñon Green Beans

This local adaptation of green beans almondine makes a simple, tasty showcase for those green, yellow, and purple beans you often find at farmers markets in midsummer. Note: The purple beans turn green when cooked, though not the same hue of green as the green beans.

Serves 6

1 pound (about 3 cups) green beans, purple beans, yellow wax beans or any combination
1 teaspoon olive oil
1 medium shallot, separated into cloves, peeled and sliced thin
3 tablespoons piñon nuts, shelled
2 teaspoons butter or butter blend (optional)
2 teaspoons gomasio (roasted, seasoned sesame seeds)

Trim the beans and slice them into 2-inch lengths. Place them in a steamer over boiling water and steam until tender, about 8 to 10 minutes.

Meanwhile, heat the olive oil in a small frying pan and sauté the shallot for about 1 minute. Add the piñon nuts and continue sautéing until the nuts begin to turn golden and the edges of the shallot slices blacken slightly. Empty the beans into a serving bowl. Immediately melt the butter or butter blend over the beans, add the *gomasio,* and stir. Spread the shallot and piñon nut mixture over the beans and toss lightly.

Grilled Eggplant and Peppers

A wonderful offering from Elena Arellano of Ohkay Owingeh Pueblo.

Serves 4 to 6

3 small eggplants
2 red bell peppers
2 green bell peppers
1 medium yellow onion
2 New Mexico green chiles
⅓ cup extra virgin olive oil
2 cloves garlic, roasted and minced
Salt to taste

Preheat a charcoal or gas grill. Rub the eggplants, bell peppers, onion, and chiles with a tablespoon or so of olive oil in a large bowl. Grill over medium/hot heat until the eggplants are soft (about 10 minutes), the skins of the peppers are blistered and charred (about 20 minutes), and the onion is soft (about 30 minutes). Remove the vegetables from the grill and let cool. When they are cool enough to handle, peel, stem, and seed the peppers and chiles, trim the eggplant, and peel the onion. Then cut all the vegetables into thick slices and put them in a medium bowl. Add ¼ cup olive oil and minced garlic and salt to taste.

Set aside to marinate at room temperature for at least 1 hour; refrigerate overnight.

Corn with Squash

This recipe comes from Elena Arellano of Ohkay Owingeh Pueblo. It is a simple version of the traditional northern New Mexico calabacitas.

Serves 4 to 6

3 small summer squashes (calabacitas mexicanas, yellow crookneck squashes, or zucchinis)
4 tablespoons olive oil
1 small yellow onion, peeled and chopped
3 cups fresh corn kernels (sliced from 3 ears of shucked corn, or substitute defrosted frozen sweet corn)
4 sprigs fresh parsley, chopped
Salt and freshly ground black pepper to taste

Cut squashes in half lengthwise, thinly slice crosswise, and set aside.

Heat olive oil in a large skillet over medium heat. Add onion and cook, stirring frequently until soft. Add sliced squash and continue cooking, stirring frequently, until soft. Add the corn kernels and cook 5 minutes more. Sprinkle with chopped parsley. Season to taste with salt and pepper.

Ajo de Mano

This old Spanish recipe comes from Kristen Davenport of Full Nest Farm, Llano San Juan.

Serves 4

4 large potatoes, cut up,
 or 12 to 20 smaller potatoes, cut in half
2 dried red chiles
5 to 10 cloves garlic, peeled
Paprika to taste
Salt to taste
Few drops vinegar
2 teaspoons olive oil

Boil the potatoes in water with a couple of dried chiles. Drain and slice the potatoes. Mash garlic with a little paprika, salt, vinegar, and olive oil. Mix with potatoes and reheat before serving.

Italian Garlic Soup

Kristen Davenport also gave us this great recipe.

Serves 4 to 6

6 cloves garlic, sliced
6 tablespoons butter or olive oil
6 cups broth, chicken or vegetable
6 slices bread, toasted
6 tablespoons grated Parmesan cheese
Minced parsley

In a soup pot, gently sauté the garlic in butter or oil until soft but not brown. Add the broth and simmer 20 minutes. Put a slice of toast in a bowl and pour soup over it. Sprinkle cheese and parsley on top.

Garden Fresh Frittata

Lisa Fox of Southwest Chutney donated this recipe to our collection.

Serves 3 to 4

2 to 3 cups fresh vegetables (such as mushrooms, red or orange bell peppers, onions, or whatever's ripe in your garden or at the farmers market), chopped into bite-size pieces
2 tablespoons olive oil, preferably lemon or orange flavored
2 tablespoons butter
6 to 8 eggs
1 medium tomato, thinly sliced
3 to 5 cloves garlic, sliced
2 to 3 scallions, finely sliced
2 large green chiles, roasted, peeled and seeded
2 teaspoons roasted whole cumin seeds
⅓ cup finely sliced and mixed marjoram, bronze fennel fronds, and cilantro
Salt and pepper to taste
⅓ cup grated provolone or hard cheese

Toss the vegetables with the olive oil, place on a cookie sheet, and roast at 400 degrees F for about 20 minutes, checking frequently, until caramelized. Heat the oil and butter in a skillet over medium heat. Carefully arrange the chopped vegetables evenly, covering the bottom of the skillet, and place a lid over it. Reduce the heat to low and cook the vegetables for 5 minutes.

Preheat the oven to 450 degrees F.

Whip the egg mixture well until frothy. Uncover the skillet and pour the eggs evenly over the vegetables. Shake the pan *gently*, allowing the ingredients to blend. Arrange the sliced tomatoes evenly around the skillet and do the same with the mixture of garlic, scallions, green chiles, cumin seeds, marjoram, fennel fronds, cilantro, salt, and pepper. Sprinkle the grated cheese on top. Again, shake the pan gently. Cover the skillet again and cook for 15 to 20 minutes over low–medium heat until the egg mixture starts to set and puff up.

Carefully place a potholder mitt on the handle and slide the skillet under the broiler, leaving the broiler door open and the skillet handle outside. Broil 10 to 12 minutes, checking frequently. If it is browning too fast, lower the heat or cover with aluminum foil and continue cooking. Remove from the oven when the frittata is browned and puffy. Serve immediately while it is puffy for the most dramatic effect. It will set and settle, collapsing as it cools. Serve with salad and garlic bread for a light dinner or brunch.

Note: Frittatas freeze beautifully. To freeze, place the frittata in a pie pan, cover first with wax paper and then aluminum foil, slip into a plastic bag and seal. To reheat, allow the frittata to come to room temperature. Remove the wax paper and recover with foil. Place in a preheated 300 degrees F to 350 degrees F oven for 15 to 20 minutes.

Stuffed Calabazas

Helen Martin of Light Bearer Herbals and Delights in Taos gave us this recipe.

Serves 4

4 medium calabazas (winter squash), or one large
1 cup water
1 onion, chopped
4 to 5 cloves garlic, chopped
1 tablespoon butter or olive oil
1 to 3 cups cooked grain (brown rice, quinoa, barley, amaranth, or millet)
1 cup roasted piñon or toasted chopped almonds
¼ cup nutritional yeast
2 to 4 teaspoons thyme ("We all need more!")
Pinch of cayenne or other ground red chile
1 teaspoon sea salt
1 cup fresh or rehydrated garenburro (wild currants)

Preheat oven to 325 degrees F. Cut the calabaza and scoop out the seeds.

Place the cut sides down in a baking dish. Add water and cook until soft. Sauté the onion and garlic in butter or oil. Add the cooked grain and stir until coated. Add the nuts, yeast, thyme, cayenne, and salt, and mix. Stuff the squash with the mixture. Bake for 25 minutes.

Garnish with *garenburros* before serving. (Cultivated currants or raisins may be substituted. Cheese may be melted on top as well.)

Sopa de Calabaza

This delicious soup recipe is provided by Loretta Fresquez of Monte Vista Organic Farm, La Mesilla.

Serves 4

2 tablespoons butter
2 tablespoons olive oil
1 medium sweet onion, chopped
3 cloves garlic, minced
2 stalks celery, diced
2 carrots, peeled and sliced
2 tablespoons minced fresh ginger
1 small dried Thai chile or similar dried hot chile pepper
4 cups puréed roasted pumpkin
1 quart chicken or vegetable broth
Heavy cream to garnish

In a stockpot, melt the butter into the oil. Add the onion, garlic, celery, and carrots, and cook until soft. Add the ginger and chile. Stir to blend, and then add the pumpkin purée and broth. Purée the soup in a blender, and then strain through a sieve. Then pour back into the pot to heat. Garnish with heavy cream when ready to serve.

Wilted Chard

Wilted chard goes with everything. Put it in frittatas or omelettes. Here's Lisa's recipe for it.

fresh chard, rainbow or regular
1 tablespoon olive oil
½ cup to 1 cup sliced almonds
2 to 3 teaspoons fruity balsamic vinegar
Juice of 1 orange
Salt and pepper to taste

Wash the chard and pat it dry. Tear it into pieces. Heat the olive oil in a large skillet. Put half the chard in the skillet, cover, and cook 3 minutes over medium-high heat. Uncover and add the rest of the chard, along with the almonds, vinegar, and orange juice. Toss, then cover again, and cook for about 5 minutes. Season to taste with salt and pepper.

Variation: Fresh herbs enhance this recipe. Add at the end of cooking. Try basil, marjoram, dill, fennel, or any combination.

Lisa's Sausage and Bean Soup with Red Chard

In the mountains of northern New Mexico, evenings are cold even during midsummer. Of course, green chile stew will chase away the chill, but harvest time offers many other options.

Serves 4 to 6

2 cups white beans
2 cups chopped fresh mushrooms
1 medium onion
2 cloves garlic
Olive oil (preferably fruit flavored—try tangerine)
1 large bunch red chard, rinsed and diced
3 or 4 bay leaves
1 package spicy chicken sausage
1 poblano chile, roasted, peeled, and seeded
1 red pepper, roasted, peeled, and seeded
1 lemon, juiced and scraped
2 to 3 tablespoons malt vinegar
2 to 3 tablespoons basil, fresh or dried
Pinch of red chile powder
Pinch of lemon pepper
Shaved Parmesan or Romano cheese

Cook the white beans and reserve the water. Sauté the mushrooms, onion, and garlic in the olive oil. Add the chard, bay leaves, and whole sausages to the reserved water the beans were cooked in. Cool until the chard begins to soften and the sausage is almost fully cooked. Take the sausage out of the liquid and dice it. Add the sausage and all other ingredients except the cheese. Heat to boiling and simmer over low heat. Don't overcook! Add water or dry white wine as needed. Garnish with cheese before serving.

Heidi's Raspberry Sopaipillas

Sopaipillas, scrumptiously calorie-packed, deep-fried pastry pillows, are traditionally served for dessert in New Mexico restaurants. You tear off one corner and squirt honey inside. Sopaipillas can also be stuffed with refried beans, meat filling, and cheese as an entrée. Since sopaipillas originated in Albuquerque about 200 years ago, we figure that they are fair game for variations using ingredients from Albuquerque-area farms. This is the ultimate jelly doughnut, New Mexico style.

Makes about 2 dozen sopaipillas

2 cups flour
1 teaspoon baking powder
1 teaspoon sugar
1 teaspoon salt
2 tablespoons vegetable oil
2 tablespoons heavy cream
½ cup warm water
Vegetable oil for frying
2 jars Heidi's Raspberry Jam (regular, red chile, or ginger)

Combine the flour, baking powder, sugar, and salt in a mixing bowl and stir until blended. Stir in the oil, cream, and water and knead it into a soft dough. Place on a lightly floured cutting board and knead more. Cover the dough with a cloth and let it rest for 30 minutes. Roll the dough into a rectangle about ⅛ inch thick. Cut into 3-inch squares.

Fill a large saucepan or deep fryer with 3 inches of vegetable oil. Heat it until a small piece of dough dropped into it sizzles and turns golden. Carefully place the squares of dough, two or three at a time, in the hot oil, pressing them down with a fork or spoon until completely immersed so they will puff up. Fry each batch until golden, turning once. Remove, drain well, and set aside to cool, and then put the next batch of dough squares in the hot oil.

Serve with Heidi's Raspberry Jam. Bite a corner off a sopaipilla to make a hole large enough to fit a soup spoon or tablespoon. Spoon one tablespoon or more of jam into the sopaipilla and tip it gently back and forth until the jam is distributed evenly inside. Eat immediately.

Champagne Apple Enchiladas

These individual dessert pies are not technically enchiladas, since they contain no chile, but we don't know of a better name for them. They look somewhat like enchiladas, and by any name they're delicious. For "true" dessert enchiladas you could (1) add a little coarse-ground red chile to the topping, or (2) top them with mole sauce instead of the sugar mixture.

The filling recipe is from Becky Mullane of Dixon's Apples, who says it originated with her grandmother, Faye Dixon, who grew her own apples for more than forty years.

Makes 6 to 8 enchiladas

Filling:
8 Dixon's Champagne apples
½ cup sugar
1½ tablespoons flour
¼ teaspoon lemon extract
2 tablespoons butter
½ cup water
6 to 8 large flour tortillas

Sauce:
½ cup butter
½ cup white sugar
½ cup brown sugar
1 teaspoon ground cinnamon
½ cup water

For the filling, core apples and slice thin. Put the slices with sugar, flour, and lemon extract in a zipperlock bag. Shake to coat the apple slices evenly. Put the mixture in a saucepan with butter and water and heat to boiling, stirring constantly. Reduce heat to low and simmer for 5 minutes.

Lay out one tortilla. Spoon about ¼ cup of filling evenly down the middle of the tortilla. Fold the ends inward, and then roll the tortilla. Place it seam down in a large greased baking dish. Repeat with other tortillas until the filling is used up.

For the sauce, combine the butter, white sugar, brown sugar, cinnamon, and water in a medium saucepan. Bring to a boil, stirring constantly. Reduce heat and simmer 3 minutes. Pour the sauce over the enchiladas and let stand 30 minutes.

Preheat oven to 350 degrees F.

Bake uncovered for 20 minutes until golden. Partially cool before serving.

Cottage Cheese Pancakes with Lisa's Fresh Fruit Compote

Make the compote ahead of time. The ingredients can vary with the season—use your imagination.

Serves 4

Fruit Compote:

3 cups diced fruit (whatever's in season; overripe or frozen fruit will also work)

1 cup juice (fruit nectar, fresh orange juice, or Grand Marnier)

¼ cup raw honey

1 banana (optional, for a thicker version)

1 to 2 tablespoons butter

Sprinkle of spices to taste (cinnamon, nutmeg, ginger, orange zest, anise)

Pancakes:

6 eggs, separated

2 cups small-curd cottage cheese

⅔ cup flour (use Sangre de Cristo or other local flour if possible)

2 teaspoons sugar

1 teaspoon salt

1 teaspoon cinnamon

⅛ teaspoon cream of tartar

For the compote, place all ingredients together in a medium saucepan. Cook over medium heat, stirring often, until reduced and thickening, about 15 to 20 minutes. Turn off heat and cover.

For the pancakes, beat the egg whites until stiff. Beat the egg yolks together and add remaining ingredients. Fold the whites gently into the egg mixture. Don't overwork it. Ladle batter onto preheated large frying pan to desired size pancakes. Fry the pancakes covered for best results, turning once. Drain cooked pancakes on a paper towel if necessary. Serve topped with warm compote.

Richard's Tomato Marmalade

Even though tomatoes are technically a fruit (as are chiles), the idea of tomato marmalade sounded strange to me the first time I saw the women from Montoya Orchard Farm in Velarde selling jars of it at the farmers market. Once I tasted it, though, I knew I had to learn how to make it. Mrs. Montoya's recipe is a family secret, of course, but by asking around I came up with this one that works for me. As with most canning projects, this recipe makes lots of marmalade. Fortunately, it makes good gifts and souvenirs.

Although this marmalade will keep in the refrigerator for a reasonable time, you'll probably want to can it in jars so you can store it at room temperature or give it away. For this, you will need a boiling water canner and about a dozen half-pint jars. Once you have the canner and learn how to use it, it will open up a wealth of possibilities for preserving farmers market ingredients.

Makes about 9 jars

5 to 6 pounds vine-ripened tomatoes
6 cups sugar
1 teaspoon salt
3 blood oranges
2 lemons
4 sticks whole cinnamon
2 whole star anise
1 tablespoon whole cloves

Score the skins of the tomatoes with an X at the blossom end and place in boiling water for 15 to 20 seconds each to loosen the skin. Move them directly into a large bowl of ice water. Slip the peel off, cut in half, and remove the seeds and any hard cores. Cut the tomatoes into small pieces. Put the tomato pieces and juice in a large cook pot. Add sugar and salt, stirring until dissolved.

Slice the oranges and lemons into very thin slices and cut each slice into quarters. Add them to the pot. Put the spices in a cheesecloth bag and put it in the pot. Bring to a rolling boil, then reduce heat and simmer for 1½ to 2 hours, stirring often to avoid scorching, until the tomatoes fall apart. When thickened to the consistency of jam, remove from heat and skim off any foam. Remove the spice bag and discard.

If canning, sterilize the canning jars. Pour the hot marmalade into the hot jars to about ¼ inch from the top. Wipe the rims of the jars with a damp paper towel. Place the two-piece canning lids on the jars according to the instructions that come with the boiling water canner.

Estofar de Carne de Baca Fantochada (Ridiculous Beef Stew)

This recipe is from John Lapin of Questa. Despite the humorous name, this is a serious dish.

Serves 6

2 pounds good-quality grass-fed stew beef
1 teaspoon each (or to taste) Spanish paprika, oregano, salt, pepper, flour
Beef fat
Olive oil
2 heaping tablespoons finely chopped garlic*
2 to 3 ounces tomato paste
2 to 3 heaping tablespoons olive tapenade
2 ounces beef or vegetable stock
1 bottle red wine, preferably Spanish
1 large yellow onion, thinly sliced and separated into rounds
Bay leaf
1 cup thinly sliced carrots

Preheat oven to 325 degrees F.

Place the beef in a large bowl and coat with herbs and spices in this order: paprika, oregano, salt, pepper, and flour. Toss until thoroughly coated. Heat a large (14-inch) iron skillet on the stovetop. Melt the beef fat with olive oil using equal parts. Brown the meat in batches without touching so the meat is crisp and brown. When cooked, move each batch to an iron pot to keep warm, sprinkle it with additional paprika, tossing lightly, and then cook the next batch.

When all the meat is browned and in the iron pot, place the pot on the stovetop over low heat. Make a hole about two inches in diameter in the center of the meat, exposing the bottom surface of the pot. In this hole, place the finely chopped garlic, tomato paste, olive tapenade, and stock. Melt these ingredients together and stir around inside the hole until they bubble. Toss the meat with these ingredients and add ⅓ to ½ bottle of red wine. Stir until all is well distributed and simmer on low.

Heat a skillet and coat the bottom with olive oil. Heat until fragrant, then turn off the heat, add the onion, and brown lightly. Add bay leaf to taste. Remove the onions from the skillet, drain them on a paper towel, put them on a plate, and keep warm.

Deglaze the skillet with the remaining wine and reduce over high heat. Add the concentrated wine to the meat and stir so the meat is evenly moist. Add the onions and bay leaf to the pot with the meat. Then add the carrots to the pot and stir.

Cover and slow-cook in the oven until tender—about 40 minutes to 1 hour.

*For best results, use heirloom Spanish Rioja Garlic from Victor Mascareñas, Costilla, New Mexico, 505-586-0148.

Bison Bearnaise

It's hard to go wrong with bison, a very forgiving meat. You can marinate a slab in red wine overnight and roast it. You can crumble buffalo sausage on top of a pizza. You can slice a sirloin thin and stir-fry it with fresh market vegetables. You can combine it with noodles and cream sauce to make buffalo stroganoff. Or you can simply cook up a batch of green chile cheeseburgers on your outdoor grill.

But if you're hosting a chic dinner party and want to serve the most elegant bison entrée ever, try this. Bison tenderloin is expensive (and worth it)—a whole one can weigh up to five pounds and cost upwards of $150. It is usually sold in smaller sizes. Because bison is so dense and high in protein, a six-ounce serving per person—one or two of these buffalo-size "medallions"—makes a generous entrée.

Bearnaise sauce is a sauce of butter and egg yolks flavored with tarragon and French shallots, cooked in wine and vinegar to make a glaze. It's like Hollandaise sauce except for the flavoring—shallots, vinegar, and tarragon instead of lemon juice. This sauce requires practice to avoid curdling the egg yolk mixture through excessive heat or separation from adding butter too rapidly, so practice in private before making it for a dinner party. This distinctive and versatile sauce can also be served with vegetables, egg dishes, asparagus, artichokes, or lobster.

Serves 4 to 6

Bearnaise Sauce:
2 tablespoons tarragon vinegar
2 tablespoons Chablis
1 French shallot, finely chopped
1 tablespoon chopped fresh tarragon
1 tablespoon fresh parsley, chilled
2 egg yolks
⅓ cup melted butter

2 pounds bison tenderloin (for 4–6 people)
3 tablespoons olive oil, divided
Salt and ground red chile to taste

Put the vinegar, Chablis, shallot, and herbs in a small saucepan; simmer until reduced to 1 tablespoon. Strain and set aside to cool. Add the egg yolks and whisk well with a balloon whisk. Place the bowl over a pan of hot water and continue whisking. Gradually add the butter, whisking until the sauce thickens and all the butter has been added. Set sauce aside.

Preheat oven to 450 degrees F.

Slice the tenderloin into 1-inch-thick medallions. Coat the bottom of a heavy cast-iron skillet with 1½ tablespoons olive oil and heat over moderately high heat. In batches, sear the bison tenderloin medallions on the stovetop until browned—about 2 minutes on each side, handling with tongs. (Don't stab them with a fork.) Remove to a baking dish. Add more olive oil and repeat with the rest of the medallions.

Arrange the medallions in the baking dish and season lightly with salt, pepper, and ground red chile. Roast the medallions in the oven for 8 minutes (medium rare) or more.

Remove the medallions from the oven and let stand about 3 minutes. Slice each medallion in half horizontally and arrange on a serving plate. Top generously with bearnaise sauce.

Peppercorn Rub

Popular belief notwithstanding, chili "peppers" are not related to the spice we know as pepper. But when you combine the two, the results can be magical. Here's the ultimate spice rub for beef or buffalo steaks.

Makes 1 ½ cups, enough for 4 large steaks

2 tablespoons crushed, dried Chimayo red chile
2 tablespoons whole peppercorns*
¼ cup brown sugar
2 tablespoons granulated garlic
¼ cup sea salt
1 tablespoon each ground cumin, dry mustard, dried oregano, dried thyme, dried basil

Place chile and peppercorns in a mortar and crush with a pestle. Add all remaining ingredients and continue crushing until well mixed.

Rub generously on beef or buffalo steaks and let stand covered or wrapped in the refrigerator for 24 hours before barbecuing or grilling the steaks.

*For best results, use three-color or four-color peppercorns, available in most natural foods supermarkets. The three-color—black, white, and green—comes from picking peppercorns from the same plant at different stages of maturity. The four-color also includes "pink peppercorns," actually the berries of another plant unrelated to pepper.

Curry with Lamb, Lentils, and Barley

This recipe is from John Lapin of Questa. To preserve the individual flavors and textures of the meat, lentils, and barley, they are partly cooked separately and added in sequence.

Serves 4 to 6

3 tablespoons clarified butter or ghee
1 cup diced onion
½ cup chopped celery greens
¼ cup finely diced garlic
1 to 2 pounds lamb or young goat, pre-rubbed with salt and pepper and cut into cubes for stew
2 heaping tablespoons Patak's Prepared Hot Curry Paste
2 tablespoons curry powder
2 cups chopped tomatoes
2 cups rich homemade chicken or vegetable stock (or one quart of store-bought, reduced by half)
1 cup barley, par-cooked
4 to 6 ounces Southwest Chutney's Peachy Green
1 cup lentils, par-cooked

Melt the butter or ghee in a stew pot or Dutch oven. Add the onion, celery greens, and garlic and sweat them over very low heat until the onions are translucent. Add the meat and brown lightly. Add the curry paste and curry powder and stir until well mixed.

Raise the heat and add the tomatoes and stock. Simmer until the meat is tender. Add the barley, adding more liquid if needed. Lower the heat and simmer. Add chutney and continue to simmer. Add the lentils, mix, and heat to near boiling. Remove from heat, cover, and let stand. Serve in bowls. This curry goes particularly well with slightly sweet Scottish ale.

Arroz con Pollo (Rice with Chicken)

Elena Arellano of Ohkay Owingeh Pueblo, sends us this recipe.

Serves 6

1 whole chicken, halved lengthwise
3 cloves garlic, peeled and crushed
Salt and freshly ground black pepper
1½ cups long-grain white rice
2 carrots, peeled, trimmed, and sliced crosswise
3 ribs celery, trimmed and chopped
1 pinch saffron threads
4 scallions, trimmed and thinly sliced

Put the chicken, garlic, and a generous pinch of salt into 8 cups cold water in a large, heavy-bottomed pot and bring to boil over high heat. Reduce heat to medium low, cover, and simmer until chicken is tender, about 1 hour. Using a slotted spoon, transfer the chicken to a plate and set aside. Strain the chicken broth into a large bowl. Discard the solids from the strainer and return the broth to the cleaned pot. Add rice, carrots, celery, and saffron and bring to a boil over high heat. Reduce heat to medium and cook uncovered, stirring occasionally, until the rice is tender, about 15 minutes.

When the chicken is cool enough to handle, peel off the skin and remove the meat from the bones, discarding the skin and bones and tearing the meat into large pieces. Add the chicken and scallions to the pot with the rice, season to taste with salt and pepper, and cook until the chicken is just heated through, about 5 minutes.

Phil's Lamb Stew with Fennel

This stew comes from Phil Loomis, president, Santa Fe Farmers Market.

Serves 4 to 6

4 tablespoons extra virgin olive oil
4 cups fennel bulb, scrubbed, trimmed, and cut into large chunks
2 to 4 small onions, chopped
12 to 14 cloves garlic, peeled and halved
1 cup coarsely chopped oyster mushrooms
2 tablespoons soy sauce
1 tablespoon sea salt
1 tablespoon freshly ground pepper
1 tablespoon coarsely ground fennel seed
3½ pounds lamb, shoulder or leg, trimmed of fat, cut into 1½-inch chunks
4 quarts vegetable stock
1 bunch baby carrots, unpeeled, and scrubbed
1½ pounds young fingerling potatoes, unpeeled, and scrubbed

In a large, heavy-bottomed stockpot of at least 10 quarts, heat olive oil to sizzling. Add fennel bulb, onion, garlic, mushrooms, soy sauce, salt, pepper, and fennel seed. Reduce flame to medium, stirring with a sturdy wooden spoon. When onions just start to turn clear, add lamb and continue to stir.

Continue browning lamb until it is cooked through. Add 3 quarts vegetable stock (use a good quality, low in salt, preferably homemade stock) and hold last quart in reserve, adding as needed to keep stew covered. Simmer for 2 to 3 hours or until lamb is tender. Add carrots and potatoes to stew. Simmer until potatoes are soft but not mushy. Ladle into large bowls and serve steaming hot.

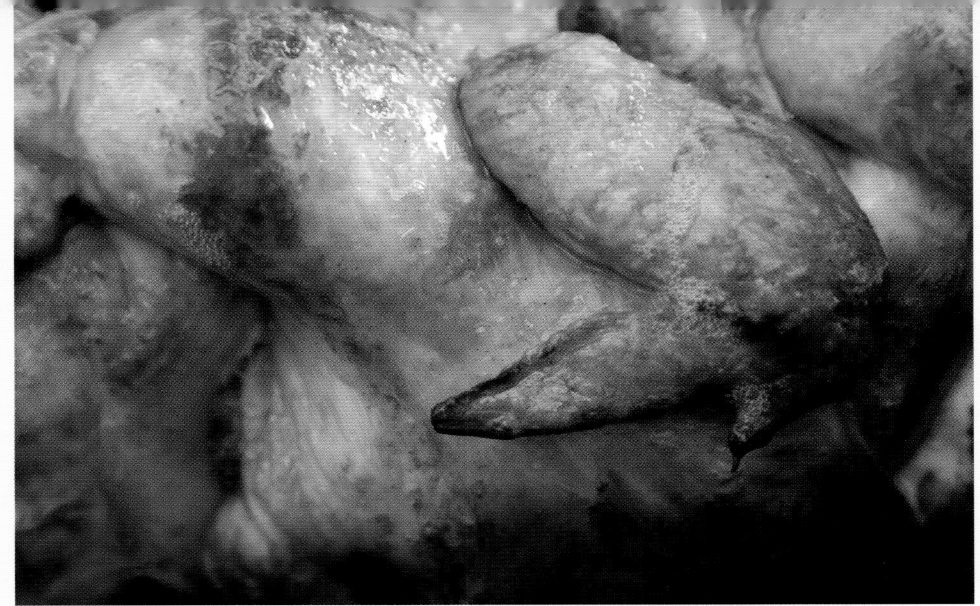

The World's Best Roast Chicken

Kate Manchester, editor, Edible Santa Fe, *gave permission for us to print her recipe.*

Serves 4

I've been roasting chickens this way for years, and it's a great way to roast Tom [Delehanty]'s flavorful, juicy Label Rouge birds. This method keeps the bird deliciously moist on the inside, and super crispy outside. You will need a cast-iron skillet large enough to hold the chicken. If your chicken is larger than 4 pounds, you may need to increase the cooking time by about 10 minutes per pound.

Rinse your bird inside and out, and then dry thoroughly with paper towels. This step is key; the bird must go into the pan dry. Season chicken all over, inside and out, with salt (¾ teaspoon sea salt per pound of chicken), pepper, and any dry seasonings you like to use. Cover and refrigerate.

When ready to roast, preheat the oven to 475 degrees F for a full 20 minutes. Place a large cast-iron skillet on top of the stove, and turn the heat to high—do not add oil. When the skillet is smoking hot, place the whole chicken in the hot skillet, breast side up. The chicken should start to sizzle immediately. Use your oven mitts and place the whole pan in the oven. Within 10 minutes you should hear the pan sizzling in the oven. If not, increase the heat by 25 degrees.

After 30 minutes, using a pair of long tongs, turn the bird over (breast side down). If the chicken has blistered, reduce heat by 25 degrees. Cook for 20 minutes, and then turn the bird back over (breast side up) and roast for another 10 minutes. Total cooking time should be approximately 45 to 60 minutes. Serve immediately!

Cilantro-Lime Marinade

Citrus fruits are not grown in New Mexico, but cilantro and chile certainly are. Somehow, about thirty years ago, limes became a popular "Santa Fe-style" ingredient, and it has been a staple in fine restaurants ever since. This is one of the most popular barbecue marinades in New Mexico today.

Makes 1½ cups, enough for 4 steaks or 1 cut-up chicken

2 cloves garlic, roasted, peeled and chopped
1 tablespoon yellow mustard
2 tablespoons lime juice
2 tablespoons extra virgin olive oil
1 tablespoon soy sauce
1 tablespoon crushed dried Chimayo red chile
¼ cup finely chopped cilantro leaves
¼ cup grated orange zest

Combine the garlic, mustard, lime juice, olive oil, and soy sauce in a blender and purée until smooth. Pour into a bowl and stir in by hand the chile, cilantro, and orange zest.

Place steaks or chicken pieces in a large airtight container. Pour the marinade over it. Close the lid tightly and shake to coat the meat thoroughly with the marinade. Place in the refrigerator for at least 8 hours before barbecuing or grilling.

Pechuga de Pollo Romero (Chicken Breast Rosemary)

Pollo Real's Label Rouge chickens are an irresistible invitation to experiment with gourmet recipes, and we've tried dozens of them. This one is a winner, with seasonings that subtly enhance the chicken's outstanding flavor without drowning it out. Best when grilled outdoors, the dish can also be made in an oven broiler during the cold months.

Serves 4 to 8

4 Label Rouge chicken breasts, split
¼ cup extra virgin olive oil
Juice of 1 dozen key limes
3 scallions, chopped, including greens
1 teaspoon chopped fresh cilantro leaves
2 teaspoons chopped fresh rosemary leaves
½ teaspoon sea salt
1 teaspoon coarse ground chile caribe
4 whole rosemary sprigs
2 key limes, cut in quarters

Skin the split chicken breasts. With a sharp knife, make crosswise slices halfway through each breast and 1 inch apart to allow the marinade to reach the inside.

Mix the oil, lime juice, scallions, cilantro, rosemary, salt, and chile in a shallow baking dish. Add the chicken breast halves, turning them so that all sides are coated with the marinade. Lay them sliced-side-up in the baking dish. Spoon the marinade remaining in the bottom of the dish over the tops of the breasts.

Cover tightly and refrigerate for 4 hours or more.

Light an outdoor grill with mesquite chips. Soak the whole rosemary sprigs in water for 30 minutes. When the mesquite wood has burned down to a bed of coals, place the sprigs directly on the coals. Place the chicken breasts bone-side-down on the grill, 4 inches above the coals, and grill them, brushing them frequently with the marinade and turning them at 10-minute intervals, until they are browned and the juices are no longer pink (about 30 to 40 minutes).

DESERT DESSERTS

Official New Mexico Bizcochitos

This widely circulated recipe for the official state cookie of New Mexico (the only U.S. state that has a state cookie), is often attributed to Gary E. Johnson, who served as governor from 1995 to 2003. While in office, the Republican governor gained national notoriety as the highest-ranking public official to advocate the legalization of marijuana, a surreptitiously grown New Mexico cash crop. It may be no coincidence that bizcochitos are the ideal answer to the munchies. Johnson himself was not known to be a pothead, though. A physical fitness and health advocate, he competed in triathalons and, after leaving office, climbed Mount Everest.

Makes 5 dozen

1 pound shortening
1½ cups sugar
2 teaspoons anise (anise seed)
2 eggs, beaten
6 cups flour
1 teaspoon salt
1 tablespoon baking powder
½ cup fresh apple cider or other organic fruit juice
1 tablespoons canela (cinnamon)

Preheat the oven to 350 degrees F.

Cream the shortening together with the sugar and anise in a large bowl. Add the eggs and beat well. Combine the flour, salt, and baking powder in another mixing bowl. Alternately add the dry mixture and the fruit juice to the shortening mixture until it makes a stiff dough; knead thoroughly.

Roll the dough to a ¼- to ½-inch thickness. Cut the dough to desired shapes using cookie cutters. Combine sugar and cinnamon in a shaker and dust the top of each uncooked cookie with a small amount of the mixture. Bake for 10 minutes or until cookies are lightly browned.

Green Tomato Pie

This recipe is from Kim Martin of Growing Opportunities in Alcalde.

Makes 8 servings

Pastry for a 2-crust pie
3 cups (1¾ pounds) sliced green tomatoes
1½ cups sugar
¼ teaspoon salt
5 teaspoons grated fresh lemon peel
½ teaspoon ground cinnamon
5 tablespoons fresh lemon juice
¼ cup melted butter

Preheat oven to 375 degrees F.

Roll out half of the piecrust pastry and line a 9-inch pie pan. In a medium-size bowl, combine the remaining ingredients. Spoon the mixture into the pastry shell. Roll out the remaining pastry and place over the filling. Flute the edges, and then cut steam vents in the top crust. Bake for 35 minutes or until the crust is golden brown and the filling bubbles.

Tesuque Pumpkin Cookies

This recipe is from Lois Ellen Frank and is reprinted by permission from Foods of the Southwest Indian Nations *(Santa Fe: Ten Speed Press, 2003).*

Most pueblos in New Mexico are relatively close to one another. Because of this, many of the women bring prepared foods over to other pueblos during feast days or other celebrations. As a result, each pueblo has developed its own version of certain recipes.

I learned this particular recipe from some of the women at Tesuque Pueblo just north of Santa Fe. If you choose, you can cut the recipe in half. But I advise you to bake the full amount. The cookies are delicious, not too sweet, and will disappear quickly!

Makes approximately 7 dozen

2 cups sugar
2 cups vegetable shortening
2 cups cooked pumpkin
2 eggs, beaten
2 teaspoons vanilla extract
4 cups all-purpose flour
2 teaspoons baking soda
1 teaspoon salt
1 teaspoon grated nutmeg
½ teaspoon ground allspice
2 cups raisins
1 cup chopped walnuts

Preheat the oven to 350 degrees F. Grease a large cookie sheet.

In a large bowl, cream together the sugar and shortening. Add the pumpkin, eggs, and vanilla and beat until smooth. In a separate bowl, combine the flour, baking soda, salt, nutmeg, and allspice. Slowly add the dry ingredients to the pumpkin mixture, small amounts at a time, until completely mixed together. Stir in the raisins and walnuts.

Drop tablespoons of the dough roughly 2 inches apart on the cookie sheet. Bake 12 to 15 minutes, until golden grown.